Get a Feel for English !

喚醒你的英文語感！

Get a Feel for English !

喚醒你的英文語感！

YBM Si-sa

TOEIC® Master
英語認證測驗國際標準版

New TOEIC® Listening

新多益大師指引

聽力滿分關鍵

登峰王牌名師 **王建民**

親傳 20 年聽力教學及命題破解秘笈

總編審 **王復國**

貝塔語言出版
Beta Multimedia Publishing

IRT 語言測驗中心
Language Testing Center

商業人士英語能力評量最具公信力的認證

　　新多益測驗（Test of English for International Communication）不但是非英語母語人士英語能力的一種評量，在國際上更是商業人士英語能力評量最具公信力的認證。事實上，新多益測驗中的聽力測驗，暫且不論 Part 1「照片描述」，Part 2「應答問題」的出題內容，可說是國際職場與日常生活中英語人士每日溝通的基本形式。而 Part 3「簡短對話」與 Part 4「簡短獨白」，更是實地取材於職場的各類主題，舉凡開會、簡報、談判、訂購商品，甚至是日常生活中的購物、用餐、看診和欣賞表演等，皆為真實生活的常見題材。因此，若能培養良好的新多益聽力應考能力，不但能讓您在國際職場更具競爭力，做為升遷和加薪的一種有利籌碼，甚至於在出差、海外居住、旅遊甚或留學進修等皆有意想不到的幫助。

新多益聽力測驗出題方向調整

　　根據新多益的命題單位美國教育測驗服務中心（ETS）所公布的情資顯示，新多益聽力測驗各大題的出題方向調整如下：

聽力測驗	傳統多益測驗	新版多益測驗	改變
Part 1	照片描述 20 題	照片描述 10 題	題數減少為 10 題
Part 2	應答問題 30 題	應答問題 30 題	維持不變
Part 3	簡短對話 30 題	簡短對話 30 題	1. 對話時間加長，題組出題 2. 題目除播放外，也會印在試題本上
Part 4	簡短獨白 20 題	簡短獨白 30 題	1. 獨白時間加長，題組出題 2. 每段獨白搭配 3 道題目

● Part 1 照片描述

1. 本大題題數減少為 10 題,但會有更多圖片細節及不同種類的混合考法,同時也會運用干擾選項來測驗考生的能力,因此讀者要訓練自己能更廣泛地掌握圖片所透露的訊息(從大重點到小細節),並覺察圖片中人物動作與場景物件的混和配置。

2. 遇到從未想到的答案選項或是聽不懂的單字時,即應靈活應用本書〈聽力滿分關鍵攻略〉Part 1 傳授的「消去法」策略,才能在第一大題致勝,拿到滿分。

3. 在練習時要特別注意人物及其動作、物品的配置、背景、介系詞及場景重點,也要留意選項中出現「相似音」、「同音異義字」、「一字多義」、「連音」、「被動語態」等干擾陷阱。

● Part 2 應答問題

1. 第二大題大致維持不變,唯獨增加了「直述句」和「直述句 + 問句」的新題型。此外,美式與英式口音的問答,更是讀者不可掉以輕心之處。Part 2 的準備要領其實並不難,只要將舊制三種高頻出題類型(詳見〈聽力滿分關鍵攻略〉Part 2「題型透析」單元及新增的直述句類型了解透徹,在應考時鎖定最重要的疑問詞、主詞與動詞、受詞等「重音字」,在配合「應試基本對策」和「破題關鍵要領」反覆練習,想要滿分過關並非難事。

2. 平時應多熟悉不同問句可能的「回答模式」或「答案選項」,並要徹底了解錯誤選項不對的原因(如:題目問何時要做某事,答案不選 (C) By bus,則要能理解 By bus 為回答交通方式,與時間毫無關聯),全盤掌握「問答配對」,這樣的學習才算一次到位。

● Part 3 簡短問答

第三大題有二大形式調整:

1. 第一項改變是,除了舊制的 A → B → A 或 B → A → B 的對話型式之外(占 20% ~ 30%),還增加了 A → B → A → B 或 B → A → B → A 的新形式,此題型為新制大宗,約占 7 ~ 8 成,當然偶爾也會有一或二段 2 男或 2 女的對話內容。無庸置疑,讀者對於不同口音的對話要有立即轉換的能力,故平日就必須熟悉各種口音、腔調甚至重音。另外,對於意思相同拼法不同的字彙轉換也要熟悉,應考時才不會成為作答的阻礙。注意,新多益 Part 2 的對話長度略微增長,有時甚至長達 130 個字左右。

2. 第二項改變是，在舊制中，一個問題只對應一個題目，但在新制中取而代之的是十段對話，每段對話搭配三道問題。這意味著，除了「對話主旨」等大方向的問題一定要聽懂之外，還要注意細節問題。另外，由於出題的順序未必與說話者所唸的順序一致，因此，「題目預測」的「速度」及「精準度」為戰勝這一大題的關鍵。有時聽懂了全部內容也不一定能夠回答題目，故必須學習針對題目所問的重點找出「答案所在」，並在最佳時間點上選取正確答案。Part 3 對話中的「特殊句型」、「特殊用字」以及重音字（動詞、名詞、形容詞、副詞）的掌握，皆會在本書〈聽力滿分關鍵攻略〉中一一揭露。讀者平日利用本書的〈Exercises〉或〈模擬測驗〉演練此單元時，一定要先做題目預測，模擬正式考試情境。在測驗結束後，務必透過「模擬測驗完全解析」了解錯誤及不懂之處，並跟著 MP3 大聲誦讀 3～5 次出題內容，甚至模仿錄音員的口音及腔調，如此一來，相信讀者的聽力及口語能力將會大幅躍進。

● Part 4 簡短獨白

　　第四大題獨白題與第三大題的題型差不多，而新舊制也大同小異。新多益中有十段獨白，各搭配三道題目，和 Part 3 一樣，出題順序不一定按照錄音內容的順序，「快速」且「精準」的預測題目是致勝關鍵。此外，獨白長度雖比舊制長一些（有時達 150 字，甚至更長）。如同準備第三大題一樣，能否正確答題，取決於是否能先熟悉常考題材內容與獨白內容的順序邏輯。一定要先做「題目預測」，因為題目內容暗示了獨白內容的走向，且若能清楚掌握各類獨白模式（比如，一聽到獨白開頭說 Good morning, welcome to this year's Employee Annual Luncheon. 就表示他們在開會（Having a meeting）），就能更快速精準地選出答案。以上之答題要領請見本書〈聽力滿分關鍵攻略〉Part 4 的「題型透析」、「基本應試對策」與「破題關鍵要領」。

　　總上所述，想考好多益聽力測驗，除了解新制出題方向及熟讀本書〈聽力滿分關鍵攻略〉的答題要領外，最好還要有足夠的單字、片語，以及熟悉英文會話常用句型。本書在〈聽力滿分關鍵攻略〉每個 Part 的後半部，皆統整列出該大題頻考的字彙、片語及常用句型，幫助讀者快速有效地厚實應考能力。最後，務必練習本書所附的二回模擬試題，熟悉出題內容及英、美、加、澳四國口音，測後一定要詳讀完整解析，徹底通透問題點，只要秉持這些終極原則，聽力必可大幅提升，挑戰 990 滿分也不再是夢！

Contnents

目　錄

Section 聽力滿分關鍵攻略

Part 1　照片描述　Photographs

Part 2　應答問題　Question-Response

Section 模擬測驗

New TOEIC 新多益測驗說明

何謂多益考試？

● 評量商業人士英語能力的標準

多益測驗 TOEIC（國際溝通英語測驗，Test of English for International Communication）是美國非營利事業組織 ETS（教育測驗服務社，Educational Testing Service）所研發製作的測驗，主要測試英語非母語人士身處國際商務環境中實際運用英語的能力，其成績常被企業使用為人員招考、升遷、技術訓練、語言訓練、海外派任的決策標準。多益測驗的分數反映受測者在國際職場環境中與他人以英語溝通的熟稔程度，測驗內容以日常使用之英語為主，應試者不需具備專業的知識或字彙。

以職場為基準點的英語能力測驗中，多益測驗為世界最頂級的考試。2007 年全球有 60 多個國家施測，大型企業、學校及政府機構使用多益測驗超過 10,000 家以上，全年應試考生超過 500 萬人以上。取得多益高分證照，就等於擁有全球職場的通行證！

● 測驗結果以得分計算

測驗的目的是為了評量英語的溝通能力，並不判定合格與否，而是透過分數來呈現考試結果。得分計算方式為：聽力測驗 5 ～ 495 分，閱讀測驗 5 ～ 495 分，合計得分範圍為 10 ～ 990 分。

ETS 台灣區代表 忠欣股份有限公司

官方網站　http://www.toeic.com.tw/

⇨ 網站上有測驗內容，測驗方式、計分說明和測驗日期等相關介紹，也有線上報名服務。

多益測驗內容為何？

　　多益測驗由「聽力測驗」和「閱讀測驗」兩部分組成，各 100 題，答題時間分別為聽力 45 分鐘、閱讀 75 分鐘。題型皆為選擇題，除 Part 2 為三選一之外，其餘都是四選一的形式。

　　多益測驗的題型每次都一樣。多益測驗會根據統計資料而調整試題的難易度，因此若實力不變，不管什麼時候參加測驗，成績應該都相同。

● **多益測驗七大題型**

聽力測驗（45分鐘）

Part 1 照片描述（**Photographs**）　**10 題**

看照片並從四個選項中選出一個最適合的答案。

答題時間：一題 5 秒

Part 2 應答問題（**Question-Response**）　**30 題**

從三個選項中找出一個最適合用來應答語音播放內容的選項。應答的選項也是由語音播放，沒印在試題本上。

答題時間：一題 5 秒

Part 3 簡短對話（**Short Conversations**）　**30 題**

一段錄音對話搭配三道題目，每題都是四選一。題目和選項都印在試題本上，題目也由語音播放。

答題時間：一題 8 秒

Part 4 簡短獨白（**Short Talks**）　**30題**

一段錄音獨白搭配三道題目，每題都是四選一。題目和選項都印在試題本上，題目也由語音播放。

答題時間：一題 8 秒

閱讀測驗（75 分鐘）

Part 5 單句填空（**Incomplete Sentences**） 40 題
從四個選項中選出一個最適合填入填空句子的詞語。

Part 6 短文填空（**Text Completion**） 12 題
從四個選項中選出一個最適合填入短文填空處的詞語。短文共有四篇，每篇搭配三道題目。

Part 7 文章理解（**Reading Comprehension**） 48 題
共有 11 到 14 篇文章，閱讀每篇文章後回答問題，必須從四個選項中選出一個最合適的答案。其中有 4 個部分為雙篇文章（Double Passage）理解題，答題時須同時參照兩篇文章。雙篇文章理解題為第 181 ～ 200 題，每部分搭配五道題目。

多益成績與英語溝通能力等級參照表

級數	分數	英語溝通能力評定
A	860	**具備充分的英語溝通能力。** 能夠理解非專業領域的話題並適切地表達意見。雖說和英語母語人士的英語程度還有一步之差，但可以確實掌握字彙、文法、句型，並流暢地溝通。
B	730	**具備以適切英語應付各種狀況的能力。** 能夠理解一般會話內容並迅速應對。可以順暢溝通特定領域的話題，並足以應付工作上的需求。在溝通的正確性和流暢性上雖有個人差異，也尚未能完全掌握正確的文法和句型，但對溝通的妨礙不大。
C	470	能夠應付日常生活的會話並滿足特定工作範圍內的需求。 能夠理解一般會話的重點並做出適當回應，但溝通內容較複雜時，就會顯得能力不足。具備基本文法、句型的知識，即使表達能力稍差，還是有堪用的字彙來表達自己的意見。
D	220	在一般會話中能做最低限的溝通。 若對方說話速度較慢或重複說話內容，或以較易理解的方式來溝通的話，就能夠理解簡單會話的內容。能夠應付個人較熟悉的話題。字彙、文法、句型等知識略嫌不足，如果對方能體諒自己是非英語母語人士而調整溝通方式的話，在傳達彼此的意見時障礙就不大。
E		**尚未具備英語溝通能力。** 即使是慢速且單純的會話，也只能理解一部分內容。具備基本字彙能力，但還無法串連成句子，對意見溝通沒有實質上的助益。

資料提供：財團法人國際商業溝通協會

新多益測驗應考注意事項

❖ 考前三日

☐ 不要念全新的內容，否則容易自亂陣腳，且不易記住。

☐ 每天至少扎實練習聽力 45 分鐘，不可中斷，並模擬實際考試自我測試一次。「聲音」的熟練度是聽力致勝的不二法門。

☐ 只複習本書「破題關鍵要領」及「大師關鍵指引」的重點，例如：指標字、訊號字，以及高頻字彙和情境用語等。

☐ 調整睡眠時間及起床時間，儘量以配合考試當天的作息時間為準。

❖ 考試當日

☐ 應考務必攜帶貼有照片之準考證、2B 鉛筆、橡皮擦及有效證件，如身分證。

☐ 務必提早 20 ～ 30 分鐘先到考試場所，並確認桌上準考證號碼與自己的准考證一致，座位桌椅無大瑕疵。考前建議先如廁，考試時不可進食或飲料。

☐ 手機切忌關機，進場之後勿東張西望以免分心，可靜坐閉目養神。

☐ 9:30 分起開始會先發放問卷表，名字、準考證號碼及一些重要個人資料切勿填錯，勿忘簽名。

☐ 填表後進行音量測試，若太大或太小聲一定要立刻舉手告知監考老師。若座位在冷氣機旁可能會受到干擾，不建議調小音量。

☐ 待監考老師說可打開試題本時，立刻先做第一大題照片題的圖片預覽，此時可略過多益測驗的 Directions。

☐ 遇到不會的題目或選項時，要善用消去法，用「會的」來找不會的，答完一題或一組題目時，務必立刻作答，千萬不要以為還有時間可以再回來檢查而留下空白，這樣很有可能漏答題目，導致後面答題全亂。

☐ 聽完一題或一組題目後，不要在意不懂的題目，應立刻忘掉該題，將注意力放在準備下一道題目。

New TOEIC

聽 力 滿 分
關 鍵 攻 略

Listening
Strategies

Part 1

Photographs
照 片 描 述

題型簡介

照片描述題共 10 題（1～10 題），每題會有一張照片，你會聽到針對每張照片所做的四個描述，必須在四個選項中選出最符合照片所見情境之描述。照片的內容包羅萬象，但多半是一些日常生活情境的照片。多數照片裡會有人物，但也有部分照片只有物件或只顯示地點而沒有人物。四個選項的描述通常都非常簡短，可能跟照片內的主題有關，也可能跟照片中某一細節有關。問題與問題之間大約間隔 5 秒，(A)、(B)、(C)、(D) 四個選項間並沒有太多停頓時間。每道題目只播放一次，且錄音內容不會印在試題本上。

答案：(B)

錄音內容

(A) He's turning the key.

(B) He's looking at the engine.

(C) He's reading a manual.

(D) He's repairing the door.

錄音翻譯

(A) 他在轉鑰匙。

(B) 他看著引擎。

(C) 他在看手冊。

(D) 他在修理門。

題型透析

Part 1「照片描述題」多為日常生活中常見的人、事、物，場景包括室內、公園、街道或辦公室等。出題重點包括人物的動作、人物所處位置、人與周圍事物或景物之間的關係，大致可分為以下幾類：

1 以「人」為主時

若照片只有出現「人」時，請注意下列重點：

⇨ 若只有一人時，注意其所做的「動作」。

⇨ 若有兩人時，注意二人的「共同點」、有無「互動關係」或「不同點」。

⇨ 若有三人（或以上）時，注意全體共同的動作，或其中一人的特別差異點。

● He's posing for a picture.

　他在擺姿勢照相。

● She's getting a haircut.

　她正在理髮。

● The man has a short-sleeved shirt on.

　男子穿著短袖襯衫。

● They're asking for direction.

　他們在問路。

● They're facing the same direction.

　他們面對著同一個方向。

● A man and a woman are sitting side by side.

　一男一女並肩坐著。

● Performers are on the stage.

　表演者在舞台上。

● A man is riding on the sidewalk.

　一名男子在人行道上騎車。

Word List
　□ pose [poz] *v.* 擺姿勢
　□ sidewalk [ˋsaɪˌwɔk] *n.*【美】人行道

● Both man are taking notes.

　兩名男子都在做筆記。

● They're using a computer.

　他們正在用電腦。

Example 1

Ⓐ　Ⓑ　Ⓒ　Ⓓ

---

1. 答案：(C)

[圖　析] 三位女人坐在桌前討論事情。

[解　析] 照片中的三位女子沒有對坐也沒在看報紙，也不是穿同樣的制服，故 (A)、(B)、(D) 皆錯，故正確答案為 (C)。

[錄音內容] (A) They are sitting across from each other.

(B) They are reading the newspaper.

(C) They are each resting an arm on the table.

(D) They are wearing matching uniforms.

[錄音翻譯] (A) 他們彼此對坐。

(B) 他們在看報紙。

(C) 他們分別把一支手擺在桌上。

(D) 他們穿著相配的制服。

---

② 以「物件」為主時

若照片只有物件時，請注意下列重點：

⇨ 物件周圍前、後、左、右、上、下有無其他相關用品。

⇨ 物件的「狀態」如何，例如：事物、東西為何？發生了什麼狀況？

● Several carts are in a row.

連續幾輛車形成一列。

● The house door is halfway open.

大門半開著。

● The bed is already made.

床已經鋪好了。

● The steps are divided by the handrail.

階梯被扶手隔開。

● The chairs are made of wood.

椅子是木頭做的。

● The glasses are stacked on the clothed table.

玻璃杯疊在鋪了布的桌子上。

● The escalator is out of service.

電梯停用。

● Chairs have been set up in a row.

椅子被排成一排。

● Curtains are covering the window.

窗簾蓋住了窗戶。

Example 2

MP3
004

Ⓐ   Ⓑ   Ⓒ   Ⓓ

Word List

☐ in a row 形成一列（或排）

☐ handrail [`hænd‚rel] *n.* 欄桿；扶手

☐ stack [stæk] *v.* 堆放；疊

2. 答案：(A)

圖 析 商店裡衣服被放在架上及櫃子上展示，但照片中並沒人。

解 析 (A) 關鍵字 shirts、on display 皆與圖片描述一致，故為正確答案。(B) 不對，因為照片中並沒有銷售助理（sales assistants）；(C) 與照片不符，衣服並不是堆在地板（floor）上；(D) 也錯，衣架（hangers）亦未出現在圖片中。

錄音內容
(A) Some shirts are on display.
(B) Sales assistants are standing near the table.
(C) Some clothes are piled on the floor.
(D) The shelves are filled with hangers.

錄音翻譯
(A) 有一些襯衫在展示。
(B) 銷售助理站在桌子附近。
(C) 有些衣服堆在地板上。
(D) 架子上擺滿了衣架。

③「人與物件」並存時

若照片同時有「人和物件」時，請注意下列重點：

⇨ 注意人與物件的「相對位置」（考介系詞）。

⇨ 注意人與物件有無「直接接觸」（考動作）。

● She's doing the dishes.
她在洗碗。

● She's using the washing machine.
她在用洗衣機。

● Passengers are boarding the aircraft.
乘客在登機。

● He has his hands on the buttons.
他的手放在按鈕上。

● Each person is rowing the boat.
每個人都在划船。

Word List
□ hanger [ˋhæŋɚ] *n.* 衣架

He's adjusting the screen.

他在調整螢幕。

They're pulling out a fire hose.

他們正在把消防水管拉出來。

A man is playing the musical instrument.

一名男子正在彈奏樂器。

Example 3

Ⓐ Ⓑ Ⓒ Ⓓ

3. 答案：(C)

〔圖析〕 實驗室裡,一名研究人員穿戴著防護衣、手套及口罩,手上握著東西。

〔解析〕 (A) 錯在動詞 walking；(B) 錯在動詞 removing；(D) 不但動詞 pushing 有誤,圖片中也沒有所見到 shopping cart（購物車）；(C) 關鍵字 wearing、protective clothing 與圖片描述一致,故為正確答案。

〔錄音內容〕 (A) She's walking to a laboratory.

(B) She's removing items from the shelves.

(C) She's wearing protective clothing.

(D) She's pushing a shopping cart.

〔錄音翻譯〕 (A) 她正走去實驗室。

(B) 她正把物品從架子上拿開。

(C) 她正穿著防護衣。

(D) 她在推購物車。

Word List

☐ fire hose [hoz] 消防水管

☐ laboratory [`læbrə͵torɪ] *n.* 實驗室 (= lab)

④ 以「場景」為主時

若照片中沒有人或特殊物件，而以場景爲主，請注意下列重點：

⇨ 所在何地？

⇨ 發生了什麼狀況？

● The buildings overlook the water.
　大樓俯瞰水面。

● A truck is parked next to the grass.
　有輛貨車停在草坪旁。

● The road is clogged with traffic.
　路上塞車。

● The wall is full of the advertisements.
　牆上貼滿了廣告。

● The platform is packed with people.
　月臺上擠滿了人。

● Buildings tower over the park.
　大樓屹立在公園旁。

● The tree is reflected in the water.
　樹影映照在水面上。

● The garden is full of flowers.
　花園裡種滿了花。

Word List

☐ overlook [͵ovɚ`luk] v. 俯瞰

☐ clog [klɑg] v. 堵塞

☐ tower [`tauɚ] v. 屹立

☐ reflect [rɪ`flɛkt] v. 反射；映出

Example 4

MP3
006

(A) (B) (C) (D)

4. 答案：(C)

圖析　一排車子停靠在路邊，圖片右邊有一排樹，但沒有人。

解析　照片中沒有花，也看不到駕駛人，也沒有人正在照料樹木，故 (A)、(B)、(D) 皆錯，(C) 的關鍵字 vehicles、parked、next to、curb 皆與圖片一致，故為正確答案。注意，(D) 句的 care for 為「照料」之意。

錄音內容　(A) Flowers are growing all along the street.
　　　　　(B) The drivers are standing next to their cars.
　　　　　(C) Some vehicles are parked next to the curb.
　　　　　(D) Some trees are being cared for.

錄音翻譯　(A) 沿路開滿了花。
　　　　　(B) 駕駛人都站在車子旁邊。
　　　　　(C) 有些車子停在路緣旁邊。
　　　　　(D) 有些樹正在被照料。

Word List
□ curb [kɜb] *n.* 路邊；（人行道的）邊欄
□ care for　照料

11

答題基本對策

① 事先做「圖片預測」

有些題目會問照片的主題是什麼，所以應考者必須了解照片的整體內容，亦即照片究竟顯示了什麼。所以，最好在錄音播放之前，事先檢視照片，對照片內容有一個整體概念，如此在聽取四個選項時，就比較容易選出正確的答案。

② 注意出題陷阱

在這個單元的測驗中，常會出現一些出題者刻意安排的陷阱，這些陷阱可能是一些發音相似的單字，也可能是人物情境的調換轉變等。需要特別注意的是一些錯誤的答案通常會包含一個聽起來像照片裡面某樣事物的字眼。這類題目主要是在測驗考生是否能正確判別類似發音的單字。例如，你在照片中看到的是：The woman is organizing her files. 但四個選項中可能會有一個答案會有 pile 這個字，而這就在測驗你是否能區別 file 和 pile 兩字的發音。所以，注意不要一聽到和題目主題有關的相似音就選，因為它們通常都是錯誤的選項。

③ 先作適當假設

有時候問題需要你針對照片的內容做出假設，例如因果關係（將會發生什麼事／已經發生什麼事）等。你需要了解照片想要表達的事情，並做出適當假設。例如，看到整個地面都是潮濕的，可以假設已經下過雨；或看到一個人站在販賣機前，可以假設他／她正要買東西。

破題關鍵要領

① 解題步驟 Step by Step

(1) 在錄音播放選項前先預覽照片，以了解大致主題。

(2) 確定照片內容為何，是只有人、只有物件，還是人與物件混合出現。

(3) 先看「最明顯」的重點，接著看「前景」、「兩邊」及「背景」。

(4) 聽錄音員在唸選項時，務必手、腦、耳並用。

眼看圖片，耳聽錄音內容，手放在答案卡紙上。

(5) 善用「消去法」來作答。

爭取時效並減少分神去聽不重要訊息的困擾。利用「消去法」來作答，有時不需聽完全部選項即可選出答案。

大師　關鍵指引

消去法原則：

1. 主詞不對 → 跳過
2. 動作不對 → 跳過
3. 介系詞不對 → 跳過
4. 受詞不對 → 跳過
5. 場景不對 → 跳過
6. 圖片中未呈現的事物（聽到圖片中沒有的字眼）→ 跳過
7. 聽到不懂單字時，利用句子其他聽得懂的線索來決定此句是對或錯。

---

(6) 利用消去法找出正確答案時，務必立即作答。

利用消去法時，手要在答案卡上跟著移動，若確定答案正確即立刻作答，若該句有一個字不對，立刻不聽完該句，立即將注意力放在下一個選項。

(7) 答完一題，爭取剩下時間預測下題圖片。

利用消去法選出最佳答案（沒有任何與圖片不符的選項）後，在錄音員唸出下一道題目之前，先去預測該題圖片。

(8) 進行下一道題目，並重複以上步驟。

大師 ┃ 關鍵指引

常見的選項陷阱類型：

1. 人物：

如，有二個人的照片中，男子在看報，女子正喝東西，但句子說成相反 → 男子在喝東西，女子在看報。

2. 動作：

如，一女子正在超市挑選商品，但句子說她正在結帳台付錢。

3. 場所：

如，一群人在室內體育場打籃球，但句子說在戶外籃球場。

4. 物體：

如，一男人旁有投影機，但句子說是電腦。

5. 天氣：

如，圖中沒看到有雨，但句子說在下雨。

6. 人物特徵：

如，兩人照片中，左邊的人有穿外套，右邊的人有戴眼鏡，但句子卻說左邊的人有戴眼鏡。

7. 有人沒人：

如，餐廳內空無一人，但句子說裡面擠滿了一群人。

8. 人物與物件的相對位置或關連：

如，一男子右邊有一瓶紅酒，但句子說在他前面有一瓶紅酒。

9. 背景：

如，一男子坐在桌前工作，背景牆上沒有壁畫，但句子卻說有壁畫。

10. 前景：

如，大廈前沒有任何棕梠樹，但句子卻說有棕梠樹在大廈前面。

② 文法時態非本大題出題重點

圖片題的選項敘述多半是以「現在進行式」、「現在簡單式」或「現在完成式」的句子來呈現，因此不用去擔心文法時態的問題。

1 現在簡單式

- A bridge crosses the waterway.

  橋跨越在河道上。

- Rows of chairs face the platform.

有好幾排椅子面對著講臺。

● Spaces are available in the parking lot.

停車場有空位。

● A ramp leads away from the road.

從道路延伸出一條斜坡。

● The bridge arches over fields and pastures.

橋拱立於田野和牧場之上。

● Her pencil needs sharpening.

她的鉛筆需要削尖。

2 現在進行式

● Someone is posting a notice.

有人在張貼告示。

● The woman is exiting the room.

女子正離開房間。

● These men are driving along the highway.

男子們在公路上開車。

● The pedestrian is walking behind the bench.

行人正從長凳後面走過。

● The bride is tossing flowers.

新娘在丟捧花。

3 現在完成式

● The paper has dropped to the ground.

報紙掉到了地上。

● A branch has fallen across the walkway.

有根樹枝掉在走道上。

Word List

☐ available [əˋveləbl] *adj.* 可利用的

☐ ramp [ræmp] *n.* 斜坡

☐ pasture [ˋpæstʃɚ] *n.* 牧草地;放牧場

☐ pedestrian [pəˋdɛstrɪən] *n.* 行人

☐ toss [tɔs] *v.* 拋;仍

● An orchestra has finished giving a performance.

交響樂團已經完成了表演。

● Food has been served to the patron.

菜已經被端給了客人。

● The players have finished their game.

球員打完了比賽。

● Some seats have been arranged on the floor.

有些椅子被擺在地上。

③ 「被動語態」是照片題的出題重點

要特別小心被動語態的用法，平時練習句子時，請試著將主動句換成被動句，如此才不會在考場上突然聽到被動用法而來不及反應。

● The tables are stacked next to each other.

桌子一張接一張地被堆放。

● The area is being evacuated.

這地區正在進行疏散。

● A row of trees has been planted.

有一排樹被種下。

● Chairs have been arranged around the table.

椅子圍繞桌子被擺放。

● The umbrellas have been folded up.

雨傘已經被收了起來。

● The table is cluttered with books and papers.

桌上堆滿了書和文件。

● The trash can has been knocked over.

垃圾桶被打翻了。

● The truck has been loaded onto the trailer.

貨車被裝進了拖車裡。

Word List

□ orchestra [`ɔrkɪstrə] *n.* 交響樂團

□ patron [`petrən] *n.* 顧客（尤指老顧客）

□ evacuate [ɪ`vækjuˌet] *v.* 從……撤離

□ fold [fold] *v.* 摺疊

□ clutter [`klʌtɚ] *v.* 堆滿

大師　關鍵指引

常用被動語態的動詞：

- be docked　停泊
- be pulled over　（車被）停靠路邊
- be parked along the street　沿著街道停靠
- be left open　開著
- be stacked up　被堆起
- be lined with　沿著……排列
- be towed away　被拖走
- be displayed　被陳列
- be piled up　被堆放

- be filled with people　充滿了人
- be crowded with people　人山人海
- be packed with people　擠滿了人
- be parked in a row　停成一排
- be seated　就座
- be made up of　由……組成
- be located at　位於
- be shaped like　形狀像
- be situated at　位於

④ 熟悉照片題出題基本句型

熟悉描述照片的基本句型，可以幫助你更快掌握解題重點。以下是照片描述題常見的基本句型：

① 主詞 + 動詞

- All the parking spaces have been taken.

  所有的停車位都滿了。

- The machinery has broken down.

  機器故障了。

- The computer is switched off.

  電腦關機了。

- All the chairs have been taken.

  所有的椅子都有人坐。

② 主詞 + 動詞 + 介系詞片語

- People are enjoying the park on a fine day.

  天氣很好，民眾在公園裡都很愉快。

- Fuel is being pumped into the vehicle.

  燃料正被加進車子裡。

Word List
- □ pump [pʌmp] *v.* 傾注；灌注

● Luggage is being loaded on the plane.

行李正被裝載上飛機。

● The luggage is lying on the carpet.

行李放在地毯上。

3 主詞 + be 動詞 + 主詞補語

● The workers are all in uniform.

工人全部穿著制服。

● The copier is out of order.

影印機壞了。

● A conference is under way.

會議正在進行。

● The area is currently unoccupied.

這個地方目前空無一人。

● They're in the middle of a meal.

他們正在用餐。

4 主詞 + 動詞／動詞片語 + 受詞

● They are both looking at the computer.

他們兩人都看著電腦。

● She's putting her telephone card into her bag.

她正把電話卡放進包包裡。

● The woman is picking up a book.

女子正拾起一本書。

● He's switching on the machine.

他正在啟動機器。

● They are enjoying the fine weather.

他們正享受著好天氣。

● Passengers are getting off the bus.

乘客正從公車上下車。

Word List
- [ ] under way 進行中
- [ ] recline [rɪˋklaɪn] *v.* 靠；躺
- [ ] intersection [ˌɪntəˋsekʃən] *n.* 十字路口

● She is putting a piece of paper on the glass.

她正把一張紙擺在玻璃杯上。

● The clerk is using the broom in the office.

職員正在辦公室裡使用掃把。

5 主詞 + 動詞 + 間接受詞（人）+ 直接受詞（事物或東西）
= 主詞 + 動詞 + 直接受詞 + 介系詞 + 間接受詞

● She is giving her boss a copy of the report.

= She is giving a copy of the report to her boss .

她正交給老闆一份報告。

● The man is passing the woman a bottle.

= The man is passing a bottle to the woman.

男子正把一個瓶子遞給女子。

6 There is/are 句型（有……）

● There is a traffic jam on the motorway.

高速公路上正在塞車。

● There are people waiting to use the copier.

有人等著使用影印機。

● There are three lanes of traffic in each direction.

每個方向都有三線道。

● There are only a few vehicles on the road.

路上只有幾輛車。

● There are many people standing up in the bus.

公車上有很多人站著。

Word List
□ broom [brum] *n.* 掃帚；長柄刷

□ motorway [`motəˏwe] *n.* 【英】高速公路

高頻字彙和情境用語

① 介系詞 & 片語介系詞

- in front of 在前面
- by 在旁邊
- on top of 在……上面
- at the top of 在……頂部
- across 在對面（橫跨）
- over 超過；在上面
- above 在上方
- close to 靠近
- underneath 在正下面
- below 在下面
- outside 在外面
- far from 離遠；完全不

- under 在下面
- toward 朝向
- behind 在後面
- at the bottom of 在……底部
- next to 在……旁邊
- beside 在旁邊
- nearby 接近
- inside 在裡面
- in back of 在……後面
- around 在周圍
- beneath 在下方
- to the right/left of 在……右／左邊

大師　關鍵指引

常考表「位置」的介系詞片語：

- near the bridge 在橋樑附近
- behind the door 在門後方
- on the girder 在主樑上
- at a construction site 在工地
- next to the shelf 在書架旁
- at the podium 在講台上
- in a hallway 走廊上
- at a service counter 在服務臺
- against the curb 靠在路邊
- in the corner 在角落
- down to the slope 下到斜坡上

- behind the man/woman 在男／女子後面
- across from the window 在窗戶對面
- on a support beam 在支樑上
- on top of the cabinet 在櫥櫃上面
- across the aisle 在走道對面
- at the table 在桌子旁；坐在餐桌座位上
- across the street 在對街
- on the other side of the road 在道路的另一側
- at the rear of the room 在房間的後面
- between the display cases 在陳列箱之間
- in front of the building 在建築物前面

Word List

- ☐ girder [ˋgɝdɚ] n.【建】大樑
- ☐ cabinet [ˋkæbənɪt] n. 櫥；櫃
- ☐ podium [ˋpodɪəm] n.（放講稿等的）講台
- ☐ slope [slop] n. 坡；斜面

② 常見工作與職稱

照片描述題常會考從照片推測照片中人物的職業,以下整理出常考的職業:

- chef 主廚
- waiter 男服務生
- bartender 酒保
- pediatrician 小兒科醫生
- optometrist 驗光配鏡師
- scientist 科學家
- veterinarian 獸醫
- newscaster 新聞廣播員
- teacher 老師
- barber 理髮師
- tailor 裁縫
- file clerk 檔案管理員
- landlord 房東
- clerk 辦事員;店員
- grocer 食品雜貨商
- baker 麵包師傅
- truck driver 卡車司機
- teller 銀行出納員
- welder 電焊工
- plumber 水電工
- police officer 警察
- fisherman 漁民
- model 模特兒
- artist 畫家
- employer 雇主
- security guard 安全警衛
- computer technician 電腦技師
- bricklayer/mason 砌磚工/泥水匠
- painter 油漆工
- assembly line worker 生產線工人

- cook 廚師
- waitress 女服務生
- doctor 醫生
- dentist 牙科醫生
- surgeon 外科醫生
- nurse 護士
- pharmacist 藥劑師
- journalist 記者
- hairdresser 美髮師
- hair stylist 髮型設計師
- seamstress 女縫紉工
- dock hand 碼頭工人
- repair personnel 維修人員
- florist 花店主
- butcher 屠夫;肉商
- sanitation worker 清潔工
- mechanic 機工/技工
- secretary 秘書
- salesperson 售貨員
- electrician 電工
- firefighter 消防員
- mail carrier 郵差
- farmer 農民
- photographer 攝影師
- colleague 同事
- employee 員工
- architect 建築師
- construction worker 建築工人
- carpenter 木匠
- window washer 洗窗工人

③ 常見背景和場所

• electronics store 電器用品店	• cafeteria 自助餐館
• concert hall 音樂廳	• hardware store 五金行
• museum 博物館	• supermarket 超級市場
• barber shop 理髮店	• clinic 診所
• daycare center 托嬰中心	• pharmacy 藥房
• travel agency 旅行社	• bakery 麵包店
• car dealership 汽車商	• grocery store 雜貨店
• movie theater 電影院	• shopping mall 購物中心
• video store 錄影帶出租店	• laboratory 實驗室
• restaurant 餐廳	• train station 火車站

④ 常考動詞

• be hanging 掛在	• be leaning against 倚靠在
• be falling into 正落入	• be drinking from a cup 正在用杯子喝（水）
• be wearing 穿（戴）著	• be vacuuming 在用吸塵器
• be pushing 正在推	• be folding one's arms 抱著雙臂
• be resting 在休息	• be making a copy 正在複印
• be performing 在表演	• be talking on the phone 正在打電話
• be staring 正在看	• be looking through a telescope 正透過望遠鏡看
• be canoeing 在划獨木舟	• be using a pay phone 正在打公共電話
• be addressing 在致詞	• be delivering a speech 在演說
• be purchasing 在採買	• be doing construction work 在進行建築工作
• be browsing 在瀏覽、翻閱	• be taking some notes 正在做筆記
• be feeding 正在餵	• be taking... down 正從……拿下
• be unloading 正在卸（貨）	• be approaching 正在接近
• be waiting 在等待	• be crossing the street 在穿越馬路
• be shaking hands 在握手	• be sitting in rows 坐了好幾排
• be chatting 在閒聊	• be having a conversation 在談話
• be installing 正在安裝	• be facing each other 互相看著對方
• be surfing 正在上網	• be taking the order 正在接受點餐
• be handing out 正在分發	• be working at the computer 正在用電腦工作
• be attending 在參加	• be studying the menu 正在看菜單
• be discussing 在談論	• be resting one's chin on one's hand 用手撐著下巴

⑤ 描述人物表情的形容詞

- disgusted 覺得厭惡的
- worried 擔心的
- shy 羞怯的
- confused 迷惑的
- pleased 喜悅的
- surprised 驚奇的
- shocked 震驚的
- displeased 不悅的

- embarrassed 尷尬的
- scared/afraid 受驚的
- bored 覺得厭煩的
- nervous 緊張不安的
- happy 高興的
- angry/mad 憤怒的
- sad 憂愁的
- confused 困惑的

⑥ 日常生活用語

❶ 家電用品

- vacuum cleaner 吸塵器
- air conditioner 冷氣機
- iron 熨斗
- dishwasher 洗碗機

- washing machine 洗衣機
- heater 暖爐
- sewing machine 裁縫機

❷ 廚房用品

- coffee maker 咖啡機
- oven 烤箱
- blender 攪拌器
- toaster 烤麵包機
- kettle 水壺
- steamer 蒸鍋
- cupboard 食物櫃；碗櫥
- sink 水槽
- food processor 食物處理機

- refrigerator 冰箱
- microwave oven 微波爐
- juicer 果汁機
- stove 爐子
- cooking pot 煮鍋
- electric cooker 電鍋
- grill 烤架
- dish rack 置盤架
- electric mixer 電動攪拌器

❸ 寢室用品

- pillowcase 枕頭套
- double bed 雙人床
- bed sheet 床單
- mattress 床墊
- quilt 棉被

- headboard 床頭板
- bunk bed 雙層床
- bed frame 床架
- blanket 毛毯
- pillow 枕頭

- hammock 吊床
- cot 小兒床；輕便帆布床
- cradle 搖籃

❹ 浴室用品
- bathtub 浴缸
- wash basin 洗手台
- faucet 水龍頭
- shower 淋浴設備
- towel rack 毛巾架
- mirror 鏡子

❺ 客廳用品
- couch 沙發
- rocking chair 搖椅
- stool 小凳子
- bookcase 書架
- wall lamp 壁燈
- carpet 地毯
- armchair 扶手椅
- bench 長椅
- end table 茶几
- curtain 窗簾
- wallpaper 壁紙
- rug 小地毯

❻ 交通工具
- automobile 汽車
- sports car 跑車
- van 廂型車
- minibus 小巴士
- bicycle (= bike) 腳踏車
- scooter 速克達（小輪摩托車）
- jet 噴射機
- chopper【俚】直昇機
- glider 滑翔機
- spaceship 太空船
- rocket 火箭
- cab/taxi 計程車
- limousine 豪華禮車
- tractor 牽引機
- double-decker bus 雙層巴士
- tricycle 三輪車
- motorcycle 摩托車；機車
- helicopter 直昇機
- airship 飛船
- parachute 降落傘
- space shuttle 太空梭

❼ 機場用語
- airliner 班機
- terminal 機場航廈
- departure lounge 候機室
- gate 登機門
- visa 簽證
- runway 跑道
- control tower 機場指揮塔；塔臺
- customs 海關
- boarding pass 登機證
- flight 航班

- duty-free shop 免稅商店
- check-in counter 報到櫃檯
- security check 安全檢查
- customs declaration card 海關申報卡
- baggage claim 行李提領處
- takeoff 起飛
- landing 降落
- captain 機長
- pilot 駕駛
- copilot 副駕駛
- flier 飛行員
- navigator 領航員
- ground crew 地勤人員
- flight attendant 空服人員
- aircrew 空勤人員
- cabin staff 客機服務人員（總稱）
- cabin 機艙
- cockpit 駕駛艙
- seatbelt 安全帶
- overhead compartment 座位上方之行李置物箱

8 飯店用語
- lobby 大廳
- receptionist 接待員
- bellhop【美口】行李員
- doorman 看門人
- concierge 門房
- reservation 預約
- booking 預訂
- vacancy 空房
- suite 套房

9 餐廳用語
- main course 主菜
- hors d'oeuvre 前菜
- appetizer 開胃菜
- starter 第一道菜
- soup 湯
- dessert 甜點
- lamb 小羊肉
- mutton 羊肉
- fowl 禽肉
- veal 小牛肉
- beef 牛肉
- poultry 家禽肉
- ham 火腿
- pork 豬肉
- mineral water 礦泉水
- bacon 培根
- champagne 香檳
- alcoholic drinks 含酒精飲料
- cider 蘋果酒
- beer 啤酒
- lemonade 檸檬水
- cocktail 雞尾酒
- coke 可樂
- (soda) pop【口】汽水；含氣飲料
- leftover 剩菜
- root beer 沙士

🔟 劇院／電影院用語

- box office 售票處
- row 排
- violin 小提琴
- trumpet 喇叭
- guitar 吉他
- aisle 走廊
- balcony 樓座
- drum 鼓
- flute 笛子
- symphony 交響曲

1️⃣1️⃣ 運動用語

- rugby 英式橄欖球
- badminton 羽毛球
- table tennis 桌球
- boxing 拳擊
- wrestling 摔角
- cricket 板球
- volleyball 排球
- football 足球

1️⃣2️⃣ 醫院用語

- cavity 蛀牙
- waiting room 候診室
- therapist 治療師
- sickroom/ward 病房
- consulting room 診察室
- flu 流行性感冒

1️⃣3️⃣ 電腦用語

- notebook/laptop 筆記型電腦
- keyboard 鍵盤
- hardware 硬體
- program 程式
- browser 瀏覽器
- modem 數據機
- printer 印表機
- version 版本
- monitor 螢幕
- mouse 滑鼠
- floppy disk 軟磁碟片
- website 網站
- homepage 首頁
- scanner 掃描器
- storage 保存
- virus 病毒

1️⃣4️⃣ 各類儀器和工具

- tool 工具
- implement 工具
- appliance 器具
- gadget 小巧的裝置
- machinery 機器（總稱）
- mechanism 機械裝置
- instrument 儀器
- apparatus 儀器
- device 裝置
- spare 備用（輪胎等）
- motor 馬達
- terminal 終端機

- beaker 燒杯
- microscope 顯微鏡
- hammer 槌子
- punch 打孔器
- screw 螺絲釘
- pocketknife 摺疊式小刀
- scissors 剪刀
- ax 斧頭

- flask 燒瓶
- knife 刀子
- drill 鑽子
- nail 鐵釘
- screwdriver 螺絲起子
- chisel 鑿子
- clippers 樹剪

⑦ 留意致命出題陷阱：相似音

照片描述題常會出現相似音的選項，要特別小心區分。出現包含圖片呈現事物之相似音的選項通常是陷阱，應避開不選。

▮ 常考相似音字詞

- lock [lɑk] 鎖 / look [lʊk] 看
- path [pæθ] 小徑 / pass [pæs] 通過
- personal [ˋpɝsn̩l] 個人的 / personnel [ˌpɝsˋn̩ɛl] 員工
- pillar [ˋpɪlə] 柱子 / pillow [ˋpɪlo] 枕頭
- rack [ræk] 架子 / wrack [ræk] 毀壞
- wrap [ræp] 包 / lap [læp] 膝部
- sew [so] 縫合 / saw [sɔ] 看（see 的過去式）
- sick [sɪk] 生病 / seek [sik] 尋找
- soar [sor] 高飛 / sore [sor] 疼痛的
- carve [kɑrv] 刻雕 / curve [kɝv] 曲線
- chef [ʃɛf] 主廚 / chief [tʃif] 首領
- cloud [klaʊd] 雲 / crowd [kraʊd] 人群
- court [kort] 法庭 / coat [kot] 外套
- desert [ˋdɛzɝt] 沙漠 / dessert [dɪˋzɝt] 甜點心
- due [dju] 應支付的 / do [du] 做
- dyeing [ˋdaɪɪŋ] 染色 / dying [ˋdaɪɪŋ] 垂死的
- firm [fɝm] 穩固的 / farm [fɑrm] 農場
- flow [flo] 流動 / floor [flor] 地板
- higher [haɪə] 較高的 / hire [haɪr] 租
- knit [nɪt] 編織 / neat [nit] 整潔的

- lunch [lʌntʃ] 午餐 / launch [lɔntʃ] 發行
- leap [lip] 跳 / reap [rip] 收割（莊稼）
- loan [lon] 借出 / lawn [lɔn] 草坪
- cost [kɔst] 花費 / coast [kost] 海岸
- weighing [ˋweɪŋ] 稱重量 / waiting [ˋwetɪŋ] 等候
- rag [ræg] 破布 / bag [bæg] 袋
- flower [flauɚ] 花 / flour [flaʊr] 麵粉
- rain [ren] 雨 / train [tren] 列車
- chair [tʃɛr] 椅子 / pear [pɛr] 洋梨
- bed 床 [bɛd] / bread [brɛd] 麵包
- stamp [stæmp] 郵票 / lamp [læmp] 燈
- lag [læg] 落後 / leg [lɛg] 腳
- broom [brum] 掃帚 / bloom [blum] 開花
- tree [tri] 樹 / three [θri] 三（的）
- walk [wɔk] 走 / work [wɝk] 工作
- firing [ˋfaɪrɪŋ] 燒毀 / wiring [ˋwaɪrɪŋ] 線路
- taste [test] 嚐 / test [tɛst] 考試
- towel [ˋtauəl] 毛巾 / tower [ˋtauɚ] 塔
- tire [taɪr] 輪胎；使疲倦 / tired [taɪrd] 疲倦的
- writing [ˋraɪtɪŋ] 書寫 / riding [ˋraɪdɪŋ] 騎
- clock [klɑk] 時鐘 / clerk [klɝk] 辦事員；店員
- coffee [ˋkɔfɪ] 咖啡 / café [kəˋfe] 咖啡廳
- water [ˋwɔtɚ] 水 / waiter [ˋwetɚ] 服務生

② 同音異義字

- blue 藍色 / blew 吹
- mail 郵件 / male 男性
- peace 和平 / piece （一）件
- eight 八 / ate 吃下（過去式）
- meet 遇見 / meat 肉
- weak 弱的 / week 週
- rain 雨水 / rein 韁繩
- pail 桶 / pale 蒼白的
- plain 樸素 / plane 平面；飛機

- pole 竿 / poll 民意測驗
- read 讀 / reed 蘆葦
- right 正確 / write 寫
- root 根 / route 路線
- sail 篷；帆 / sale 出售
- scene 一場 / seen 看（see 的過去分詞）
- hole 洞 / whole 全部的
- heard 聽（hear 的過去式和過去分詞）/ herd 畜群
- stair 樓梯 / stare 盯
- peer 凝視 / pier 碼頭
- cent 一分值的硬幣 / sent 送（send 的過去式和過去分詞）
- site 地點 / sight 視覺
- fair 公正的 / fare （交通工具的）票價
- heal 治癒 / heel 腳後跟
- tail 尾巴 / tale 從事
- close 關閉 / clothes 衣服

3 詞性改變而意義不同的單字

- present [prˋzɛnt] v. 呈現 / present [ˋprɛzṇt] n. 禮物
- object [əbˋdʒɛkt] v. 反對 / object [ˋɑbdʒɪkt] n. 物體
- record [rɪˋkɔrd] v. 錄音 / record [ˋrɛkəd] n. 記錄；唱片
- contract [kənˋtrækt] v. 收縮；感染 / contract [ˋkɑntrækt] n. 合約
- progress [prəˋgrɛs] v. 前進 / progress [ˋprɑgrɛs] n. 進步
- produce [prəˋdjus] v. 生產 / produce [ˋprɑdjus] n. 農產品

⑧ 頻出字彙英美說法比較

美式用法	英式用法	字義
truck	lorry	卡車
gas (gasoline)	petrol	汽油
sidewalk	pavement/footpath	人行道
traffic circle	roundabout	圓環
overpass	flyover	高架橋；天橋
intersection	junction/crossroads	十字路口

street car	tram	路面電車
subway	underground/tube	地下鐵
sweater	jumper/jersey	毛衣
underwear	pants	內褲（內衣）
bathrobe	dressing gown	浴袍
purse	handbag	（女性用）手提包
drapes	curtains	窗簾
couch	sofa/settee	沙發
crib	cot	嬰兒床
stroller	pushchair	嬰兒推車
tub	bath	浴缸
flashlight	torch	手電筒
yard	garden	庭院
apartment	flat	公寓
elevator	lift	電梯
mail	post	郵件
zip code	post code	郵遞區號
downtown	city centre	市中心
can	tin	罐頭
eraser	rubber	橡皮擦
soccer	football	足球
football	American football	美式足球
intermission	interval	中場休息
movie theater	cinema	電影院

Exercises

①

②

③

④

詳解

1. 答案：(D)

圖 析 一個工人站在梯子上，並在檢查紅綠燈訊號裝置。

解 析 (A) 不對，梯子並非靠在 pole（柱子）上；(B) 與照片不符，場地並沒有用繩子圍住（roped off）；(C) 也不對，照面中並無車流（traffic）。(D) 關鍵字 worker、checking、signal 皆與圖片一致，為正確答案。

錄音內容 (A) The ladder is leaning against the pole.
(B) The area has been roped off.
(C) Traffic is moving in one direction.
(D) The worker is checking the signal.

錄音翻譯 (A) 梯子靠在柱子上。
(B) 場地被繩子圍住。
(C) 車流單向前進。
(D) 工人正在檢查號誌。

□ pole [pol] *n.* 柱；竿　　　　□ signal [ˋsɪɡn̩] *n.* 號誌

2. 答案：(A)

圖 析 可眺望海洋的戶外露台上有幾張桌椅排成一排，但照片中並沒有人。

解 析 (A) 關鍵字 tables、arranged、line 皆與圖片敘述一致，為正確答案。(B) 露台被幾棵樹遮蔽、(C) 椅子被推靠著牆壁和 (D) 用餐的人坐在太陽下皆與照片不符。

錄音內容 (A) The tables are arranged in a line.
(B) The patio is shaded by several trees.
(C) The chairs are pushed against the wall.
(D) The diners are sitting in the sun.

錄音翻譯 (A) 桌子被排成一列。
(B) 露台被幾棵樹遮蔽。
(C) 椅子被推靠著牆壁。
(D) 用餐的人坐在太陽下。

□ patio [ˋpatɪo] *n.* 露臺　　　　□ diner [ˋdaɪnɚ] *n.* 用餐的人

3. 答案：(D)

圖 析 一名女子在超市挑選水果，身前有一個推車，裡面有一些商品。

解 析 照片中的女子並非在付錢，也沒有在提籃子，更不是在做菜，故 (A)、(B)、(C) 皆錯。(D) 中的關鍵字 selecting 及 produce 與圖片敘述一致，故為正確答案。注意此處的 produce 是名詞，為「農產品」之意。

錄音內容 (A) She's paying for some groceries.
(B) She's picking up a basket.
(C) She's preparing a meal.
(D) She's selecting some produce.

錄音翻譯 (A) 她正在付一些雜貨的帳。
(B) 她正提起一個籃子。
(C) 她正在做菜。
(D) 她正在挑選一些農產品。

□ grocery [ˋɡrosərɪ] *n.* 食品雜貨　　　□ produce [ˋprɑdjus] *n.* 農產品

---

4. 答案：(C)

圖 析 旅館房間內有二張鋪有床單及枕頭的單人床，床的兩側各有一盞壁燈。

解 析 (A) 有誤，因為燈在床頭而非床尾；(B) 不能選，因為房間裡並沒有客人（guest）；(D) 則錯在房間並沒有掛畫（painting）。本題應選 (C)，關鍵字 pillows、placed、beds 皆與圖片敘述一致。

錄音內容 (A) There's a pair of lamps at the foot of the bed.
(B) The guests are relaxing in the room.
(C) Pillows have been placed on the beds.
(D) There's a painting hanging on the wall.

錄音翻譯 (A) 床尾有一對燈。
(B) 客人在房內休息。
(C) 有枕頭被擺在床上。
(D) 牆上掛著一幅畫。

5. 答案：(D)

圖 析 火車停靠在月台旁邊，但月台空無一人。

解 析 (A)不對，因為圖中並無乘客；(B) 有誤，因為圖中並未見車掌（conductor）；(C) 不可選，因為看不出火車是進站還是離站。(D) 關鍵字 platform、nearly、deserted 皆與圖片吻合，故為正確答案。

錄音內容 (A) Passengers are boarding the train.

(B) The conductor is checking tickets.

(C) Trains are departing the station.

(D) The platform is nearly deserted.

錄音翻譯 (A) 乘客正在上車。

(B) 車掌正在查票。

(C) 火車正駛離車站。

(D) 月台幾近空蕩。

□ conductor [kən`dʌktə] *n.* （電車、巴士的）車掌

□ deserted [dɪ`zɝtɪd] *adj.* 空寂無人的；被遺棄的

Part 2

Question-Response
應 答 問 題

題型簡介

Part 2「應答問題」共 30 題（11 ～ 40 題），每題會聽到一個問題及三種不同的回應，問題及三個選項只播放一次，且錄音內容不會印在試題本上，因此沒有任何視覺線索。考生必須專心聆聽問題和選項，並在三個選項中選出一個最適合回答問題的答案。通常進行方式是男生提問，女生回答；或女生提問，男生回答。在多益測驗中，只有這個部分是三選一的形式。

出題預覽

Mark your answer on your answer sheet. Ⓐ Ⓑ Ⓒ

答案：(B)

錄音內容

How was your vacation?

(A) I never go on vacation.

(B) I had a lot of fun.

(C) I'm going on vacation next week.

錄音翻譯

你的假期過得如何？

(A) 我從未去度假。

(B) 我玩得很盡興。

(C) 我下週將去度假。

✥ 題型透析

類型一

1 資訊題：Wh 問句

由 what/when/where/who/why/how/which 開始的問句，要根據問題（Wh...）所問的重點回答明確的資訊。

● A: <u>Where</u> can I rent a van for a couple of weeks?

B: You should try the agency next to the hotel.

A：我可以去哪裡租用小貨車幾個星期？

B：你應該去飯店隔壁的租賃公司試試看。

● A: <u>When</u> can we pick up our reimbursement check?

B: <u>As soon as</u> purchasing approves it.

A：我們什麼時候可以來拿退款支票？

B：經採購部核准即可。

● A: <u>How many</u> copies should I make?

B: Ten should be <u>plenty</u>.

A：我應該印幾份？

B：十份應該就夠了。

● A: <u>How often</u> does the CEO visit this office?

B: Sorry, I'm a <u>newcomer</u> here.

A：執行長多久來這間辦公室一次？

B：抱歉，我是這裡的新人。

● A: <u>Why</u> didn't you accept their job offer?

B: I <u>already got hired</u> somewhere else.

A：你為什麼沒有接受他們的工作？

B：我已經應徵上別處的工作了。

Word List

□ reimbursement [ˌriɪmˈbɜsmənt] *n.* 償還；退款

□ newcomer [ˈnjuˈkʌmə] *n.* 新人

● A: <u>Who</u>'s going to be responsible for the new department?

B: <u>Mr. Duncan</u> from the accounting department.

A：這個新部門會由誰負責？

B：會計部的鄧肯先生。

● A: <u>How</u> would you like to take a vacation next week?

B: I'd like to, but <u>I'm too busy</u>.

A：你下星期想不想去度個假？

B：我很想，可是我太忙了。

● A: <u>What</u> is the subject of your report?

B: <u>How we can improve sales</u>.

A：你的報告主題是什麼？

B：我們可以如何改善銷售。

● A: <u>Whose</u> duty is it to organize the annual conference?

B: It's <u>Nina's</u> job.

A：籌備年會是誰的職責？

B：那是妮娜的工作。

Example

MP3 013 ▶▶ MP3 016

1. Mark you answer on your answer sheet.   Ⓐ Ⓑ Ⓒ

2. Mark you answer on your answer sheet.   Ⓐ Ⓑ Ⓒ

3. Mark you answer on your answer sheet.   Ⓐ Ⓑ Ⓒ

4. Mark you answer on your answer sheet.   Ⓐ Ⓑ Ⓒ

---

1. 答案：(C)

[破題] Why/office chairs/lobby? ⇨ 問「原因」。

[解析] (A) 不對，因為用 Why 問的句子，不可用 Yes 或 No 回應。(B) 答非所問，原問句問的是 office chairs，回答時說的是「人」。(C) They 代表問句之 chairs，而 cleaning the carpets 則解釋了椅子在 looby 的原因。

录音内容 Why are all the office chairs in the lobby?

(A) No, there are also some in the meeting room.

(B) He must be waiting to see the general manager.

(C) They're cleaning the carpets this weekend.

录音翻译 辦公室的椅子為什麼都在大廳裡？

(A) 不，也有一些在會議室裡。

(B) 他一定是等著要見總經理。

(C) 他們本週末要清理地毯。

2. 答案：(C)

破 題 Who/ready/dessert? ⇨ 問「人」。

解 析 (A) 主詞錯誤，The cake 不是人。(B) 動詞錯誤，read 跟題目無關。(C) I 回應了問題重點，而 couldn't eat another bite（一口都吃不下）則說明了原因。

录音内容 Who's ready for dessert?

(A) The cake is delicious.

(B) I read it this morning.

(C) I couldn't eat another bite.

录音翻译 誰準備要吃甜點了？

(A) 蛋糕很好吃。

(B) 我今天早上看了。

(C) 我一口都吃不下了。

3. 答案：(B)

破 題 What/Mr. Park's suggestion? ⇨ 問「建議內容」。

解 析 (A) 錯誤，因 Wh 問句不用 yes 或 no 回答。(B) He wanted to close the downtown location（他想要結束市區的據點）回答了 Mr. Parker 的意見，故為正確選項。(C)答非所問，問句問的是 Mr. Park，與 we 無關。

録音內容 What was Mr. Park's suggestion for lowering costs?
(A) No, he wasn't able to reduce the price.
(B) He wanted to close the downtown location.
(C) Perhaps we should consider buying one too.

録音翻譯 帕克先生對降低成本有什麼建議？
(A) 不，他沒辦法降價。
(B) 他想要結束市區的據點。
(C) 也許我們也應該考慮買一個。

4. 答案：(B)

破 題 How much/to the airport? ⇨ 問「價錢」。

解 析 (A) 的 45 minutes 表「時間」，答非所問。(B) 的 between 20 and 25 euros（20～25 歐元之間）答出價錢，故為正確答案。(C) Head north 表「進行方向」，與題目毫不相關。

録音內容 How much is it to the airport?
(A) About 45 minutes if there's no traffic.
(B) It should be between 20 and 25 euros.
(C) Head north on Highway 15 and follow the signs.

録音翻譯 到機場要少多錢？
(A) 如果沒有車陣，大約要 45 分鐘。
(B) 應該是 20～25 歐元之間。
(C) 由 15 號高速公路往北，然後依循標示。

類型二

② 以 Yes/No 回答的問句

通常是由 Are you... / Is he... / Can they... / Would you... / Did she... / Do we... / Does it... / Have you... 等「be 動詞」開頭或「助動詞」開頭的問句，回答時一般以 yes 或 no 來回答。

● A: <u>Is</u> there any space in the storage room for these files?

B: <u>No</u>, but I can make some room for you.

A：貯藏室裡有沒有任何空間可以放這些檔案？

B：沒有，不過我可以挪一些空間給你。

● A: <u>Have</u> you filed your income taxes yet?

B: <u>No</u>, the accountant is working on them now.

A：你申報所得稅了沒？

B：還沒，會計師目前正在處理。

● A: <u>Am</u> I late for the meeting?

B: <u>Yes</u>, but no one will notice.

A：我開會是否遲到了？

B：是的，不過沒有人會注意。

● A: <u>Can</u> you finish editing report for me?

B: <u>Yes</u>, I can look at it.

A：你能幫我把報告編輯完嗎？

B：好，我可以幫你看看。

不過，回答時也常省略 yes 或 no：

● A: <u>Did</u> you receive the contracts yet?

B: We will receive them later today.

A：你們收到合約了嗎？

B：我們會在今天稍晚收到。

● A: <u>Do</u> you have a pen I can borrow?

B: Sorry, this is my only one.

A：你有筆可以借我嗎？

B：抱歉，這是我唯一的一枝。

● A: <u>Is</u> your air conditioner going to be fixed soon?

B: In a few days, I hope.

A：你的空調會很快修好嗎？

B：幾天就會修好，希望如此。

Word List
☐ file [faɪl] *v.* 提出（申請）

● A: <u>May</u> I take these documents later?

B: You can have them now, if you want.

A：我晚點可以帶走這些文件嗎？

B：假如你想要的話，現在就可以帶走。

Example

 MP3 017

5. Mark you answer on your answer sheet. Ⓐ Ⓑ Ⓒ

 詳 解

5. 答案：(A)

[破 題] Can/you/recommend/place/lunch? ⇨ 請對方推薦。

[解 析] (A) There's deli around the corner.（轉角有家熟食店）回應了問題，為正確選項。(B) 答非所問，No, thanks 為回答對方「提供」或「邀請」的答案。(C) 與原問句毫無關聯。

[錄音內容] Can you recommend a good place for lunch?

(A) There's a deli around the corner.

(B) No, thanks. I've already eaten.

(C) My favorite gallery has a new exhibit.

[錄音翻譯] 你能不能推薦一個用午餐的好地方？

(A) 轉角有一家熟食店。

(B) 不了，謝謝。我已經吃過了。

(C) 我最喜歡的藝廊有新的展覽。

☐ deli [ˋdɛlɪ] *n.* 熟食店　　　　　　　☐ exhibit [ɪgˋzɪbɪt] *n.* 展覽（品）

❸ 附加問句

在句尾常會聽到 ..., are you? / ..., don't they? / ..., aren't they? / ..., doesn't he? / ..., isn't it? / ..., wouldn't you? / ..., haven't you? 等這類的問句形式，一般回答的重點在於「同意」或「不同意」說話者的敘述。

● A: Johnny needs to pay a fee before he can become a member, <u>doesn't he</u>?

B: That's what he told me.

A：強尼需要付費才能成為會員，不是嗎？

B：他是這樣告訴我的。

● A: The new model is more expensive, <u>isn't it</u>?

B: No, the price is about the same.

A：新款比較貴，不是嗎？

B：不會，價錢差不多。

● A: You bought a new copy machine, <u>didn't you</u>?

B: No, I just had the old one repaired.

A：你買了一台新的影印機，不是嗎？

B：沒有，我只是拿舊的去修。

● A: You plan to give your presentation next Friday, <u>right</u>?

B: I haven't decided on a schedule yet.

A：你打算下星期五要提報，對吧？

B：我還沒有決定時間。

大師 | 關鍵指引

附加問句句尾可能出現的其他句型：

- ..., don't you think?
- ..., right?
- ..., OK?
- ..., would you say?

Example

6. Mark you answer on your answer sheet.　　ⒶⒷⒸ

---

6. 答案：(A)

> **破　題**　You haven't seen.../have you? ⇨ 為附加問句，問對方「有沒有看到」。

> **解　析**　(A) Not since + 時間，表自從那個時間點開始就沒有，故為正確答案。(B) 問句詢問有沒有看到 my address book（我的通訊錄），回答 Mike's phone number，答非所問。(C) 要對方 put it anywhere you like（愛放哪就放哪），文不對題。

> **錄音內容**　You haven't seen my address book anywhere, have you?
> (A) Not since the meeting yesterday.
> (B) Yes, I need Mike's phone number.
> (C) Just put it anywhere you'd like.

> **錄音翻譯**　你都沒看到我的通訊錄，有嗎？
> (A) 從昨天開會後就沒看到了。
> (B) 對，我需要麥克的電話號碼。
> (C) 你愛放哪就放哪。

④ 否定問句 = 助動詞 + not

通常是由 Wasn't... / Aren't... / Don't... / Hasn't... 等開頭，可能以 Yes/No 或其他說法來回答。

● A: <u>Aren't</u> you coming to our Christmas party, Monica?
　　B: I'm not sure yet.
　　A：莫妮卡，妳不來我們的耶誕派對嗎？
　　B：我還不確定。

● A: <u>Can't</u> he speak Chinese?

B: Unfortunately, he can't.

A：他不會說中文嗎？

B：很遺憾，他不會。

● A: <u>Don't</u> you want to bring a bigger suitcase on the trip?

B: Maybe you're right.

A：你不想帶大一點的手提箱去旅行嗎？

B：或許你說得對。

● A: <u>Didn't</u> you hear that the conference has been postponed?

B: Really? For how long?

A：你沒聽說會議延期了嗎？

B：真的嗎？要延多久？

大師 關鍵指引

常聽到的否定問句句型：

- Can't you...?
- Didn't you...?
- Weren't you...?
- Wasn't he...?
- Haven't they...?

- Don't you...?
- Does he...?
- Isn't she...?
- Aren't they...?
- Hasn't he...?

Example

7. Mark you answer on your answer sheet.　　　　Ⓐ Ⓑ Ⓒ

Word List
□ unfortunately [ʌn`fɔrtʃənɪtlɪ] *adv.* 遺憾地；可惜

□ postpone [post`pon] *v.* 使延期

7. 答案：(C)

> **破題** Don't you/want/hire? ➪ 否定問句，詢問對方「不想嗎」。

> **解析** (A) followed the instructions 與原句毫無關聯；(B) 牛頭不對馬嘴；故 (C) 為正確答案。

錄音內容 Don't you want to hire an assistant?
　　　　　(A) I just followed the instructions.
　　　　　(B) On the shelf above the copier.
　　　　　(C) Yes, but not right now.

錄音翻譯 你不想雇用一位助理嗎？
　　　　　(A) 我只是照指示。
　　　　　(B) 在複印機上頭的櫃子。
　　　　　(C) 想啊，但不是現在。

⑤ 選擇性問句

這類問句是以 or 連接兩個選項，要回答者選擇前者或後者。

● A: Can you install this program, <u>or</u> do you want me to call the help desk?
　 B: I could use some help, I think.
　 A：你會安裝這個程式嗎，還是你要我找服務窗口？
　 B：我可能需要一些協助。

● A: Should we send this document by overnight mail <u>or</u> bring it in person?
　 B: Whichever you think is better.
　 A：我們應該用隔夜郵件寄出這份文件，還是親自帶去？
　 B：看你覺得怎樣比較好。

● A: Do you want to work overtime <u>or</u> do it first thing in the morning?
　 B: The latter is better.
　 A：你希望加班，還是明天一大早做？
　 B：後者比較好。

Word List
　　□ in person　親自

● A: Would you prefer the blue model <u>or</u> the yellow one?

　B: Either one is fine with me.

　A：你喜歡藍色的還是黃色的款式？

　B：我哪一款都可以。

Example

8. Mark you answer on your answer sheet.　　　Ⓐ　Ⓑ　Ⓒ

---

8. 答案：(B)

　破　題 Would/you/call/or/someone else? ➡ 希望對方回答 A 或 B。

　解　析 (A) 重覆題目字 Tina，而 nickname 與問題毫無關係。(B) Let's... 表建議，give Janice a chance 表示讓 Janice 來做，回話者選擇了 someone else，故為正確選項。(C) 答非所問。

　錄音內容 Would you like to call Tina, or ask someone else to work on it?
　　　　(A) Tina is just her nickname.
　　　　(B) Let's give Janice a chance.
　　　　(C) I'll let her know it's already done.

　錄音翻譯 你想找提娜，還是請別人來做？
　　　　(A) 提娜只是她的小名。
　　　　(B) 我們給珍妮絲一個機會吧。
　　　　(C) 我會通知她說已經做完了。

---

⑥ 插入句

這類問句的詢問重點在於句子中的「間接問句」，回答者需針對這個問題回答。

● A: Does anyone know <u>when</u> the train for Tokyo arrives?

　B: It'll be here in twelve minutes.

　A：有沒有人知道開往東京的火車何時會到？

　B：12 分鐘之內就會到站。

● A: Can you tell me <u>where</u> the meeting is held?

B: I haven't seen the agenda.

A：你可不可以告訴我會議在那裡召開？

B：我還沒看到議程。

● A: Would you mind <u>if</u> I skip this workshop?

B: No, you don't have to be here.

A：你介不介意我不出席這場研討會？

B：不會，你不必參加。

● A: Do you know <u>where</u> the company picnic will be held?

B: It hasn't been announced yet.

A：你知不知道公司要在哪裡辦野餐？

B：還沒有宣布。

● A: Does anyone know <u>where</u> Mr. Williams is?

B: I haven't seen him.

A：有沒有人知道威廉斯先生在哪裡？

B：我沒有看到他。

大師　關鍵指引

常考的插入句句型：

• Do you know why...?
• Can you tell me how...?
• Do you know why...?

• Would you mind if...?
• Do you know when...?

Example

9. Mark you answer on your answer sheet.　

Word List

☐ agenda [əˋdʒɛndə] *n.* 議程；待議事項

☐ skip [skɪp] *v.*（故意）不出席；不參加

☐ workshop [ˋwɜkˌʃɑp] *n.*

9. 答案：(A)

> 破題 Do you think/Julie/could/take over? ⇨ 為插入句，重點在 Do you think 之後的子句。

> 解析 (A) I don't see why not（我看不出有何不可），表「同意」對方的意見，為正確答案。(B) At 7:30 表「時間」，答非所問。(C) 原句問的是 Julie，不應用 I 回答。

> 錄音內容 Do you think Julie could take over for Frank while he's on leave?
> (A) I don't see why not.
> (B) At about 7:30.
> (C) No, I'll send it myself.

> 錄音翻譯 你認為茱莉可以在法蘭克休假時接手嗎？
> (A) 我看不出有何不可。
> (B) 大約 7:30。
> (C) 不會，我會親自送過去。

☐ take over 接管

7 表「建議」、「請求」或「邀請」的問句

這類問句一般是希望回答者表明「要」或「不要」的意願。

● A: <u>Could you</u> please send up some fresh towels?
B: Certainly, they will be sent up right away.
A：能不能麻煩你送幾條新毛巾上來？
B：好的，馬上就送去。

● A: <u>Could I</u> use your phone, please?
B: Sure, go ahead.
A：我可以用你的電話嗎？
B：當然可以，請用。

● A: <u>Why don't we</u> spend the afternoon at the park?
B: That sounds like a good idea.
A：我們下午何不去公園走走？
B：聽起來似乎是個好主意。

● A: **Shouldn't you** fill in the registration form and send it in?

　B: Right. Thanks for reminding me.

　A：你不是應該填寫並繳交登記表嗎？

　B：對，謝謝你提醒。

● A: **Wouldn't you like** some sandwiches for lunch?

　B: Yes, that would be great.

　A：你午餐不想來點三明治嗎？

　B：好啊，太好了。

● A: **Would you like** some bread with your soup?

　B: Yes, that sounds good.

　A：您要不要來一些麵包配湯？

　B：好，聽起來不錯。

● A: **Would you mind if** I sat next to you in the conference?

　B: Not at all.

　A：你介不介意我在開會時坐你隔壁？

　B：完全不介意。

大師　關鍵指引

常考表「建議」或「邀請」的直述句問句：Let's + V + ...

這類句子通常要對方去做說話者要求的動作。

- A: Let's talk about this over lunch .

  B: That's a good idea. Where should we go?

  A：我們在午餐時談談這件事吧。

  B：這是個好主意。我們應該去哪裡好呢？

- A: Let's ask the CEO for an autograph.

  B: I think we need to wait in a long line, then.

  A：我們去請執行長簽個名吧。

  B：那我想我們得排隊等很久。

Word List

　　□ registration [ˌrɛdʒɪˋstreʃən] *n.* 登記；註冊

　　□ autograph [ˋɔtəˌgræf] *n.* （尤指名人的）親筆簽名

大師 關鍵指引

常考表「建議」、「請求」、「邀請」的問句：

- How about...?
- Why don't you...?
- Should we...?
- Would you...?

- What about...?
- Could you...?
- Can I...?
- Would you mind...?

Example

10. Mark you answer on your answer sheet.   Ⓐ Ⓑ Ⓒ

 詳 解

10. 答案：(A)

破 題 Why don't you/extend/deadline? ⇨ 表「建議」。

解 析 (A) I don't think（表個人看法），that 指 extend the deadline 這件事，故整句話表不接受對方建議，為正確答案。(B) 文不對題。(C) 答非所問。

錄音內容 Why don't you extend the deadline by a day or two?
   (A) I don't think that will be necessary.
   (B) Ms. Lawry asked you to call her tomorrow.
   (C) It's on my table next to the calendar.

錄音翻譯 你何不把截止期限延個一、兩天？
   (A) 我認為沒那個必要。
   (B) 羅瑞女士要你明天打電話給她。
   (C) 它在我桌上的行事曆旁。

類型四

8 直述句

此爲多益的新型考題，難度在於須從直述句中聽出說話者的意圖或目的。

● A: <u>The memo says that</u> several people will be absent from the meeting.

B: In that case, we should change the seating arrangement.

A：備忘錄上說，有幾個人不會參加會議。

B：這樣的話，我們應該調整一下座位安排。

● A: <u>I think</u> the seminar will be held near our office.

B: Actually, I heard it was across town.

A：我想研討會會在我們辦公室附近舉行。

B：事實上，我聽說是在城的另一邊。

● A: <u>Julia was</u> late for the meeting again.

B: I'm not surprised.

A：茱麗亞開會又遲到了。

B：我並不意外。

● A: <u>I managed to</u> find the missing copies.

B: I've been looking for those for hours.

A：我總算找到了遺失的文件。

B：我找了好幾個小時。

大師　關鍵指引

常考的直述句句型：

- It seems as if....
- I love....
- It's....
- I heard....

- There's a....
- I'd like you to....
- Sb. is... again.

Word List
□ seminar [ˈsɛmənar] *n.* 研討會；討論會

Example

11. Mark you answer on your answer sheet.   Ⓐ Ⓑ Ⓒ

11. 答案：(A)

破題 You/too busy/to discuss/proposal ⇨ too busy to... 說明對方「沒空」作某事。

解析 (A)「我現在有一點時間」為合理回答。Actually... 通常用來說明實情。(B) 不知所云。(C) minimum charge（最低消費）與問題無關。

錄音內容 You're probably too busy to discuss Kathy Wagner's proposal.
(A) Actually, I have some time now.
(B) I've been here for two years.
(C) There's no minimum charge.

錄音翻譯 你大概太忙沒空討論凱西‧韋格納的提案。
(A) 事實上，我現在有一點時間。
(B) 我在這裡兩年了。
(C) 沒有最低消費。

☐ minimum [ˈmɪnəməm] *n.* 最小量；最低限度

⑨ 直述句 + 疑問句

「直述句」後面加「疑問句」的考題必須兩個句子的重點都要聽到，才能判斷答案。

● A: It's too crowded in this café. How about going to another place?
B: Yeah, let's go somewhere else.
A：這家咖啡店太擠了。去別的地方怎麼樣？
B：好啊，我們就去其他地方吧。

● A: <u>I need</u> to go home. <u>How</u> should I go?

B: Take the train to 2nd and then go south 3 blocks to Kim Avenue.

A：我必須回家。我該怎麼走？

B：搭火車到第二街，然後往南走三個街區到金恩大道。

● A: <u>Human resources approved</u> the position. <u>Are</u> you going to apply?

B: Unfortunately, I am not qualified so I don't think I will.

A：人力資源部核准了這個職位。你要不要申請？

B：很不幸，我不符合資格，所以我想我不會去。

Example

12. Mark you answer on your answer sheet.　　Ⓐ　Ⓑ　Ⓒ

---

12. 答案：(C)

破 題 How about/launching/product? ⇨「建議」產品在五月上市。

解 析 (A) reasonable priced 指「定價合理」，並未回應題目重點。(B) 回答的是「地方」，答非所問。(C)「不太確定到時是否已做好準備」為合理回應，即指不太會接受說話者的建議。

錄音內容 The factory will be operational in April. How about launching the product in May?

(A) I think it's reasonably priced.

(B) At the Italian restaurant across the street.

(C) I'm not sure we'll be ready by then.

錄音翻譯 工廠在四月就會啓用。產品在五月上市如何？

(A) 我覺得這是合理的定價。

(B) 在對街的義大利餐廳。

(C) 我不確定到時我們是否已做好準備。

☐ operational [ˌɑpəˋreʃənḷ] *adj.* 操作上的；啓用的

☐ launch [ˋlɔntʃ] *v.* （產品）上市；推出

☐ price [praɪs] *v.* 定價

⑩ 由平述句直接形成的問句

這類問句要注意問句的上升語調，回答者則需回答「要」或「不要」。

● A: Lucy <u>can't</u> go to the movies tomorrow?

B: No, she has plans with Billy.

A：露西明天不能去看電影嗎？

B：對，她跟比利有約。

Example MP3 025

13. Mark you answer on your answer sheet.

詳 解

13. 答案：(A)

破 題 You can't join us for lunch? ⇨ 表驚訝並希望對方說明原因。

解 析 本題原問句是問「對方為何不能一起吃午餐？」，(A) I am expecting a call（我在等電話）說明了無法一起用餐原因，為正確答案。(B) Why don't we... 常用於邀請或給予建議，無法回應原問句，不選。(C) 答非所問。

錄音內容 You can't join us for lunch?

(A) I'm expecting a call from Ms. Greene.

(B) Why don't we invite the new accountant?

(C) I brought a small printer from home.

錄音翻譯 你不能和我們一塊吃午餐嗎？

(A) 我在等葛林先生的電話。

(B) 我們何不邀請新來的會計？

(C) 我從家裡帶來一部小型的印表機。

☐ expect sb's call 等某人電話

答題基本對策

① 先掌握題型

充分了解「問題類型」，有助於聽出問題的重點及目的。

② 對症下藥

針對「問題重點」，選擇「最合適」的答案。與題目重點無關的選項，立刻「不聽」下去並跳至下個選項。

③ 先聽疑問詞

播放錄音內容時，先聽問題的疑問詞，接著為主詞、動詞及受詞。

④ 留心「重音字」

聆聽錄音內容時，留心問句和選項的「重音字」，例如：動詞、名詞、形容詞、副詞等字。

⑤ 注意「連音」及「美式口語辨音」

因為試題本不會列出任何錄音內容，所以必須注意「連音」及「美式口語辨音」概念（例如：弱音、省音、縮音、變音）。

⑥ 不懂不停留

聽到不懂的單字，立即跳過。只要掌握問題重點，仍可選出正確答案。

⑦ 先下手為強

拿筆的手放在答案卡上，跟著聲音的 (A)、(B)、(C) 選項移動。若認為其中一個選項即為正確答案，立刻塗滿；但若沒十足把握時，覺得是 (A)，即先在 (A) 的空格上輕點一下，全部聽完確定後再回來將輕點的答案塗滿；但若已在 (A)點了一下，聽到 (C)時，發現才是正確答案，則立刻將 (C)答案格塗滿，並回去將 (A) 輕點的地方擦乾淨。

⑧ 善用「消去法」

利用 Part 1 所提之「消去法」，通常可順利選出答案。

⑨ 完全通透才是正確選項

只要選項中有「一個字」或「一個點」不能呼應問題重點即跳過不選。要圈選的答案，一定要完全聽完，並確定沒有任何瑕疵。

⑩ 過題即忘

聽完該題後立刻忘掉內容。趕快將注意力及手上的筆移到下一題；若有不會的題目，則從兩個較可能的答案中擇一，答對的機率較高。

破題關鍵要領

① 答非所問

錯誤選項常會出現答非所問的情形，比方說：重點轉移（問地點卻回答時間）、無中生有、主詞錯誤（人稱代名詞錯誤）或開頭字有誤等。

● A: <u>Where</u> can I find a projector for my presentation?

B: Three days ago. （×）

A：我可以在哪裡找到投影機來作簡報？

B：三天前。

② 相似音

作答時，遇到包含與題目重點字之相似音的選項通常是錯誤選項，需特別留意。

● Frank's <u>filed</u> a report.

法蘭克已經提出了報告。

Frank's reading the <u>file</u>.

法蘭克正在看那份檔案。

大師	關鍵指引

常考相似音：

age [edʒ] 年齡	edge [ɛdʒ] 邊緣
bill [bɪl] 帳單	bell [bɛl] 鈴
board [bord] 木板	bold [bold] 大膽的
boss [bɔs] 老闆	bus [bʌs] 公車
box [baks] 盒子	bucks [bʌks] 美元（複數）
came [kem] 來（過去式）	cane [ken] 藤杖
cash [kæʃ] 現金	crash [kræʃ] 撞毀
chair [tʃɛr] 椅子	share [ʃɛr] 分享
color [ˋkʌlə] 顏色	collar [ˋkalə] 領子

cut [kʌt] 切	cot [kɑt] 鄉下小屋；嬰兒床
duck [dʌk] 鴨子	dock [dɑk] 碼頭
endorse [ɪnˋdɔrs] 背書	indoors [ˋɪndorz] 室內
face [fes] 臉	phase [fez] 階段
gel [dʒɛl] 凝膠	jail [dʒel] 監獄
glue [glu] 膠水	grew [gru] 長大（grow 的過去式）
gross [gros] 總體	growth [groθ] 成長
hire [haɪr] 僱用	hare [hɛr] 野兔
hitting [ˋhɪtɪŋ] 打	heating [ˋhitɪŋ] 加熱
later [ˋletə] 晚一點	latter [ˋlætə] 後者
let [lɛt] 讓……	late [let] 遲到
list [lɪst] 清單	wrist [rɪst] 手腕
loose [lus] 寬鬆的	lose [luz] 失敗
luck [lʌk] 幸運	rack [ræk] 架子
order [ˋɔrdə] 訂單	older [ˋoldə] 較年長的
pan [pæn] 平底鍋	pen [pɛn] 筆
pocket [ˋpɑkɪt] 口袋	packet [ˋpækɪt] 小包
quiet [kwaɪət] 安靜的	quit [kwɪt] 辭職
raw [rɔ] 生的	law [lɔ] 法律
remit [rɪˋmɪt] 匯款	emit [ɪˋmɪt] 放射
renew [rɪˋnju] 更新	revenue [ˋrɛvənu] 收益
rug [rʌg] 地毯	rag [ræg] 破布
sew [so] 縫	soul [sol] 靈魂
stock [stɑk] 股票	stuck [stʌk] 刺（stick 的過去式）
steep [stip] 陡峭	sleep [slip] 睡覺
toll [tol] 通行費	tall [tɔl] 高的
win [wɪn] 贏	wing [wɪŋ] 翅膀

③ **同音異義字**

同音異義字也是多益聽力測驗 Part 2 經常出現的混淆選項，須特別留意。

● She's <u>working out</u> at the gym.

　　她在健身房運動。

　　She's <u>working out</u> a solution.

　　她正在設法找到解決辦法。

大師 | 關鍵指引

常考同音異義字：

brake 剎車	break 打破	⇨	[brek]
fare（交通工具的）票價	fair 博覽會；公正的	⇨	[fɛr]
site 地點	sight 視力	⇨	[saɪt]
right 右邊	write 寫	⇨	[raɪt]
sail 帆	sale 銷售	⇨	[sel]
wait 等	weight 體重；重量	⇨	[wet]
pail 桶	pale 蒼白的	⇨	[pel]
heal 治癒	heel 腳後跟	⇨	[hil]
hole 洞	whole 全部的	⇨	[hol]
mail 郵政	male 男性的	⇨	[mel]
meat 肉	meet 遇見	⇨	[mit]
flew 飛（fly 的過去式）	flu 感冒	⇨	[flu]

④ 一字多義

有些單字有多種意義，必須仔細聆聽句子的其他重點字來判斷是否符合題目所問。

● When can you finish the tour of the plant?

你何時會結束參觀工廠？

I bought a plant yesterday.

我昨天買了一株植物。

大師 | 關鍵指引

常考一字多義的單字：

字彙	動詞	名詞
change	變化、改變、交換、替換	改變、零錢
miss	想念、錯過、遺漏	失敗、未中
figure	計算、動腦筋	數字、輪廓、人物、計算、外型
bill	開帳單	帳單、法案、紙幣票據

⑤ 字義隨詞性不同而改變的單字

● Would you mind if I <u>watch</u> you operate the new printer?

你介不介意我<u>看</u>你操作印表機？

My <u>watch</u> is brand new.

我的<u>手錶</u>是全新的。

大師 關鍵指引		
常考字義隨詞性而改變的單子：		
字彙	動詞	名詞
book	預約	書
charge	索價；控訴；充電	責任；充電；費用
break	打破	休息；損壞
interest	對……感興趣	利息

⑥ 文法錯誤

1 時態混淆

● A: <u>Did</u> you see that?

B: <u>Until</u> next week.（×）

A：你有沒有看到那個？

B：直到下星期。

● A: Should we <u>leave</u> tonight at 9:00 or at 10:00?

B: We <u>left</u> at 10:00.（×）

A：我們應該在今晚九點還是十點離開？

B：我們在十點就離開了。

2 介系詞誤用

● A: <u>How soon</u> can you finish this report?

B: <u>For</u> a few days.（×）

A：你能多快完成這份報告？

B：幾天之久。

3 助動詞誤用

● A: Weren't you suprised that I passed the test?

B: No, I didn't.（×）

A：你不訝異我通過測驗了嗎？

B：沒有，我沒有。

● A: Have you sent your application to other schools?

B: No, I wasn't.（×）

A：你把應徵資料寄到其他學校了嗎？

B：不是，我不是。

⑦ 主詞或受詞異位（主客異位）

● A: How long has Ted been working on this project?

（主詞）　　　　　　　　　　（受詞）

B: The project should be finished soon.（×）

（原受詞）

A：泰德處理這個案子多久了？

B：這個案子應該很快就會完成。

⑧ 運用題目重點字以假亂真（「音」曾相似）

1 借用問句中的重點字

● A: Does Frank like the new furniture?

B: It's brand-new furniture.（×）

A：法蘭克喜歡新家具嗎？

B：它是全新的家具。

● A: Does your sister know any language tutors?

B: She knows six languages.（×）

A：你妹妹有沒有認識任何語言家教？

B：她懂六種語言。

● A: Why didn't you go to Cily's party?

B: I like parties a lot.（×）

A：你為什麼沒去參加希莉的派對？

B：我非常喜歡派對。

Word List
☐ tutor [`tjutɚ] *n.* 家庭教師；私人教師

2 借用問句重點字的一個音節

　　● A: Do you know where my pass<u>port</u> is?

　　　B: To the air<u>port</u>. （×）

　　　A：你知道我的護照在哪裡嗎？

　　　B：去機場。

⑨ 詞性變化陷阱

　　● A: Did Tom finish the <u>report</u>?

　　　B: He's a <u>reporter</u>. （×）

　　　A：湯姆完成報告了嗎？

　　　B：他是個記者。

⑩ 線索不明確，未完全表達題目重點

　　● A: <u>Should</u> I submit the report today <u>or</u> tomorrow?

　　　B: Yes, you <u>should</u>. （×）

　　　A：我應該今天還是明天提報告？

　　　B：對，你應該。

⑪ 答案前後矛盾

　　● A: Do you have an English tutor?

　　⇨ B: No, I <u>already have</u> one. （×）

　　⇨ B: Yes, <u>I'll have</u> some. （×）

　　　A：你有沒有英文家教？

　　⇨ B：沒有，我已經有一位了。

　　⇨ B：有，我會有幾位。

⑫ 跳躍式回答

　　● A: <u>Why don't we get</u> something to eat before the test?

　　　B: <u>I'll have</u> an apple pie and some tea, please. （×）

　　　A：我們何不在考試前先吃點東西？

　　　B：我要一塊蘋果派和一些茶，麻煩你。

⑬ 聯想陷阱

● A: How are you going to spend your summer <u>vacation</u>?

B: The <u>resort</u> is near the beach.（×）

A：你要怎麼過暑假？

B：那家度假村靠近海灘。

● A: Where did you learn to <u>speak French</u>?

B: It's an easy <u>language</u>.（×）

A：你是在哪裡學會說法語的？

B：它是種易學的語言。

Word List————————————————————————————
□ resort [rɪ`zɔrt] *n.* 休閒度假勝地

高分必通法則

① 簡答法

Part 2「應答問題」有些題目的答案選項常省略與問句中相同的字眼,即以「簡答」來回應,如:

● A: What time does the guided tour start?

B: Every hour on the hour.（省略 The guided tour starts）

A：導覽何時開始?

B：每個整點。

● A: What time are you leaving?

B: At eight.（省略 I am leaving）

A：你什麼時候要離開?

B：八點。

● A: How long have you lived in this country?

B: Nine months.（省略 I have lived in this country）

A：你在這個國家住多久了?

B：九個月。

● A: Have all the applicants finished the survey?

B: Just about .

A：所有的申請人都填完調查表了嗎?

B：差不多了。

② 第三種可能的答案

有些問題一般人會用 Yes 或 No 來回答,但多益考試中卻常會有第三種可能的回答。

● A: Did you finish the report, Sam?

B: I left it on your desk.

A：你的報告完成了嗎,山姆?

B：我把它放在你桌上了。

Word List
　□ just about　差不多

● A: Mrs. Williams is on the phone. May I take a message?

B: I need to speak to her.

A：威廉斯太太正在講電話。您要不要留言？

B：我需要跟她談談。

③ 換句話說

多益考試常會在正確答案中安排與題目重點字意思相近的「同義字」，考驗應試者對同義字彙的理解力。

● A: Do you <u>like</u> pizza?

B: Yes, I <u>love</u> it.

A：你喜歡吃披薩嗎？

B：喜歡，我很愛吃。

④ 省略 Yes/No 的回答

● A: Can you finish this job in time?

B: I think so.

A：你能夠及時完成這項工作嗎？

B：我想可以。

⑤ 不可能選擇的答案

(1) or 問句 ⇨ 不能用 Yes 或 No 回答。

(2) Wh 開頭的問句 ⇨ 不能用 Yes 或 No 回答。

(3) 用 Why 問的問句 ⇨ 通常不選用 because 回應的答案。

高頻情境用語

下列用語經常出現在多益測驗 Part 2「應答問題」中，平時多熟悉這些生活或商業用語，臨場就能立刻反應，迅速找出正確選項。

1 詢問意見 Asking for Opinions

- How about...? ……怎麼樣？
- How was...? ……如何？
- What do you think about...? 你認為……如何？
- How'd you like...? 你想不想……？

2 回應對方的意見 Responding to Opinions

1 表贊同

- Me too. 我也是。
- I don't either. 我也沒有。
- Why not? 為什麼不？
- OK. 好。
- Sure! 當然！
- Right on. 說得好。
- You said it. 你說對了。
- I'll say! 我同意！
- You can say that again. 你說得真對。
- Neither do I. 我也沒有。
- So do I. 我也是。
- By all means. 當然。
- Sounds good to me. 聽起來不錯。
- That's a great idea. 那是個好主意。
- No problem. 沒問題。
- Who wouldn't？ 誰不會呢？
- You bet! 你說對了！
- I couldn't agree more. 我非常同意。
- I feel the same way you do. 我跟你有同感。

2 表反對

- I don't think so. 我不這麼認為。
- That's not what I think. 那不是我所認為的。
- I can't say I agree. 我不能苟同。
- That's not the way I see it. 那不是我的看法。
- I couldn't agree with you less. 我非常不同意你的看法。
- I'm afraid I don't agree. 我恐怕不同意。
- I'm afraid not. 恐怕不行。
- Not really. 不盡然。
- Not likely. 不太可能。
- Maybe you're right, but.... 也許你說得對，可是……。
- I really don't know. 我真的不曉得。
- I'm not sure if.... 我不確定是不是……。
- I'm not so sure. 我不是那麼確定。
- No, let's.... 不，我們……吧。
- Sorry, but.... 很抱歉，可是……。
- Thanks anyway, but I can't. 總之很謝謝，可是我不行。
- No, thanks. 不了，謝謝。
- Probably not. 大概不會。
- Not necessarily. 不一定。

③ 要求 Making Requests

- Do you think you could...? 你覺得你可不可以……？
- Could you...? 您可不可以……？
- Will you...? 你願不願意……？
- Would you like...? 您要不要……？
- Could you please...? 可不可以麻煩您……？
- Would you please...? 能不能麻煩您……？
- Is there...? 有沒有……？
- Would it be OK. if...? 要是……可不可以……？
- Can you...? 你可不可以……？
- Would you mind...? 您介不介意……？
- Do you mind if...? 您會不會介意如果……？

④ 回應要求 Responding to Requests

① 同意要求

- I'd be delighted to. 我很樂意。
- Certainly. 當然。
- Be my guest. 請便。
- Sure thing. 當然可以。
- Why not? 有何不可？

② 拒絕要求

- I wish I could, but.... 我希望可以，不過……。
- I'm afraid not. 恐怕不行。
- I don't think so. 我不認為可以。
- Actually, I do mind. 事實上，我會介意。
- Of course not. 當然不行。

⑤ 建議 Making Suggestions

- You'd better.... 你最好……。
- Shouldn't we/you...? 我們／你不是應該……嗎？
- What do you think about...? 你認為……如何？
- How would you feel about...? 你覺得……如何？
- How about...? ……如何？
- How does ... sound? ……聽起來怎麼樣？
- What would you say to...? 你覺得……如何？
- Why don't I...? 我何不……？
- Why don't we/you...? 我們／你何不……？
- Why bother...? 何必……？
- Why not...? 何不……？
- Shall we...? 我們要不要……？
- Let's.... 我們……吧。
- Try.... 試試……。
- We'd better.... 我們最好……。
- Do you think...? 你是不是認為……？
- Shouldn't you...? 你不是應該……？
- Have you ever thought of...? 你有沒有想過……？

- You/We could always.... 你／我們可以一直……。
- Perhaps we should.... 或許我們應該……。
- If I were you, I'd.... 假如我是你的話，我會……。
- If I were in your shoes.... 假如我碰到你這種情況……。
- May I suggest...? 我可不可以建議……？
- Maybe you/we could.... 也許你／我們可以……。
- Would you like to...? 您要不要……？
- Maybe you should.... 也許你應該……。
- You might want to.... 你可能希望……。
- What about...? ……怎麼樣？
- What if you/we...? 要是你／我們……呢？
- You/We might want to.... 你／我們可能希望……。
- Why don't you...? 你何不……？
- You ought to.... 你應該……。

⑥ 回應對方的建議 Responding to Suggestions

1 贊同
- Why not? 有何不可？
- Sounds good to me. 聽起來不錯。
- That's an idea. 那是個好點子。
- That's worth a try. 那值得一試。

2 不贊同
- I don't think so. 我不這麼認為。
- I don't think that will work. 我不認為那樣會有用。
- Don't look at me! 別看我！
- I don't believe so. 我不相信是這樣。

⑦ 提供協助 Offering Help

- Here, I'll give you a hand with.... 來，我來幫忙你……。
- Let me.... 讓我來……。
- Would you like...? 您要不要……？
- Can I...? 我能不能……？
- May I...? 我可不可以……？

- Should I...? 我該不該……？
- Do you want me to...? 你要不要我……？
- Would you let me to...? 您願不願意讓我……？
- Shall I...? 我要不要……？
- I could.... 我可以……。

⑧ 回應對方提供的協助 Responding to Favors

❶ 接受對方協助

- Yes, please. 好，麻煩了。
- If you wouldn't mind. 假如你不介意的話。
- That would be nice. 這樣不錯。
- Sure, thanks. 好，謝謝。

❷ 拒絕對方協助

- No, ... 不用了，……。
- That's OK; I can handle it. 沒關係，我可以自己處理。
- Don't bother. 不用麻煩了。
- That won't be necessary. 那沒有必要。

⑨ 邀請 Making Invitations

- Shall we...? 我們要不要……？
- Let's.... 我們……吧。
- Can you...? 你能不能……？
- Could you...? 您可不可以……？
- Do you want to...? 你要不要……？
- Would you like to...? 您要不要……？
- Would you care to...? 您想不想要……？
- Would you be able to...? 您是不是能……？

⑩ 回應邀請 Responding to Invitations

❶ 接受邀請

- All right, I'd love to. 好，我十分樂意。
- What a great idea! 真棒的主意！
- Sure. Thanks for inviting me. 好啊。謝謝你邀請我。

- I'd like that. 我很願意。

2 拒絕要請

- I'll pass. 我不用了。
- Can I take a rain check? 我可以改天嗎？
- I don't think I'll make it this time. 我想我這次沒辦法。
- I'd love to, but.... 我十分樂意，可是……

Word List
- ☐ rain check 延期；改期

實用對話短句

• A piece of cake!	輕而易舉。
• A real knockout!	真行！
• After you.	你先請。
• All set.	都準備好了。
• All you can eat.	吃到飽。
• Anything you say.	隨你便。
• Bad news travels fast.	壞事傳千里。
• Beats me.	可難倒我了。
• Behave yourself!	規矩一點！
• Big deal.	有什麼了不起的？
• Can you give me a rain check?	我們約下次好嗎？
• Can't complain.	還不錯。
• Can't say.	很難說。
• Certainly not.	絕不。
• Close call!	好險！
• Come on!	少來了！／來吧！／拜託！
• Could be better.	可以再更好。
• Could be.	說不定。
• Count me out.	別把我算在內。
• Cut it out!	停止！
• Definitely not.	絕不。
• Do as you like.	隨便你。
• Do I make myself clear?	你了解我的話了嗎？
• Do you have a minute?	耽誤你一點時間可以嗎？
• Doesn't that sound great?	那不是很好嗎？
• Don't be so hard on me.	別這樣嚴厲地對我。
• Don't count on it.	別指望了。
• Don't I know you?	我們是不是在哪裡見過面？
• Don't you get it?	你還是不懂嗎？
• Drop it!	停止！
• Easier said than done.	說是容易，做可就難了。

• Face it.	認了吧！
• Fair enough.	很公平。
• Forget it.	算了。
• Get a clue?	知道了嗎？
• Get dressed.	穿好衣服。
• Get off that phone!	不要再講電話了！
• Get over it.	忘了吧。
• Get real!	面對現實吧！
• Get to the point.	說重點。
• Give it a shot.	試試看。
• Go easy!	放輕鬆！
• Good buy!	物美價廉！
• Good choice!	好眼光！
• Good for you!	真替你高興！
• Good guess!	答對了！
• Good question!	問得好！
• Got a minute?	耽誤一點時間好嗎？
• Got it!	知道了！
• Guess what?	你猜怎麼樣？
• Guess who?	猜看看是誰？
• Hang on!	別掛斷！／別放手！／撐住！
• Have you lost your mind?	你瘋了嗎？
• Hope not.	希望不是那麼回事。
• How come?	怎麼會？
• How did it go?	還順利嗎？
• How many more?	還有幾個？
• How nice!	真好！
• I blew it.	我搞砸了！
• I can hardly wait!	我等不及了！
• I got it.	我懂了。
• I guess it will do.	我想應該沒問題。
• I have a hangover.	我宿醉。
• I have to draw the line somewhere.	事情得有個限度。
• I knew it.	我早料到了。

- I need my space.　　　　　　　　　我需要有自己的空間。
- I owe you one.　　　　　　　　　　我欠你一個人情。
- I see your point.　　　　　　　　　我懂你的意思。
- I swear.　　　　　　　　　　　　　我發誓。
- I want to make this work.　　　　　我要這件事做得成。
- I went too far.　　　　　　　　　　我太過分了。
- I'd better not.　　　　　　　　　　我最好不要。
- I'd rather not.　　　　　　　　　　我寧可不要。
- I'll cross my fingers.　　　　　　　我希望能順利進行。
- I'll get it.　　　　　　　　　　　　我來！（如電話響時說或門鈴響時）
- I'll get right on it.　　　　　　　　我馬上開始做。
- I'll give it a try.　　　　　　　　　我會試試看。
- I'll have the usual.　　　　　　　　我還是照舊要一樣的。
- I'll leave it up to you.　　　　　　我就把它交給你了。
- I'm a little rusty.　　　　　　　　　我有點生疏。
- I'm flattered.　　　　　　　　　　　我受寵若驚。
- I'm had it.　　　　　　　　　　　　我受夠了。
- I'm half dead.　　　　　　　　　　我快累死了。
- I'm in!　　　　　　　　　　　　　　我加入！
- I'm moved.　　　　　　　　　　　　我好感動。
- I'm not in the mood.　　　　　　　我沒那個心情。
- I'm on your side.　　　　　　　　　我站在你那一邊
- I'm out of shape.　　　　　　　　　我的身體狀況很差。
- In your dreams.　　　　　　　　　　你在作夢！
- Is it on you?　　　　　　　　　　　你請客嗎？
- Isn't that something?　　　　　　　很了不起吧！
- It doesn't quite do it for me.　　　那對我沒什麼用。
- It just goes on forever.　　　　　　沒完沒了的。
- It makes no difference to me.　　　對我沒什麼差別。
- It was enlightening.　　　　　　　　那真是發人省思。
- It's getting out of hand.　　　　　事情變得難以收拾。
- It's no big deal.　　　　　　　　　那沒什麼大不了的。

Word List
□ rusty [ˋrʌstɪ] *adj.*（知識、能力等）荒廢的；生疏的

• It's up to you.	由你決定。
• I've tied up.	我一直脫不開身。
• Just checking.	只是問一下。
• Kind of.	有那麼點。
• Know what?	你知道嗎？
• Let me think it over.	讓我好好想想！
• Let's get this straight.	咱們把話說清楚。
• Let's go Dutch.	我們各付各的吧！
• Let's play it safe.	咱們小心行事。
• Let's split it.	我們平分吧！
• Like this?	像這樣嗎？
• Look here.	喂！／注意！
• Love it!	真棒！
• Maybe some other time.	下次吧！
• Me neither.	我也不。
• My feet are killing me.	我的腳痛死了。
• My treat.	我請客。
• Never say never.	絕不說不。
• Nice try.	白費力氣。
• No doubt.	不必懷疑！
• No need to rush.	不必急！
• No sweat.	小事一樁。
• No way!	不會吧！／不行！
• Nobody told me that.	沒聽人說過。
• Not exactly.	不盡然。
• Not likely.	不可能。
• Not quite.	不全然。
• Not really.	不盡然。
• Not this time.	這次不行。
• Nothing much.	沒什麼特別的。
• Ow what?	又怎麼啦？
• Oh, yeah?	喔？是嗎？
• Please don't get off track.	請別離題了。
• Pull yourself together.	振作一下！

- Same as usual.   照舊。
- Same here.   我也一樣。／我有同感。
- Save it.   少來了！／省省吧！
- Since when?   我怎麼沒聽說？
- Sleep tight.   祝你好睡。
- So far, so good.   到目前為止都還好。
- So what?   那又怎樣？
- Sorry, something's come up.   對不起，我突然有事。
- Spare me.   饒了我吧。
- Stay put.   不要動。
- Suit yourself!   隨你便。
- Sure thing.   當然可以。
- Take it or leave it.   要不要隨你便！
- Take my word for it.   相信我，不會錯的。
- Tell you what.   我跟你說。
- Thank you for your time.   謝謝您撥空。
- That can't be!   那不可能！
- That is a must-buy.   那是絕對要買的。
- That/It depends.   看情形。
- That suits you.   那很適合你。
- That's enough!   夠了！
- That's how I got started.   我就是這樣起步的。
- That's it.   就這樣。
- That's neat.   真不錯。
- That's something!   太棒了！
- That's what I say.   我就是這個意思。
- That's what I thought.   跟我想的一樣。
- There you go again.   你又來了。
- Things couldn't be better.   形勢大好。／一切都很順利。
- Think twice.   請三思！
- Told you.   早跟你說了！
- Tomorrow is another day.   明天又是新的一天！
- Watch out!   小心！
- We are set.   我們準備好了！

- Well said. 說得好。
- We've got chemistry! 我們很合得來。
- What a pain! 真煩！
- What a relief! 總算鬆了口氣。
- What a waste! 真是浪費！
- What do you say? 你覺得怎麼樣？
- What for? 為什麼？
- What is it for? 你這是幹什麼？／這東西做什麼用？
- Whatever you say. 隨便你怎麼說。／你說了算。
- What's it to you? 這跟你有關係嗎？
- What's keeping him? 他怎麼這麼慢啊？
- What's on? 電視在播什麼節目？
- Where were we? 我們剛剛說到哪了？
- Who cares? 誰在乎？
- Why's that? 為什麼會那樣？
- You are (really) something! 你真行！
- You asked for it. 你自找的。
- You can count on me. 放心交給我吧！
- You don't mean that. 你該不是認真的吧？
- You don't say. 不會吧！
- You're driving me crazy. 你快讓我發瘋了。
- You're driving me nuts! 你快讓我抓狂了。
- You got it! 你說對了！
- You know what? 你知道怎樣嗎？
- You made my day! 你讓我很開心！
- You mean it? 你說真的嗎？
- You see? 你看吧！
- You tell me. 說來聽聽。
- You told me. 你告訴過我了！
- You'll see . 到時候你就知道。
- You've got me. 被你逮到了！
- You're telling me! 還用你說！
- You've got it wrong. 你誤會了。

Exercises

MP3 026 ▶▶ MP3 040

1 Mark you answer on your answer sheet. Ⓐ Ⓑ Ⓒ

2 Mark you answer on your answer sheet. Ⓐ Ⓑ Ⓒ

3 Mark you answer on your answer sheet. Ⓐ Ⓑ Ⓒ

4 Mark you answer on your answer sheet. Ⓐ Ⓑ Ⓒ

5 Mark you answer on your answer sheet. Ⓐ Ⓑ Ⓒ

6 Mark you answer on your answer sheet. Ⓐ Ⓑ Ⓒ

7 Mark you answer on your answer sheet. Ⓐ Ⓑ Ⓒ

8 Mark you answer on your answer sheet. Ⓐ Ⓑ Ⓒ

9 Mark you answer on your answer sheet. Ⓐ Ⓑ Ⓒ

10 Mark you answer on your answer sheet. Ⓐ Ⓑ Ⓒ

11 Mark you answer on your answer sheet. Ⓐ Ⓑ Ⓒ

12 Mark you answer on your answer sheet. Ⓐ Ⓑ Ⓒ

13 Mark you answer on your answer sheet. Ⓐ Ⓑ Ⓒ

14 Mark you answer on your answer sheet. Ⓐ Ⓑ Ⓒ

15 Mark you answer on your answer sheet. Ⓐ Ⓑ Ⓒ

1. 答案：(B)

破 題 Whom/I say/calling? ⇨ 問「人」。

解 析 (A) 主詞有誤，不應用 I 回應，且 extension（電話分機）是 calling 的聯想陷阱。(B) Ted Kline（名字）回答了問題重點，而 from marketing 代表所屬的工作部門，故為正確答案。(C) Please 開頭的祈使句表建議或動作，答非所問。

錄音內容 Whom shall I say is calling?
(A) I'd like extension 558, please.
(B) This is Ted Kline from marketing.
(C) Please have him call me back.

錄音翻譯 我應該說是誰打來的？
(A) 麻煩你，我要接分機 558。
(B) 我是行銷部的泰德‧克萊恩。
(C) 麻煩請他回電給我。

□ extension [ɪk`stɛnʃən] n.（電話的）分機；內線

2. 答案：(A)

破 題 When/you/moving/new building? ⇨ 問「時間」。

解 析 (A) A week from yesterday. 表時間，且回應了問題重點，故為正確答案。(B) 文法錯誤，問句重點為未來的動作，ago 指的是過去。(C) 不知所云，用 my first time 與時間字 when 混淆。

錄音內容 When are you moving into the new building?
(A) A week from yesterday.
(B) About two years ago.
(C) It's actually my first time.

錄音翻譯 你什麼時候要搬進新大樓？
(A) 從昨天開始的一週之內。
(B) 大概兩年前。
(C) 其實我是頭一遭。

3. 答案：(B)

破 題 How long ⇨ 問「時間長度」。

解 析 (A) 答非所問，twice 表「倍數」。(B) three or four years 表「時間長度」，故為正確答案。(C) 也答非所問，That's why... 表「原因」。

錄音內容 How long has it been since we switched to the new system?
(A) It's twice as fast as the old one.
(B) At least three or four years.
(C) That's why we had to shorten it.

錄音翻譯 我們改用新系統到現在有多久？
(A) 它是舊的速度的兩倍
(B) 起碼三、四年了。
(C) 那正是為什麼我們必須縮短時間。

4. 答案：(C)

破 題 Who/going/take over/Mr.Diller/retire? ⇨ 問「人」。

解 析 (A) 雖然提到 this week，但並未回答問題的重點。(B) 雖然重複題目字 retire，但答非所問。(C) I don't think 表看法，而 it 指接替 Mr. Diller 這件事，故為正確答案。

錄音內容 Who's going to take over for Mr. Diller when he retires?
(A) I'm not too busy this week, so maybe I can help.
(B) He's planning to retire in December.
(C) I don't think it has been announced yet.

錄音翻譯 迪勒先生退休時，誰要去接替他？
(A) 我這星期不太忙，所以也許我可以幫忙。
(B) 他打算十二月退休。
(C) 我想這件事還沒有宣布。

☐ take over 接管

5. 答案：(A)

破 題 Where/you/going/vacation? ⇨ 問「地方」。

解 析 (A) To... 表去某地，而 To southern Mexico. 則回答了問題的重點。(B) 答非所問，At the end of the month 說的是「時間」。(C) 也答非所問，「by + 交通工具」表方法。

錄音內容 Where are you going on your vacation?
(A) To southern Mexico.
(B) At the end of the month.
(C) By rental car.

錄音翻譯 你休假要去哪裡？
(A) 去南墨西哥。
(B) 月底的時候。
(C) 租車。

6. 答案：(C)

破 題 What/you/do/after work? ⇨ 問「特定事情」。

解 析 (A) Sure 表「確定」，但 that sounds great 答非所問。(B) After seven（大約七點），不知所云。(C) do housework（做家事）則回答了題目重點。

錄音內容 What do you usually do after work?
(A) Sure, that sounds great.
(B) About seven, I think.
(C) I often do housework.

錄音翻譯 你下班後通常做什麼？
(A) 當然，那聽起來很棒。
(B) 我想大約七點。
(C) 我常做家事。

7. 答案：(B)

破題　How/you/like/hotel/they choose ⇨ 問「喜好」。

解析　(A) 答非所問，presentation（簡報）與原句 conference（會議）為聯想陷阱。(B) 的 not close enough to the airport（離機場不夠近）表「缺點」，亦即代表不太滿意此選擇，故為正確答案。(C) We'll staying there... 並未回答問題重點。

錄音內容　How do you like the hotel they chose for the conference?
(A) The presentations were all excellent.
(B) It's not close enough to the airport.
(C) We'll be staying there for two nights.

錄音翻譯　你覺得他們為討論會所選的飯店如何？
(A) 簡報都非常精彩。
(B) 飯店離機場不夠近。
(C) 我們會在那裡停留兩晚。

8. 答案：(A)

破題　How/your interview/go? ⇨ 問「事情進展」。

解析　(A) I'll know by the end of the week.（本週結束前會知道結果。）為合理回應，故為正確答案。(B) got back from Hawaii（從夏威夷回來）答非所問。(C) right there on the desk（就在書桌上）不知所云。

錄音內容　How did your interview go?
(A) I'll know by the end of the week.
(B) We just got back from Hawaii.
(C) It's right there on the desk.

錄音翻譯　你的面試結果如何？
(A) 我週末結束前會知道結果。
(B) 我們剛從夏威夷回來。
(C) 它就在書桌上。

9. 答案：(A)

破 題 Have/you/been/helped ⇨ 詢問「是否」得到協助。

解 析 (A) No 回答了問題，而且說 but I like to try these on 表示「仍然需要幫忙」，故為正確答案。(B) Sure 表肯定，但 be happy to 表「主動」想去做……，和題目重點不符。(C) Thank you very much. 表「感激不盡」，但並未回答問題重點。

錄音內容 Have you been helped yet, sir?
(A) No, but I'd like to try these on.
(B) Sure, I'd be happy to.
(C) Thank you very much.

錄音翻譯 有人幫你了嗎，先生？
(A) 沒有，不過我想試穿這些。
(B) 當然，樂意之至。
(C) 感激不盡。

10. 答案：(A)

破 題 Would/it/move economical/by train? ⇨ 問搭火車「是否」比較划算。

解 析 (A) I'll have to look into that. 表說話者不確定，需進一步去了解，為正確答案。(B) improving all the time（一直在進步），答非所問。(C) 用 training（訓練）與原句的 train 混淆，不可選。

錄音內容 Would it be more economical for us to go by train?
(A) I'll have to look into that.
(B) It's improving all the time.
(C) Yes, let's start training immediately.

錄音翻譯 我們搭火車去會比較省錢嗎？
(A) 我必須研究一下。
(B) 它一直在進步。
(C) 好，我們立刻開始訓練。

☐ economical [ˌikəˈnɑmɪkl] *adj.* 經濟的；節省的

11. 答案：(B)

破 題 Is/Michael/at/meeting/next week ⇨ 問某人「是否」會參加開會。

解 析 (A) 題目問的是 Michael，與 I 毫無關係。(B) No，Bob will take his place. 回應題目問句，也說出重點，故為正確答案。(C) 答非所問，plans（設計圖）為混淆題目 planing meeting 一詞。

錄音內容 Is Michael going to be at the planning meeting next week?
(A) Next week is convenient for me.
(B) No, Bob is going to take his place.
(C) Don't worry. I'll bring the plans.

錄音翻譯 麥可下星期會去參加規畫會議嗎？
(A) 我下星期可以。
(B) 不會，鮑伯會代替他去。
(C) 別擔心，我會把設計圖帶著。

□ plan [plæn] *n.*（建築物、花園等的）設計圖

---

12. 答案：(A)

破 題 Would you mind/helping/pick out? ⇨ 問「是否」介意。

解 析 (A) Who's it for? 指說話者需要知道更進一步的訊息，代表「不介意幫忙」，為正確答案。(B) I would appreciate it. 應該是提出要求的人說的話，不可選。(C) 答非所問，題目並沒問「有或沒有」某物。

錄音內容 Would you mind helping me pick out a present?
(A) Who's it for?
(B) I would appreciate it.
(C) I don't have one.

錄音翻譯 你介不介意幫我挑個禮物？
(A) 要給誰的？
(B) 我會很感激。
(C) 我沒有禮物。

13. 答案：(C)

破 題 You've/submitted/haven't you? ⇨ 附加問句，問對方「是否」已遞交申請書。

解 析 (A) 答非所問；(B) 用相關字 applying 混淆題目的 application，文不對題；(C) 省略 No, 回答 It's not due until the tenth.（它到十日才截止。）符合問題重點，為正確答案。

錄音內容 You've already submitted your application, haven't you?
(A) Yes, I've been there twice.
(B) I'm applying for both positions.
(C) It's not due until the tenth.

錄音翻譯 你已經提出申請了吧，還沒嗎？
(A) 是的，我去過兩次。
(B) 我同時應徵兩個職位。
(C) 到十日才截止。

□ due [du] *adj.* 到期的

14. 答案：(C)

破 題 Is/this/Wendy's/or/yours? ⇨ 要對方在 A 或 B 之間做選擇。

解 析 (A) 不對，有 or 的問句，不可用 yes 或 no 回答。(B)句重點在 "color"，但與問題毫不相關。(C) I think it belongs to Marsha 以「既非 A 也非 B」而是「第三者」的來回應，故為正確答案。

錄音內容 Is this Wendy's jacket or is it yours?
(A) Yes, don't forget to dress warmly.
(B) We don't have any more in that color.
(C) Well, I think it belongs to Marsha.

錄音翻譯 這是溫蒂的外套還是你的？
(A) 對，別忘了穿暖一點。
(B) 我們已經沒有那種顏色的了。
(C) 嗯，我想它是瑪莎的。

15. 答案：**(B)**

> 破題　I /hope/calculations/accurate ⇨ 直述句，I hope... 表希望某事成真。

> 解析　(A) 單數主詞 it 有誤，且文意不通。(B) Mary double-checked them 表示有人再次檢查計算結果，故為正確答案。(C) 不知所云。

> 錄音內容　I hope these calculations are accurate.
> (A) It's not what I ordered either.
> (B) Don't worry. Mary double-checked them.
> (C) I just bought it a year ago.

> 錄音翻譯　我希望這些計算無誤。
> (A) 那也不是我訂的東西。
> (B) 別擔心，瑪莉複算過了。
> (C) 我一年前才買的。

□ calculation [ˌkælkjəˋleʃən] *n.* 計算（的結果）

Part 3

Short Conversations
簡 短 對 話

題型簡介

Part 3「簡短對話」共有 30 題，每題會聽到兩人的簡短對話，通常是 A ⇨ B ⇨ A ⇨ B 或 A ⇨ B ⇨ A 的對話模式，對話之後，必須回答三個問題，問題與選項都會印在試題本上。每個題目會有四個選項，考生必須從中選出一個最適合的答案。

出題預覽

1. Why is the man concerned?
   (A) He needs to be trained to use the computer.
   (B) His boss told him that he was not ready for work.
   (C) He may have forgotten some important information.
   (D) His computer will not be ready tomorrow.   Ⓐ Ⓑ Ⓒ Ⓓ

2. Why didn't the man use a computer to take notes?
   (A) He has an excellent memory.
   (B) His computer didn't work.
   (C) He didn't want to look unprepared.
   (D) He didn't have access to one.   Ⓐ Ⓑ Ⓒ Ⓓ

3. How did the woman offer to help the man?
   (A) By lending him some stationery.
   (B) By buying him something to eat.
   (C) By letting him use her computer.
   (D) By giving him some advice.   Ⓐ Ⓑ Ⓒ Ⓓ

---

1. 答案：(C)　　**2. 答案：(D)**　　**3. 答案：(A)**

錄音內容

M: I hope I can remember everything from this morning's training session.

W: It's your first day at work! Didn't you take notes?

M: I was told we'd each be issued a laptop computer first thing in the morning, but they won't be ready until tomorrow. I thought about borrowing a pen from someone, but I didn't want to look unprepared.

W: Well, I have some paper and pens you can borrow. Let's stop by my office after lunch.

録音翻譯

男：真希望我能記住今天早上訓練講習的每一點。

女：你才上班第一天耶！你沒做筆記嗎？

男：有人跟我說，每個人一早來就會發一台筆電，可是要明天才會準備好。我想過跟別人借筆，可是又不想看起來毫無準備的樣子。

女：嗯，我有一些紙筆可以借你。吃完午飯後，到我辦公室去吧。

題目&選項翻譯

1. 男子為什麼要擔心？

(A) 他需要接受使用電腦的訓練。

(B) 老闆告訴他，他沒有做好上班的準備。

(C) 他可能忘了一些重要的訊息。

(D) 他的電腦明天沒辦法準備好。

2. 男子為什麼沒有用電腦來做筆記？

(A) 他擁有絕佳的記憶力。

(B) 他的電腦故障了。

(C) 他不想看起來毫無準備。

(D) 他沒有電腦可用。

3. 女子提議要如何幫助男子？

(A) 借他一些文具。

(B) 買東西給他吃。

(C) 讓他使用她的電腦。

(D) 給他一些建議。

Word List
- [ ] access [ˋæksɛs] *n.* 接近；使用；存取
- [ ] stationery [ˋsteʃənˌɛrɪ] *n.* 文具；信紙

題型透析

① 考「人名、職業或部門單位」

出題關鍵 Who/profession/job/occupation

全真題 <u>Who</u> will be buying a house?

<u>Who</u> will the man talk to next?

<u>Who</u> are the speakers?

破解重點 a. 注意聽問題所問的人名，不用擔心是否聽得懂對話內容，只要看著答案，找發音最相近的名字，通常就是答案。

b. 若是問職稱時，有時對話不會提到該人物的工作職稱，但對話可能會提到二到三個與該職務有關的詞彙，只要稍微推測一下，即可知道該人的工作職稱。

大師 關鍵指引

多益常考的職業或職稱：

- manager 經理
- supervisor 主管
- CEO 執行長
- travel agent 旅行社職員
- mechanic 技工
- flight attendant 空服員
- surgeon 外科醫生
- editor 編輯
- cashier 收銀員
- baker 麵包師傅
- supplier 供應商

- president 總經理
- head of department 部門主管
- consultant 顧問
- dentist 牙醫
- technician 技術人員
- pharmacist 藥劑師
- physician 內科醫生
- assistant 助理
- chef 主廚
- receptionist 接待員
- distributor 經銷商

---

② 考人物的「動作」

出題關鍵 **What...will do / going to do / probably do / happening / did... do**

全真題 <u>What</u> are the speakers probably <u>doing</u>?

<u>What</u> does Tommy have to <u>do</u>?

<u>What</u> will the woman probably <u>do next</u>?

破解重點　a. 要注意題目問的是「過去」、「現在」還是「未來」，留心正確的動詞時
　　　　　態。

　　　　b. 此類題目通常在下列句型之後，會出現表動作的字眼：

- I'll / I'm going to / I'd rather / I might
- I prefer to / I may / I'd like to
- I want to / I need to / I can
- I could / I would / I have to / I've got to

　　　　c. 注意題目是問「誰」做什麼：亦即，人名與動作需完全對應。

③ 考「地點」

出題關鍵　**Where...?**

全真題　<u>Where</u> are the speakers?

　　　　<u>Where</u> will the plants be placed?

　　　　<u>Where</u> is this conversation mostly probably taking place?

破解重點　a. 通常若是整段對話只提到一個地點，很有可能就是答案所在。

　　　　b. 若提到二個或三個地點，則要聽清楚所問的地點是哪一個。（如：題目
　　　　　問男子現在人在那裡，但對話中提到了其中一個地點，是男子之後處理
　　　　　某件事要去的地方）。

　　　　c. 若沒有直接唸出地點名稱，則會提到與該地點相關的字眼，可由此推知
　　　　　地點名稱為何。比方說若提到 track, platform, board 即可推知地點為
　　　　　train station（車站）。

大師　關鍵指引

常考的場所名稱：

- conference room　會議室
- hotel　飯店
- airport/flight　機場／班機上
- restaurant　餐廳
- plant/factory　工廠
- concert　音樂會
- department store　百貨公司
- bus/train station　公／火車站
- library　圖書館
- theater　戲院／劇院
- drugstore　藥局
- cafeteria　自助餐館
- supermarket　超市
- shopping mall　購物中心

④ 考「原因、理由」

出題關鍵 **Why...?**

全真題 <u>Why</u> did the man miss the training session?

<u>Why</u> do the speakers need to talk to Linda?

<u>Why</u> will they go into the shop?

破解重點 a. 原因通常與所在場所有關：如在 farewell party（離別派對）中表示有人 resign（辭職），或 start one's own business（自行創業）。

b. 若場所在 luncheon（午餐會）中，表示可能為年度員工犒賞午餐會議，表揚某位員工的 achievements（成就）、宣告 sales figures（銷售額）增加，或是報告某項與公司或部門有關的產品的 performance（表現）。

c. 若題目中 why 和有「否定」意涵的字眼連用，如 not，則表示有 problem（問題），則要去聽對話中具「否定、負面」字眼的句子。

⑤ 考「發生問題」

Part 3「簡短對話」常出現的對話內容是談論某件事引發的問題及解決方法。若考發生的問題，答案通常在對話中帶有「負面」或「否定」字眼之處。

出題關鍵 **poblem / the matter with / wrong with / upset about / concerned about / worried about**

全真題 <u>What</u> was probably the <u>problem</u> with the <u>printer</u>?

<u>What</u> is the woman <u>concerned about</u>?

<u>What</u> is the <u>problem</u> with the <u>party</u>?

<u>Why can't</u> the woman help?

破解重點 通常聽到詢問發生問題的問句後，對方接續的回答通常就是答案所在。

大師 關鍵指引

常考詢問「發生問題」的句型：

• What's with you?

• What's the matter with Ann?

• What's bothering you?

• What's wrong with you?

• What happened to Mary?

• Is everything all right with the computer?

⑥ 考某人提出的「建議」

出題關鍵 **suggest sb. to do sth. / suggestion / advice to V.**

全真題 <u>What</u> does the <u>woman</u> <u>want</u> the <u>man</u> to <u>do</u>?

<u>What</u> does the <u>woman</u> <u>suggest</u>?

<u>What</u> <u>advice</u> does the <u>man</u> <u>give</u>?

破解重點 a. 此題型通常在聽到表「建議」的訊號字眼之後，即是答案。

b. 要注意出題句型；若是主動問句，在對話中可能以被動唸出，反之亦然。

c. 當聽到祈使句／命令句的句子時，通常該句為首的動詞即為答案，如：
Make sure...。

| 大師 | 關鍵指引 |

常考表「建議」的句型：

- Let's...
- Perhaps you could + V....
- Why not + V?
- What about + N/V-ing?
- Why don't we/you + V...?
- You'd better + V....
- You really ought to + V....
- Have you ever thought of + Ving?

- Maybe you should + V....
- If I were you, I'd + V....
- How about + N/V-ing?
- Shall we + V...?
- Try +Ving....
- You may/might as well + V....
- You should + V....

---

⑦ 考「細節問題」

出題關鍵 **When / How long / What time / How often / numbers**
這類問句要問的是明確的細節問句，一聽到與該句問題有關的「數字」，應立刻選取答案。

全真題 <u>When</u> does the <u>conversation</u> take place?

<u>When</u> will the <u>tour</u> <u>begin</u>?

<u>How many</u> <u>tablets</u> is the man going to buy?

破解重點 要注意對話中與該細節問題相關的數字詞（如：問 what time...? 在對話中卻提到 2 ～ 3 個不同的時間點），一定要確定所選取的數字答案是問題所問的重點。在 Part 3「簡短對話」中，要小心題目是問男子還是女子。基本上，問有關男子的問題，在男子的話中找答案；反之，有關女子的問題，以女子的話來破題。不過要注意，有時答案也會出現在對方的回答中。

大師　關鍵指引

常見的細節問題例句：

• Peter will be out of town <u>until Friday afternoon</u>.
• Our project proposal is due <u>next Tuesday</u>.
• The board meeting is set for <u>Monday</u>.
• We're running <u>one hour behind</u> schedule.
• The flight is delayed for <u>three hours</u>.
• My hair stylist's appointment had to be <u>rescheduled</u> for tomorrow at <u>5 P.M.</u>
• The reunion has to be put off <u>until next Sunday</u>.
• Virtually everyone's sales figures are up <u>this month</u>.

❽ 考「請求」、「提供協助」、「邀請」

出題關鍵　**need to V / want to V / be asked to V / offer to V / hope to V**
以上句型有表「請求」、「提供」、「邀請」等概念，通常要聽取包含同義詞或近意詞的選項。

全真題　<u>What</u> does the woman <u>want</u> the man to <u>do</u>?
<u>What</u> does the man <u>offer</u> to <u>do</u>?
<u>What</u> is the <u>woman</u> <u>asked</u> to <u>do</u>?

破解重點　a. 本類型的考題，答案以選動詞為主。
b. 當聽到 need + N（名詞）或 want + N（名詞）時，答案則選名詞（東西或事物）。
c. 要留心題目問句與對話句型主、被動互換的考法。
d. 祈使句也會出現在「請求」類的考題中，如：Please + V....。

大師　關鍵指引

1. 常考表「請求」的用語：

• I wonder if you could + V...?
• Is it all right for you to + V...?
• Do you mind if I + V...?
• May I + V...?

• Would it be OK if I + V...?
• Would you mind + Ving...?
• Can/Could I + V...?
• Will/Would you + V?

2. 常考表「提供協助」的句型：

• Would you like me to + V...?

• Do you want me to + V...?

• Let me know if I can be of any help to sb.

• Is there anything I can help you with?

• Is there anything I can get you?

• May I give you a hand with sth.?

• Shall I help you with sth....?

• Can I get you anything to eat/drink?

3. 常考表「邀請」的句型：

• Do you want to come over to my birthday party?

• Would you like to come over to my birthday party?

• Will you come over to my birthday party?

• You want to come over to my birthday party?

• Won't you come over to my birthday party?

⑨ **考對話「主旨」**

出題關鍵　**discuss / talk about / topic / subject**

全真題　<u>What</u> are the woman and the man <u>discussing</u>?

<u>What</u> are they <u>discussing</u>?

<u>What</u> is the conservation <u>about</u>?

破解重點　a. 這類考題以聽對話者二人共同提出的「名詞」為主（鎖定對話的前半段），但有些題目必須聽名詞與動詞方可找出答案。

b. 有些對話會在最後一句再提到主旨（亦即名詞），因此若剛開始無法聽懂或選不出答案時，應堅持到最後一秒；但若一開始即聽到二者提及的名詞，則應立刻圈選答案。

大師 關鍵指引

常考表「主旨」的句型：

- Welcome to....
- As you know....
- Today, we're going to talk about....
- I'm calling to ask....
- I hear....
- Did you hear...?
- I was wondering if we received....
- This is + 〈人名〉 with + 〈公司名〉. I'm calling to verify....
- Let's move on to the final item on our agenda, ...

- I'm calling to tell you that....
- As I mention....
- I'd like to announce that....
- So, have you checked out that...?
- I heard....
- Have you heard...?
- How's + 主題 + going?

Example

MP3 042 ▶▶ MP3 046

1. Where does this conversation take place?
   (A) In a bank
   (B) In a police station
   (C) In an airport
   (D) In a train station
   (A) (B) (C) (D)

2. What is the woman looking for?
   (A) A currency exchange counter
   (B) A security guard
   (C) A telephone
   (D) A boarding gate
   (A) (B) (C) (D)

3. What will the woman probably do next?
   (A) Call the relevant authorities
   (B) Contact a security officer
   (C) Make an official report
   (D) Leave her address and phone number
   (A) (B) (C) (D)

4. Who most likely is the woman?
   (A) A professor
   (B) A doctor
   (C) A receptionist
   (D) A student
   Ⓐ Ⓑ Ⓒ Ⓓ

5. What does the man want to do?
   (A) Change a doctor's appointment
   (B) Apply for medical school
   (C) Attend a college lecture
   (D) Leave a message for Dr. Ting
   Ⓐ Ⓑ Ⓒ Ⓓ

6. When was this call made?
   (A) January
   (B) February
   (C) March
   (D) April
   Ⓐ Ⓑ Ⓒ Ⓓ

7. What is the woman concerned about?
   (A) Rising office space costs
   (B) Extending a deadline
   (C) Unanswered correspondence
   (D) Unfilled invoices
   Ⓐ Ⓑ Ⓒ Ⓓ

8. What does the woman hope to do?
   (A) Move to a cheaper location
   (B) Prioritize the man's work
   (C) Avoid a rent increase
   (D) Receive Mr. Fish's assistance
   Ⓐ Ⓑ Ⓒ Ⓓ

9. What will the man probably do next?
   (A) Respond to customers' e-mails
   (B) Negotiate the rent
   (C) Contact Mr. Fish
   (D) Call a real estate agent
   Ⓐ Ⓑ Ⓒ Ⓓ

10. Where does the conversation take place?
    (A) At a movie theater
    (B) At a travel agency
    (C) At a music school
    (D) At a concert hall   Ⓐ Ⓑ Ⓒ Ⓓ

11. Who is Marcus?
    (A) A ticket agent
    (B) An usher
    (C) A piano teacher
    (D) A performer   Ⓐ Ⓑ Ⓒ Ⓓ

12. What does the man imply?
    (A) He won't be able to purchase tickets.
    (B) He could have gotten better seats.
    (C) The tickets went on sale some time ago.
    (D) He has a music lesson every Sunday.   Ⓐ Ⓑ Ⓒ Ⓓ

13. What are the speakers discussing?
    (A) A technology conference
    (B) A computer program
    (C) An employee orientation
    (D) A management trainee   Ⓐ Ⓑ Ⓒ Ⓓ

14. What does the woman ask the man to do?
    (A) Join her for brunch
    (B) Report to the chief technology officer
    (C) Introduce her to Dr. Hampton
    (D) Give her directions   Ⓐ Ⓑ Ⓒ Ⓓ

15. What does the man say?
    (A) All employees should go to the Rosewood Room.
    (B) Joseph Hampton is a respected computer scientist.
    (C) The woman is lucky to have found the right place.
    (D) He will accompany her to the meeting.   Ⓐ Ⓑ Ⓒ Ⓓ

Questions 1~3

MP3
042

1. 答案：(C)

破題 Where/conversation ⇨ 聽取「地點」字眼，或該地點有關的「特性字眼」來推論（聽「名詞」）。

解析 由男子第一次發言的 terminal 及女子第二次發言的 flight 及 boarding，可推知此處為機場，故本題選 (C)。

2. 答案：(C)

破題 What/woman/look for ⇨ 聽取女子說的話，找「名詞」。

解析 由女子第一次發言的 have left my cell phone...，可知答案為 (C) telephone。

3. 答案：(D)

破題 What/woman/probably/do/next ⇨ 原則上聽女子說的話，注意聽未來可能會做的「動作」。

解析 本題是「特殊考法」，因為一、三句女子說的話並沒有此題的相關線索。而男子第二次發言 Why don't you... 表建議，後面所接之動作 leave your contact information with me 即為答案。注意，此處以 address and phone number 代替原句中的 contact information。

(錄音內容)
Questions 1 through 3 refer to the following conversation.

W: Hi, I think I may have left my cell phone here while I was exchanging money.

M: I'm sorry. Nobody has turned one in to us. There are security officers stationed at the far end of the terminal. Perhaps you should report this to them.

W: I would, but my flight has already started boarding and I really can't miss it.

M: Why don't you leave your contact information with me and I'll pass it on to the relevant authorities.

題目 1~3 請參照以下對話。

女：嗨，我想我剛才在換錢的時候可能把手機掉在這裡了。

男：抱歉，沒有人交手機給我們。在航空站走到底的地方有駐守的警衛，或許妳應該向他們反映這件事。

女：我很願意，可是我的班機已經開始登機了，我真的不能錯過。

男：妳何不把妳的聯絡方式留給我，我會轉交給相關單位。

題目&選項翻譯

1. 這段對話發生在什麼地方？
   (A) 在銀行
   (B) 在警察局
   (C) 在機場
   (D) 在火車站

2. 女子在找什麼？
   (A) 匯兌櫃台
   (B) 警衛人員
   (C) 電話
   (D) 登機門

3. 女子接下來大概會怎麼做？
   (A) 打電話給相關單位
   (B) 聯絡警衛
   (C) 正式報案
   (D) 留下她的地址和電話號碼

☐ station [ˋsteʃən] v. 部署；配置；駐紮

☐ terminal [ˋtɝmənl] n. 航空站

☐ authorities [əˋθɔrətɪz] n. 當局；官方

Questions 4~6

4. 答案：(C)

破題 Who/woman ⇨ 問女子的工作。可由對話中提到女子工作性質的字眼來推論。

解析 由男子第一次發言說的... physical exam scheduled... but... not... able... make 及女子第一次發言說的 ... If you cancel, I won't be able to reschedule...，可推知答案為 (C)。

5. 答案：(A)

破題 What/man/want/do ⇨ 聽男子說的話，注意聽「動作」。

解析 由男子第一次發言說的 ... scheduled... not... able... make...，加上第二次發言說的 I was hoping to see Dr. Ting sometime next week.，可推知他想要 reschedule，故選 (A)。

6. 答案：(A)

破題 When/was/call/made ⇨ 聽與「時間」有關的字眼。

解析 由男子第二次發言 That's more than a month away.（指上一句 reschedule 後的時間），加上女子第二次發言說的 Dr. Ting... lecturing... for the entire month of February.，可推知打電話的時間為 January，故選 (A)。

録音内容

Questions 4 through 6 refer to the following conversation.

M: Hi, this is Rob Preston calling. I have a physical exam scheduled for this afternoon, but I'm not going to be able to make it.

W: OK Mr. Preston, but Dr. Ting's schedule is quite full. If you cancel, I won't be able to reschedule your appointment until the first week of March.

M: That's more than a month away. I was hoping to see Dr. Ting sometime next week.

W: I'm sorry. Dr. Ting is going to be lecturing at the medical college for the entire month of February.

題目 4~6 請參照以下對話。

男：嗨，我是羅布‧普雷斯頓。我約好了今天下午體檢，可是我沒辦法赴約。

女：沒關係，普雷斯頓先生。不過丁大夫的行程相當滿，假如你取消的話，我要到三月的第一週才能幫你重約時間。

男：那要過一個多月囉。我希望下星期能有時間看丁大夫。

女：抱歉，丁大夫整個二月都要去醫學院教課。

題目&選項翻譯

4. 女子最可能是什麼人？
   (A) 教授
   (B) 醫生
   (C) 接待員
   (D) 學生

5. 男子想做什麼？
   (A) 跟醫生改約時間
   (B) 申請醫學院
   (C) 去大學上課
   (D) 留話給丁大夫

6. 這通電話是什麼時候打的？
   (A) 一月
   (B) 二月
   (C) 三月
   (D) 四月

☐ physical exam 身體檢查

☐ make it 到達；趕上

☐ lecture [ˋlɛktʃɚ] v. 向……演講；對……授課

Questions 7~9

MP3
044

7. 答案：(A)

破題 What/woman/concerned ➭ 聽女子話中表「關切」的「強烈字眼」。

解析 由女子發言的 ... landlord... planning... increasing the rent. Could you... listing... average rates... different parts... 可知，答案為 (A)。注意，此處用 rising 取代原句的 increasing。

8. 答案：(C)

破題 What/woman/hope/do ➭ 聽女人所說未來可能的相關「動作」字眼。

解析 由女子第二次發言的 If we can find a few less expensive locations，以及 ... I may be able... persuade... landlord not to raise our rent.，可知答案為 (C)。注意，此處用 avoid a rent increase 代替原句的 persuade... landlord not to raise our rent。

9. 答案：(C)

破題 What/man/do/next ➭ 聽男人所說未來可能的相關「動作」字眼。

解析 由男子第二次發言的 I'll let Mr. Fish know about...，可推知答案為 (C)。注意，本句中 and 前後皆有動作字眼，但以第一個提到的動作優先選擇。

錄音內容
Questions 7 through 9 refer to the following conversation.

W: Ben, our lease is almost up and the landlord is planning on increasing the rent. Could you write a short report listing the average rates for office spaces in different parts of the city?

M: Sure, but when do you need it by? Mr. Fish asked me to reply to all of the Customers' e-mails by the end of the day.

W: The rent survey takes priority. If we can find a few less expensive locations, I may be able to persuade the landlord not to raise our rent.

M: OK, I'll let Mr. Fish know about your request and then start calling real estate agents.

録音翻譯

題目 7~9 請參照以下對話。

女：班，我們的租約快到期了，房東打算調漲房租。你能不能寫篇簡短的報告，列出市內不同區域的辦公據點的平均租金？

男：好的，可是妳什麼時候要？費雪先生要我在下班前回覆所有顧客的電子郵件。

女：租金調查先做。假如我們能找到比較便宜的地點，我或許就有辦法說服房東不要調漲我們的房租。

男：好，我會把你的要求告訴費雪先生，然後開始打電話給房仲業經紀人。

題目&選項翻譯

7. 女子關切的是什麼事？
   (A) 辦公據點的費用上漲
   (B) 延長期限
   (C) 尚未回覆的信
   (D) 未開立的發票

8. 女子希望做什麼？
   (A) 搬到比較便宜的地方
   (B) 把男子的工作排出優先順序
   (C) 避免調漲房租
   (D) 得到費雪先生協助

9. 男子接下來大概會做什麼？
   (A) 回覆顧客的電子郵件
   (B) 協商房租
   (C) 聯絡費雪先生
   (D) 打電話給房仲業經紀人

- [ ] lease [lis] n. 租約
- [ ] landlord [ˋlænd‚lɔrd] n. 房東
- [ ] priority [praɪˋɔrətɪ] n. 優先；優先權
- [ ] persuade [pɚˋswed] v. 說服
- [ ] real estate [ɪsˋtet] 不動產
- [ ] invoice [ˋɪnvɔɪs] n. 發票
- [ ] correspondence [‚kɔrəˋspɑndəns] n.（總稱）信件
- [ ] negotiate [nɪˋgoʃɪ‚et] v. 協商；談判

Questions 10~12

10. 答案：(D)

破　題 Where/conversation ➡ 問「地點」，由地點的相關字眼來推知答案。

解　析 由男子第一次發言的 I'd like two tickets for the... show...，可推知為 At a concert hall，答案為 (D)。

11. 答案：(D)

破　題 Who/Marcus ➡ 問「職稱」，由和 Marcus 相關的字眼來推知其工作。

解　析 由男子第一次發言中的 the Marcus Dupree show 及第女子第一次發言中的 ... show are sold out，可知答案為 (D)。因為一個人若有 show，表示他是 performer。

12. 答案：(C)

破　題 聽What/man/imply ➡ 聽男人的話中之意來推論。

解　析 由男子第二次發言中的假設語氣 I knew I should've bought tickets as soon as they went on sale. 可推知，正確答案為 (C)。

(錄音內容)

Questions 10 through 12 refer to the following conversation.

M: Hi. I'd like two tickets for the Marcus Dupree show next Friday.

W: I'm sorry. Both that show and the following night's show are sold out. We do have excellent seats available for the Sunday afternoon show though. That's the one on the tenth.

M: I knew I should've bought tickets as soon as they went on sale. Oh well, I guess I can postpone my piano lesson.

W: So, that'll be two tickets for the matinee, right?

(錄音翻譯)

題目 10~12 請參照以下對話。

男：嗨，我要買兩張馬可斯‧杜普利下週五演出的票。

女：抱歉，那一場和隔天晚上演出的票都賣光了。不過星期天下午倒是有非常棒的位子，就是十號那一場。

男：我就知道我應該在票一開賣的時候就買。嗯，好吧，我想我可以把我的鋼琴課延後。

女：那就是日場票兩張囉，對吧？

(題目&選項翻譯)

10. 這段對話發生在什麼地方？
    (A) 在電影院
    (B) 在旅行社
    (C) 在音樂學校
    (D) 在音樂廳

11. 馬可斯是什麼人？
    (A) 售票員
    (B) 引座員
    (C) 鋼琴老師
    (D) 演奏家

12. 男子暗示什麼？
    (A) 他沒辦法買票。
    (B) 他本來可以買到更好的位子。
    (C) 票在前一段時間就開賣了。
    (D) 他每星期日都要上音樂課。

☐ postpone [post`pon] *v.* 將……延後

☐ matinee [ˌmætə`ne] *n.* 日戲；日場

☐ usher [`ʌʃɚ] *n.* （劇場等）引座員

Questions 13~15

13. 答案：(C)

破題 What/speakers/discuss ⇨ 問「主旨」，聽二者的談話主題，以「名詞」為主。

解析 由女子第一次發言說的 I'm here for the new employee orientation brunch...，及男子第一次發言說的 ...actually two brunches. 可推知，正確答案為 (C)。

14. 答案：(D)

破題 What/woman/ask/man/do ⇨ 聽女子要男子做的「動作」字眼。

解析 由女子第一次發言說的 Could you tell me how to get there（there 代表上句所指的地方）可知，她希望男子 Give her directions，故選 (D)。

15. 答案：(B)

破題 What/man/say ⇨ 聽男人說的「特殊訊息」。

解析 男子第二次發言時提到 Dr. Hampton is one of the leading computer programming experts in the world，可知答案為 (B)。男子說 Dr. Hampton is a respected computer scientist. 即代表他是 one of the leading computer programming experts。

[錄音內容]

Questions 13 through 15 refer to the following conversation.

W: Hi, I'm here for the new employee orientation brunch, but I can't find the right room. Could you tell me how to get there?

M: Well, there are actually two brunches. Are you in the engineering division or are you a management trainee?

W: Engineering, I guess. I'm supposed to report to Joseph Hampton, the chief technology officer.

M: Oh, you're lucky. Dr. Hampton is one of the leading computer programming experts in the world. You'll want to head upstairs to the Rosewood Room. Go up that escalator; it's the first door on the right.

錄音翻譯

題目 13~15 請參照以下對話。

女：嗨，我來這裡參加新進員工早午餐訓練營，可是我找不到該去的廳。你可不可以告訴我要怎麼走？

男：嗯，早午餐其實有兩場。妳是工程部的還是管理部的見習生？

女：我想是工程部的。我應該要向科技長約瑟夫‧漢普敦先生報到。

男：噢，妳很幸運。漢普敦博士是全世界屬一屬二的頂尖電腦程式專家。妳要上樓到紫檀廳。搭手扶梯上去，右邊第一扇門就是了。

題目 & 選項翻譯

13. 說話者在討論什麼事？
    (A) 科技大會
    (B) 電腦程式
    (C) 員工訓練營
    (D) 管理見習生

14. 女子要男子做什麼？
    (A) 跟她一起去用早午餐
    (B) 向科長技報到
    (C) 把她介紹給漢普敦博士
    (D) 告訴她方向

15. 男子說了什麼？
    (A) 所有的員工都應該去紫檀廳。
    (B) 約瑟夫‧漢普敦是可敬的電腦科學家。
    (C) 女子很幸運，找到了對的地方。
    (D) 他會陪她去開會。

☐ orientation [ˌorɪɛnˋteʃən] *n.* 對新生或新進員工的訓練
☐ brunch [brʌntʃ] *n.* 早午餐（早、午餐合在一起的一餐）
☐ trainee [treˋni] *n.* 新兵；見習生
☐ head [hɛd] *v.*（向特定方向）出發

答題基本對策

① 先瀏覽題目

務必在播放錄音內容前先瀏覽題目，看題目前、中、後的重點字，即「疑問詞」、「主詞」和「動詞」，來預測對話可能出現的內容。

② 聽重點，找重點

聽到對話出現與題目相關的內容時，立即去看該題目的選項；看到正確選項時，並立即圈選答案。

③「同義字」或「同義片語」常是答案所在

多益考試的正確答案常會以「同義字詞」或「同義片語」取代錄音內容中的用字，考生務必多熟悉同義字彙或片語的轉換。

④ 問什麼，聽什麼：

(1) 問題若是問有關男子的事情，專心聽取男子的對話內容；反之，若問有關女子的問題，則專心聽取女子的對話。

(2) 題目問「地點」（Where），則注意聽「地方」字（如 library），或是注意聽與地方相關但不直接告訴你地方的關鍵字（如內容提到 to cash a check，地點應該為 bank）。通常由兩到三個關鍵字即可推論出正確地點名稱。

(3) 題目問「動作」時，注意聽「動作」。

(4) 若題目問說話者討論什麼（discussing），就必須 注意聽主旨句或名詞。

⇨ 常見句型：I heard... / Did you hear... / Have you heard...

⑤ 真人不露相

題目中有時會問到並未真正在對話中出現的人名，（亦即該人士並未真正說話），而是由其他人來「代言之」，因此「聽到」對話中提及題目所問的「人名」時即立刻去找答案。

⑥ 務必要聽清楚對話的第一句

尤其是第一句話中加重音的字詞（動詞、名詞、形容詞、副詞），因為它可能是主旨，更有可能為下一句對話會提出的問題。

⑦ 注意每句對話中出現的名詞

對話中提到的名詞，在下一句對話再提到時，通常會用代名詞 that 或 it 來代替，而該名詞通常不會再出現，所以在一開始出現時就要留意這些重點名詞。

⑧「重音字」、「數字」、「時間」字眼常是出題關鍵

整段對話中，不是答案所在的句子仍要注意聽其中的「重音字」、「數字」、「時間」等字眼，因為它們可能是下一句對話的線索。

破題關鍵要領

① 問「why」的問題

注意聽說明「原因」或「理由」的句子。

② 問「who」的問題

這類問題的答案可能要問的是「人名」、「職稱」或「部門單位」。

③ 問「專有名詞」問題

比方說 sprinkler system（灑水系統），若選項有包含該專有名詞的相關線索字，即為標準答案。

④ 問「負面概念」問題

例如，題目問對話主角為何 upset 時，聽到對話中有對應的負面字眼，通常就是標準答案。

⑤ 問「聽者是誰」的問題

題目若出現 To whom is + 人 + speaking? 的句型時，要注意聽聽眾是誰。

⑥ 問「特定時間」的問題

若題目問 before + 特定時間（如：before 2001），通常對話會先講到 after + 特定時間的事情，需要稍加推論才能知道正確答案。

⑦ 問「事實」、「確定的事」、「要做的事」或「已發布的公告事項」

這類問題的答案通常不會在有 probably、maybe、perhaps 等「不確定」字眼的句子中。

⑧ 暗示性問題

題目問到某人或某事暗指（imply）何事時，不以聽到的「事實陳述」來作答，而要從聽到的「相關線索或資訊」來推測。

⑨ 注意聲東擊西的陷阱

題目問有關「主角」的事情，卻常先講「配角」，如題目問 Ann，卻先講 Amy 的事情。因此，要注意聽對話中討論的人名。

⑩ 不該聽的不聽

聽到不是題目重點的敘述或句型時，立刻不再聽下去。例如：題目問男子的電腦，對話中的女子一直說自己電腦的狀況，則不須聽下去；或是題目是女子有問題去問男子，男子若回答：I'm not sure、probably、maybe、perhaps，則立刻不聽下去，因為此類用語為不確定的概念。

⑪ 出現〈What does the man learn?〉的問句

若問男子得知何事，通常要聽女子的發言，反之亦然。若為兩個男子的對話，題目則會問：What does the first man learn?，要從第一個男子的發言找答案。

⑫ 出現〈Why isn't + sb. + going to...〉的問句

出現這類問題，則表示某人沒有做某件事或去某個地方，答案通常會出現在表「原因」的連接詞（如：beacause、as、since）等或介系詞片語（如：due to、owing to、as a result of）之後的敘述。

⑬ 出現〈What will Sb. probably do...?〉的問句

聽到這類問題時，要注意聽此人的所做的「動作」。

⑭ 出現〈What does the man <u>want</u> from the woman?〉的問句

(1)看到這類問句，要聽男子的發言，若男子的發言中也有 Do you think you could + V... 的句型，could 後面的動作字眼即為答案。如：

Do you think you could feed my dog while I am away next Monday?

⇨ To feed his dog 即為需要對方幫忙的動作。

(2) want ⇨ 表示想要去做的「動作」（want to + V）或想要得到的「東西」（want + N），可大概瀏覽選項，若皆為動作字，則聽動詞；若皆為物品名稱，則聽名詞。

⑮ 出現〈What does the man <u>want to know</u>?〉的問句

看到這類問句，要去聽男子的發言中所問的問題。want to know 表原來不知或不了解的事情，因此要注意聽男子所說的問句。

⑯ 出現〈How has the building <u>changed</u>?〉的問句

看到這類問句時，要注意 Have you noticed / found out... 這類句型，後面的敘述即爲答案。對話中聽到的問句內容和題目所問的重點一樣，答案通常就是緊跟在重點後的字眼或下一句話。此爲利用句型破解的一種方法。

⑰ 出現〈What is the woman's <u>problem</u>?〉的問句

看到這類問句，要聽到女人提及的「負面」字眼。如：terrible、never... again、too bad 等字，後面的敘述常是答案所在。這些關鍵字即暗示「問題點」要出現了。

⑱ 注意「轉承語」

Part 3「簡短對話」和 Part 4「簡短獨白」中經常可透過一些特殊用字，來預測出題重點所在或答案位置。

(1) 表前後相反：but, yet

(2) 否定字眼：not, barely, hardly, scarcely, never, no, none

(3) 比較級：-er... than, more... than...

(4) 獨一性：only, exclusively, except

(5) 強烈字眼：definitely, absolutely, certainly, especially

(6) 假設語氣：If, I wish...

(7) 因果關係：so, because, since, therefore

(8) 表目的：to V, in order to V, so as to V

(9) 讓步子句：although, though

(10) 轉折語：however, otherwise

(11) 附加字眼：besides, in addition, also

大師　關鍵指引

多益測驗常見的轉承語：

1. 表順序

• First(ly) / first of all / to begin with　首先

• Second(ly)　第二點

• Third(ly)　第三點

• next/then　其次／然後

• finally / at last / at length / eventually / in the end　最後

- in the first place 第一點
- last but not east 最後，但不是最不重要的

2. 舉例或說明

- for example / for instance 譬如說
- take sb./sth. for example 以……為例來說
- including 包括……
- in other words 換句話說
- that is (to say) / in other words / namely 也就是說
- especially 特別是
- in particular 尤其是

3. 對照

- on the contrary / conversely 相反的
- in spite of this 儘管如此
- by contrast 對照起來
- conversely 相反地
- yet 但是
- still 仍然
- notwithstanding 儘管
- on the one hand 從一方面來說
- instead 不……而……，反而……
- for all that 儘管如此
- in contrast to/with 與……相反
- although/though 雖然
- however 然而
- nevertheless 雖然……但是
- in spite of / despite 縱使
- on the other hand 從另一方面來說

4. 表目的

- for this purpose 為此目的
- to this end 為此目的
- with this object in mind 心裡懷此目的

5. 表因果關係

- as a result / in consequence 結果
- consequently 因而
- therefore/hence 因此
- for this reason 因為此理由
- and so / so 所以
- as a consequence 後果是
- accordingly 從而
- under such circumstances 在此情況下
- for the sake of 因……之故
- thus 如此；於是

6. 作比較

- similarly/likewise 同樣地
- at the same time 同時
- in a like manner 以同樣的方式
- in much the same way 以幾乎相同的方式

7. 增加或更進一步

- besides / in addition 此外
- furthermore / moreover / what's more 再者
- by the way 順便一提
- on the top of that 而且
- equally important 同樣重要的是
- in other words 換句話說

8. 確定

- no doubt / doubtlessly / undoubtedly 無疑地
- of course 當然
- to be sure 的確
- certainly/definitely/absolutely 確實地

9. 結論或綜結

- in brief / in short 簡言之
- in conclusion / to conclude 總而言之
- to sum up / to summarize / in summary 總結來說
- on the whole / by and large 大體上說來
- in a word 一言以蔽之

高頻字彙和情境用語

① 旅遊用語

1 行前規劃

- accommodations 膳宿設備
- advance payment 預付
- book/booking 預約
- package tour 套裝旅遊
- confirmation 確認
- ID card 身分證
- itinerary 旅程

- admission 入場費
- advance ticket 預售票
- on-season price 旺季價格
- personal effects 個人物品
- group-inclusive tour 整團旅遊
- insurance 保險
- advance booking 預訂

2 機場

- terminal 航空站
- baggage claim 行李領取處
- direct flight 直達班機
- transit passenger 過境旅客
- vacant 有空位的
- validate 使……有效
- currency exchange 貨幣兌換
- destination airport 目的地機場
- detour 繞道
- carry-on baggage 隨身行李

- aviation 航空
- boarding pass 登機證
- ticket counter 售票處
- unaccompanied baggage 託運行李
- valid 有效的
- carrier 航空公司；從事運輸業的公司
- departure lounge 離境大廳；候機室
- description of articles 攜帶物品說明書
- duty-free 免稅的
- claim tag 行李牌

3 海關

- security check 安全檢查
- quarantine 檢疫
- yellow card 國際預防接種證明書

- customs 海關
- immigration 入境（檢查）

4 飯店食宿

- hotel classification 旅館分級
- meal voucher 餐券
- safety box 保險箱

- hotel reservations 旅館預訂處
- meeting service 接送服務
- Continental breakfast 歐陸式早餐

5 交通運輸

- metro 地下鐵
- bus depot 長程巴士站
- expressway 高速公路
- fare 車費
- conductor 車掌
- ground transport 地面運輸

6 觀光遊樂

- souvenir 紀念品
- full fare 全額票價
- general store 百貨店；雜貨店
- entertainment area 娛樂區
- general information 綜合服務處
- hot spring resort 溫泉勝地

7 通訊

- overseas call 國際電話
- local call 國內電話

② 商業用語

1 公司營運

- head office 總公司
- listed company 上市公司
- subsidiary company 子公司
- joint-stock company 股份有限公司
- first-rate firm 一流公司
- reliable 可信賴的
- line of business 業務種類
- be well accepted 很受歡迎
- have a good reputation 有好名聲
- branch office 分公司
- parent company 母公司
- affiliated company 關係企業
- limited company 有限公司
- leading 主要的
- well-established 信譽卓越的
- be warmly received 受好評
- be highly estimated 評價很高
- enjoy a high reputation 享有佳評

2 董事運作

- managing director 常務董事
- convene the board 召開董事會
- the board + approve 董事會同意
- the board + ratify 董事會批准
- board approval 董事會的認可
- board meeting 董事會議
- member of the board 董事會成員
- be elected to the board 獲選為董事
- sit on the board 擔任董事
- the board + meet 董事會召開會議
- the board + reject 董事會拒絕
- board level 董事會層級
- board resolution 董事會決議

❸ 銷售目標與業績

- achieve the target 達成目標
- exceed the target 超越目標
- lower the target 降低目標
- meet/reach the target 符合／達到目標
- miss the target 未達目標
- raise the target 提高目標
- set a target 設定目標
- fall short of the target 未能達成目標
- budget target 預算目標
- stay within the target 維持在目標之內
- growth target 成長目標
- sales target 營業目標；銷售目標
- achieve sales 達成營業額
- sales amount to 總計銷售額為……
- sales + decline/fall 銷售額下降
- sales + rise/grow 銷售額增加
- sales analysis 銷售分析
- sales drive 推銷活動
- sales plan 銷售計畫；營業計畫
- sales promotion 促銷
- sales quota 銷貨配額
- sales tax 營業稅
- annual sales 年銷售額
- gross sales 銷售總額
- net sales 銷售淨額
- open the export section 開設出口部
- expand one's business 拓展業務
- expand market 拓展市場

❹ 價格

- best price 最佳價格
- lowest price 最低價格
- competitive price 具競爭力價格
- market price 市價
- current price 時價
- unit price 單價
- fixed price 定價
- net price 淨價
- sale price 售價
- price level 物價水準
- price stabilization 價格穩定
- retail price 零售價
- wholesale price 批發價
- lower/reduce a price 降價
- make a price reduction 減價
- mark down the price 降底價格
- cut the price 削價
- slash the price 砍價
- raise the price 漲價
- under quote 報出低於……的價格
- bargain down the price 殺價
- haggle over the price down 討價還價
- price tag 價碼牌
- pay a high price for sth. 高價購買某物
- a good price 划算的價格
- a moderate/reasonable/right/fair price 合理的價格
- a low price 便宜的價格
- a reduced price 降低的價格
- a high price 昂貴的價格
- an exorbitant price 離譜的價格
- an outrageous price 過分的價格
- a steep price 過高的價格
- the wholesale price 批發價

5 處理訂單

- initial order 初次訂購
- trial order 試購
- regular order 定期訂購
- firm order 確定訂購
- minimum order 最低訂購
- be on order 已訂購
- place an order 下訂單
- receive an order 接到訂單
- confirm an order 確認訂單
- fulfill/supply an order 履行訂單
- order + be down 訂單減少
- order + come in 訂單到達
- bulk order 大批訂購
- repeat order 再訂購

- sample order 樣品訂單
- telephone order 電話訂購
- scheduled order 計畫訂購
- large order 大量訂購
- place an order with... 向……訂購
- get/obtain/secure orders 取得訂單
- process/execute an order 處理訂單
- win an order 獲得訂單
- cancel an order 取消訂單
- decline an order 婉拒訂單
- rush in 湧現
- order + be up 訂單增加
- back order 未交清訂單

6 折扣

- offer a discount 提供折扣
- negotiate a discount 協商折扣
- cash discount 現金折扣
- quantity discount 大量購買折扣
- deep discount 大幅度折價

- be entitled to a discount 有權給予折扣
- give a discount of X percent 給予百分之X的折扣
- discount price 折扣價
- basic discount 基本折扣
- at a discount 以折扣價

7 商品

- goods 貨品
- article （一項）商品
- commodity 商品
- the latest product 最新產品
- replacement 替換品
- defective goods 瑕疵品
- good buy 買得便宜的東西
- seasonal goods 季節品

- item （一項）商品
- merchandise 貨品
- product 產品
- main lines of business 主要營業項目
- newly-developed product 新（開發的）產品
- substitute 替代品
- rejected goods 不合格品
- insured goods 被保險商品

8 存貨

- old stock 陳貨
- goods in stock 庫存貨品
- be sold out 售罄
- in short supply 供給短缺
- stock 存貨
- goods to arrive 將到貨
- be out of stock 無存貨

9 品質

- best quality 最佳品質
- superior quality 優良品質
- inferior quality 低劣品質
- recall 回收
- put on the market 上市
- highest quality 最高品質
- poor quality 劣等品質
- handle 處理
- market 行銷

10 郵遞業務

- enclose 隨函附上
- by return 立即回郵
- by air parcel post 航空小包裹
- outgoing 寄出的
- special delivery 限時專送
- confidential 親展；機密
- post office box 郵政信箱 (= POB)
- enclosure 附件 (= enc.)
- validity 有效性
- receipt 收據
- stamp 郵票
- package 包裹
- attach 附加
- by airmail 航空郵件
- by surface mail 陸上或海運郵件
- incoming 到達的
- registered mail 掛號郵件
- forward 轉交；轉寄
- postscript 附筆 (= P.S.)
- printed matter 印刷品
- voucher 憑證
- envelope 信封
- mailbox 郵筒
- scale 秤

11 生產與物流

- manufacturer 製造廠商
- importer 進口商
- wholesaler 批發商
- packer 食品包裝商
- sub-agent 次代理商
- sole agent 獨家代理商
- connection 關係
- distributor 經銷商
- exporter 出口商
- retailer 零售商
- agent 代理人
- exclusive selling agent 獨家銷售代理商
- ad agent 廣告代理商
- customer/client 顧客

- producer 生產者
- maker 製造者
- competitor 競爭者
- supplier 供應商

12 經濟現況

- market trend 市場動向
- strong 堅強的
- firm 堅實的
- weak 疲弱的
- quiet 清淡的
- jump 急升
- slump 暴跌
- decline 下跌
- sag 軟化
- consumer reaction 消費者反應
- bullish 看漲的
- stiff 堅挺的
- bearish 看跌的
- soft 疲軟的
- advance 上揚
- soar 暴漲
- collapse 崩跌
- stiffen 硬化
- price trend 價格動向
- economic recovery 景氣復甦

13 投資

- stock market 股票市場
- asset allocation 資產配置
- long-term 長期的
- dividend 紅利；股息
- loss 虧損
- yield 收益
- bull market 牛市（股市行情看漲）
- risk tolerance 風險承擔
- portfolio 投資組合
- short-term 短期的
- principal 資本；本金
- tax 稅金
- gain 獲利
- volatility 波動
- bear market 熊市（股市行情看跌）

14 銀行業務

- open an account 開戶
- traveler's check 旅行支票
- write a check 開支票
- cash a check 將支票兌現
- bounce a check 跳票
- bank account 銀行帳戶
- checking account 支票帳戶
- security guard 保全人員
- ATM card 提款卡
- have an account 擁有帳戶
- transfer to sb.'s account 轉帳到某人的帳戶
- deposit a check 將支票存入
- sign a check 在支票上簽名
- endorse a check 在支票背面簽名（背書）
- savings account 儲蓄帳戶
- teller 出納員
- foreign exchange counter 國際匯兌櫃臺
- ATM 自動提款機 (= automatic teller machine)

- keypad 鍵盤
- credit card bill 信用卡帳單
- water bill 水費帳單
- phone bill 電話費帳單
- deduct sth. from your account 從你的帳戶扣除……的款項

- electricity/power bill 電費帳單
- gas bill 瓦斯帳單
- utility bill 水電費帳單
- check sb.'s account balance 查詢某人的帳戶餘額

15 工作

- keep late hours 工作到很晚
- work short hours 工作時間短
- flexible working hours 彈性工時
- regular hours 固定的工作時間
- short hours 短工時
- after hours 下班後或打烊後

- put in long hours 長時間工作
- office business hours 辦公時間；營業時間
- opening hours 營業時間；開放時間
- irregular hours 不固定的工作時間
- working hours 工作時數

16 退休

- approach retirement 接近退休年齡
- go into retirement 正式退休
- take retirement 退休
- retirement benefits 退休福利
- early retirement 提早退休
- in retirement 退休後

- extend retirement 延後退休
- mark one's retirement 慶祝某人退休
- retirement age 退休年齡
- retirement pension 退休金
- ahead of retirement 退休前

③ 高頻情境用語

1 表達意見

- As far as I'm concerned 就我而言
- From my point of view 就我的觀點
- If you ask me 假如你問我的話
- It seems to me 就我看來
- What I like about... is... 我喜歡……的地方在於……

表達強烈意見

- It's impossible to deny that... 不容否認的是……
- ...is/are definitely/absolutely... ……肯定／絕對……
- Without a doubt... 無疑……

表達中立意見

- Generally speaking, I think that... 大致來說，我認為……
- Basically, I believe/think that... 基本上，我相信／認為……
- In most cases, I'd have to say that... 在大多數的情況下，我必須說……

表達較弱意見

- ...is/are/should probably... ……八成應該……
- I suppose... 我推測……
- I'm not sure one way or the other, but I guess... 總之我不確定，但我猜……

2 表達支持

- It's quite clear that... 很清楚的是……
- There's no doubt that... 無庸置疑的是……
- The best thing about... is that... ……最棒的地方在於……
- The problem with... is that... ……的問題在於……
- Most importantly... 最重要的是……
- An even important reason is... 更重要的理由是……

3 舉例

- For one thing 一則……
- And another thing is... 再則……
- Let's take... 我們以……
- Let's take... as an example. 我們以……為例。
- Remember? 還記得嗎？
- How/What about...? ……如何？

4 表達困難

- I don't know what to do with... 我不曉得該怎麼處理……
- I can never make sense of... 我完全不能理解……
- I have trouble with... 我搞不定……
- I'm having difficulty doing... 我做不來……
- I'm having a problem... 我處理不了……
- I'm having a hard time with... 我應付不了……
- I can never understand... 我完全搞不懂……
- ... turned out to be hard. ……相當棘手。

5 給予鼓勵

- Stick with it. 堅持下去。
- Why don't you get some help from...? 你何不去向……尋求一點協助？
- Don't give up. It always seems hard when you are just starting out.
  別放棄。萬事總是起頭難。

6 表達不理解

- I'm lost. 我沒搞懂。
- I've lost you there. 我不懂你的意思。
- It's over my head. 我一頭霧水。
- It's beyond me. 我不懂。
- I wonder why you didn't wait for me. 我不曉得你為什麼沒等我。
- I can't make heads and tails of it. 我被它搞得莫名其妙。
- It doesn't make any sense to me. 它對我沒有任何意義。
- I didn't quite catch what you said just now. 我不太明白你剛才所說的話。

7 給予建議

- How about the whole week? 整個星期怎麼樣？
- It's time we cleared off the desk. 我們該把書桌清理一下了。
- If I were you, I'd apply for that position.
  假如我是你的話，我就會應徵那個職位。
- How does tomorrow sound? 明天聽起來怎麼樣？
- Why not do it now? 為什麼不現在就做？
- You'd better wrap it up before Friday. 你最好在星期五以前把它結束掉。
- Wouldn't it be better if you do it now? 你現在做不是比較好嗎？
- It won't hurt if you give him a ring now. 你現在打個電話給他不會有什麼損失。
- You might as well as do it tomorrow. 你不如明天再做。

8 提供協助

- Need a hand with...? 需不需要幫忙……？
- Do you want me to...? 你要不要我……？
- I can give you a hand with... 我可以幫忙你……
- Do you need a hand with...? 你需不需要人幫忙……？

9 請求協助用語

- Could you...? 你能不能……
- Could I ask you...? 我能不能請你……？

10 期限用語

- I don't know whether I can make the deadline.
  我不曉得我能不能趕上截止期限。
- I don't know whether I can get an extension. 我不曉得我能不能獲得延期。
- The deadline has been extended for THREE weeks.
  截止期限延長「三週」了。
- There is a two-day extension. 可以延長兩天。

11 總結用語

- All in all, ... 總的來說，……
- Overall, ... 整體而言，……
- Generally speaking, ... 一般來說，……
- In a nutshell, ... 概括來說，……
- The bottom line is... 總結來說，……
- When you look at the big picture, ... 綜觀全局，……
- The key point is... 重點在於……

4 同義詞語互換

片語	定義	同義字彙與片語
all of a sudden	突然	all at once; suddenly
break down	故障	stop functioning; malfuction
bring forward	提前	move to an earlier time
call it a day	今天到此為止	stop working for the day
calm down	冷靜	relax; take it easy; settle down
can't complain	無可抱怨	the situation is good or acceptable
clear up	1. 澄清	1. clarify; explain; make clear
	2. 放晴	2. become nice and sunny
cross out	刪除	eliminate; discard; get rid of; throw out; dispose of
deal with	處理	manage; handle

drop by	造訪	stop for a casual visit
every now and then	有時	sometimes; occasionally; from time to time
fall behind	落後	not move as quickly as; lag behind
fill in for	代替	substitute for; take the place of
get along with	與……和睦相處	live or work harmoniously with
get around	到處跑	move from place to place
get back	1. 返回	1. return
	2. 取回	2. recover a possession
get down	使沮喪	depress; discourage
get mixed up	混淆	confused; complicate
get rid of	擺脫	discard; dispose of
get used to	習慣	become used to; be accustomed to
give a hand	1. 鼓掌	1. applaud; clap
	2. 幫忙	2. help; assist
give away	贈與	give as a gift
give up	放棄	cease, stop trying; abandon
go down	下跌	reduce, lessen, fall, drop
go on	1. 繼續	1. continue; proceed
	2. 發生	2. happen; occur
go through	1. 經歷	1. endure; suffer
	2. 溫習	2. review; go over
go up	上漲	rise; increase
go with	1. 陪伴	1. accompany
	2. 相配	2. look good together
hang on	1. 等候	1. wait
	2. 堅持	2. persist; persevere
hang up	1. 掛（電話）	1. put the receiver back; stop talking (on the phone)
	2. 擱置	2. delay; put off; postpone
have to do with	與……有關	to be related ; to be relevant
head up	統籌	manage; lead; supervise
hold over	延期	postpone; put off
in fact	事實上	as a matter of fact; actually; in reality

in the long run	終究	over the long term; in the end
in time	1.及時	1. not late
	2.有朝一日	2. sooner or later; eventually
in view of	有鑑於	taking something into account; considering something
jump to conclusions	驟下結論	form opinions without sufficient evidence
keep in mind	記住	don't forget; remember
keep track of	追蹤	to keep or maintain a record of
lag behind	落後	fall behind; fall back; fail to keep up
leave out	省去	omit, exclude; skip
look for	尋找	try to locate; search for
look out	注意	be careful; watch out
look up	查閱	find information
make ends meet	收支平衡	balance a budget; meet one's expenses
make out	理解	understand
make sense (of)	有道理	be logical and clear
no doubt about it	無疑	certainly; definitely; absolutely
now and then	偶爾	occasionally; once in a while
on purpose	故意	deliberately; intentionally
on time	準時	punctual; not late
out of the question	不可能	definitely not; impossible
pay off	成功	bring good results; be successful
pick up	1. 取得	1. get
	2. 買	2. buy
put off	延遲	delay; postpone
put up	建造	build
read over	讀完	go over; run over
rule out	排除	say something is impossible; eliminate
see eye to eye	看法一致	have the same opinion; be in agreement
set off	1. 出發	1. head for; depart for
	2. 展開	2. start (events); set out; commence
sign up for	註冊	enroll; register for
stand for	代表	symbolize; represent

take advantage of	利用	utilize; make use of; exploit
take off	1. 脫去	1. remove (clothes)
	2. 嶄露頭角	2. become successful; popular or well-known quickly
take up	開始從事	begin to study some topic or engage in some activity
try on	試穿	try clothing before buying
turn down	回絕	reject (an offer); refuse
turn out	1. 結果是	1. happen to be; end up
	2. 生產	2. produce
use up	用盡	use completely; exhaust
wait for	等待	expect; await
wear down	耗損	erode; lessen
work out	1. 健身	1. exercise
	2. 解決	2. bring to a successful conclusion; solve; settle; fix

⑤ 同義字彙互換

字彙	字義	同義字彙
acclaim	喝采	applaud; praise
achieve	達成	accomplish; complete; fulfill
acknowledge	承認	recognize; concede; admit; grant
additional	額外的	supplementary; extra; spare
adjust	調整	modify; adapt
alter	改變	change; vary; deviate
alternative	替代方案	choice; substitute; replacement
anticipate	預期	expect; await; foresee
appreciate	感激	respect; admire; be grateful
ban	禁止	prohibit; forbid
banquet	盛宴	feast
beneficial	有益的	advantageous; favorable; conducive; useful
bias	偏見	prejudice; partiality
bonus	紅利	extra; premium

brochure	宣傳冊	pamphlet; booklet
browse	翻閱	look through; read
capacity	能力	ability; capability
cease	中止	discontinue; halt; end; quit
characteristic	特徵	feature; quality; attribute
circumstance	情況	condition; situation
classify	分類	organize; categorize; sort
compensate	補償	reward
competent	能幹的	effective; able; capable; qualified; fit
compromise	妥協	settle; concede; recocile
consult	商量	confer; discuss
crucial	重要的	important; critical; decisive; urgent
defeat	打敗	overcome; win; triumph; beat; conquer
defect	缺點	fault; flaw; weakness; blemish
deplete	耗盡	exhaust; drain; use up
device	裝置	apparatus; appliance
display	展示	show; exhibition; exhibit
eligible	合格的	qualified; entitled; fit for; suitable
endure	忍耐	bear; tolerate; stand
enterprise	企業	business; venture; firm; company
equivalent	相當於	equal; same; like
examine	檢查	inspect; investigate; scrutinize
excess	多餘	surplus; extra; overabundance; additional
expand	擴大	extend; enlarge
expense	開銷	expenditure; payment; consumption
fad	時尚	fashion; vogue
fatigue	疲憊	tiredness; exhaustion; weariness
feasible	可行的	possible; practicable; achievable; workable
fiscal	會計的	financial; economic; monetary
graph	圖表	diagram; chart
hamper	阻礙	impede; obstruct; hinder; block
hazard	危險	risk; danger; jeopardy; peril
highlight	凸顯	mark; stress; high point

honor	榮耀	glory; respect; esteem; fame
identify	分辨	recognize; distinguish
imitate	仿效	copy; counterfeit; mimic
immense	巨大的	vast; huge; enormous
implement	實行	apply; enforce
incentive	誘因	motive; motivation; inducement
income	收入	profits; earnings
increase	增加	enlarge; extend; rise; multiply
initial	起初的	first; beginning
inspire	啟發	motivate; stimulate; prompt
integrate	整合	unite; unify
journey	旅程	trip; voyage; tour; travel
launch	推出	take off; hurl; initiate
legal	合法的	lawful; legitimate
liability	負債	debt
link	連結	join; connect
logical	合理的	reasonable; sensible
luxury	奢華	comfort; profusion
maintain	維持	continue; sustain; retain; uphold
manufacture	製造	make; produce; construct
material	材料	substance; stuff
merit	長處	virtue; value; excellence
modify	修改	vary; change; adjust; alter
negotiate	協商	bargain
normal	正常的	regular; routine; typical
novice	新手	beginner; newcomer; rookie
obstruct	阻絕	block; hinder; impede; hamper
occur	發生	happen; appear
omit	省略	exclude
onset	開始	start; beginning; commencement
opponent	敵人	adversary; competitor; rival; enemy; foe
ordinary	尋常的	usual; common; normal; typical
outdated	過時的	old-fashioned; obsolete; outmoded

outstanding	傑出的	prominent; noticeable; exceptional
overcome	克服	conquer; surmount
overlook	忽略	ignore; neglect
oversee	監督	supervise; watch; monitor
partial	偏袒的	prejudiced; biased; unfair
peak	顛峰	top; pinnacle; summit; apex; zenith
perform	執行	execute; do
permit	允許	allow; let; authorize
plague	折磨	annoy; trouble; bother; disturb
plentiful	大量的	ample; abundant; larish
precious	珍貴的	expensive; costly; valuable; priceless
prominent	顯著的	noticable; outstanding; distinguished; eminent
property	財產	possessions; holdings; belongings
prosper	繁榮	succeed; flourish; thrive
purpose	目的	aim; intention; goal; objective; target
recommend	建議	advise; suggest
region	區域	area; territory; zone
reject	拒絕	refuse
relevant	相關的	pertinent; related; germane
reluctant	不情願的	unwilling; disinclined
renovate	修繕	renew; restore; refurbish
restore	恢復	recover; mend; renovate
reveal	顯示	disclose; unveil; uncover
revoke	撤銷	cancel; recall
seek	尋求	search; hunt
shortcoming	短處	fault; defect; flaw; weakness; imperfection
significant	重大的	important; meaningful; substantial; vital
skillful	有技巧的	skilled; adept; proficient
status	地位	standing; position
straightforward	直率的	frank; direct
striking	引人注意的	dramatic; conspicuous; spectacular
suffer	遭受	experience; tolerate
supervise	監管	oversee; manage; monitor

tedious	乏味的	dull; boring; tiring; monotonous
thrifty	節儉的	frugal; economical
unattainable	達不到的	unreachable; unachievable
uneasy	不安的	anxious; nervous
upgrade	升級	enhance; elevate
vital	必需的	crucial; essential; indispensable
watchful	小心的	cautious; wary; vigilant
withstand	反抗	resist
worsen	惡化	decline; deteriorate
yield	產生	produce; generate
zeal	熱忱	enthusiasm; eagerness

:> Exercises

1. What are the speakers discussing?

   MP3 047 ▶▶ MP3 051

   (A) Taking a business trip
   (B) Cutting costs overseas
   (C) Opening a branch office
   (D) Purchasing a building

   Ⓐ Ⓑ Ⓒ Ⓓ

2. What does the man imply?

   (A) The proposal is too costly to consider.
   (B) Jeremy's calculations may not be correct.
   (C) The company has a strong presence in Europe.
   (E) An accountant should be brought in.

   Ⓐ Ⓑ Ⓒ Ⓓ

3. What does the woman suggest?

   (A) Moving the office
   (B) Financing the investment
   (C) Hiring a consultant
   (D) Accepting the proposal

   Ⓐ Ⓑ Ⓒ Ⓓ

---

4. Who most likely is the woman?

   (A) A student
   (B) A recruiter
   (C) A financial researcher
   (D) An office assistant

   Ⓐ Ⓑ Ⓒ Ⓓ

5. What does the woman ask about?

   (A) The working hours
   (B) The response time
   (C) The paid position
   (D) The job requirements

   Ⓐ Ⓑ Ⓒ Ⓓ

6 When will the woman probably be contacted?

(A) At the end of the day

(B) Tomorrow

(C) The day after tomorrow

(D) In one week

Ⓐ Ⓑ Ⓒ Ⓓ

7 When is the woman going on a trip?

(A) Thursday

(B) Friday

(C) Saturday

(D) Sunday

Ⓐ Ⓑ Ⓒ Ⓓ

8 What does the man imply?

(A) The company retreat will be tiring.

(B) He would like the woman to give a speech.

(C) The company retreat could help her career.

(D) He has never been to New York.

Ⓐ Ⓑ Ⓒ Ⓓ

9 Why is the woman going to New York?

(A) To take care of some business

(B) To relax with her coworkers

(C) To attend a personal event

(D) To plan a family reunion

Ⓐ Ⓑ Ⓒ Ⓓ

10 What are the speakers discussing?

(A) Arranging to meet someone

(B) Scheduling an overseas flight

(C) Preparing for a training session

(D) Making a dinner reservation

Ⓐ Ⓑ Ⓒ Ⓓ

11 What does the woman ask the man to do?
   (A) Make a reservation
   (B) Change his schedule
   (C) Greet a client
   (D) Drive her to the airport   Ⓐ Ⓑ Ⓒ Ⓓ

12 What time does the training session end?
   (A) At 5:00 P.M.
   (B) At 6:00 P.M.
   (C) At 7:00 P.M.
   (D) At 8:00 P.M.   Ⓐ Ⓑ Ⓒ Ⓓ

13 What is the man doing?
   (A) Mailing a package
   (B) Taking an order
   (C) Making a delivery
   (D) Scheduling a meeting   Ⓐ Ⓑ Ⓒ Ⓓ

14 What does the woman imply about Nancy Porter?
   (A) She has already received a package.
   (B) She has been extremely busy.
   (C) She has stepped out of the office.
   (D) She has another appointment scheduled.   Ⓐ Ⓑ Ⓒ Ⓓ

15 What will the woman probably do next?
   (A) Ask the man to explain the situation
   (B) Bring a package to Nancy Porter's office
   (C) Sign a document for Nancy Porter
   (D) Get in touch with Nancy Porter   Ⓐ Ⓑ Ⓒ Ⓓ

Questions 1~3

1. 答案：(C)

> 破題 What/speakers/discuss ⇨ 聽取二人所談的「主旨」，以名詞及動詞為主。

> 解析 由男子第一次發言中的 ... what do you think about... proposal? 及女子第一次發言中的 ... opening an office in Paris... 可知，答案應選 (C) Opening a branch office（設立分處）。

2. 答案：(B)

> 破題 What/man/imply ⇨ 聽取男子所說的「特殊字眼」。

> 解析 由男子第二次發言中的 I'm not sure that Jeremy's numbers are accurate... 可知，本題應選 (B)。答案中的 may... be 呼應原句中的 not sure，而 calculations 則取代原句的 numbers，correct 取代原句的 accurate。

3. 答案：(C)

> 破題 What/woman/suggest ⇨ 聽取女子表「建議」字眼之後的動作。

> 解析 由女子第二次的發言中的 I suppose we could hire a consultant to... 可知，本題答案為 (C)。

(錄音內容)

Questions 1 through 3 refer to the following conversation.

M: So, what do you think about Jeremy's proposal? Should we consider it?

W: Well, opening an office in Paris would help with sales in France, but it would also be quite costly.

M: Yes, you're right. I'm not sure that Jeremy's numbers are accurate, but there's no doubt it would be a big investment. On the other hand, it would give the company a foothold in the European market.

W: I suppose we could hire a consultant to conduct a detailed financial analysis. So, yes, let's tell Jeremy that we're considering it.

錄音翻譯

題目 1~3 請參照以下對話。

男：那你覺得傑若米的提案怎麼樣？我們應該考慮嗎？

女：嗯，在巴黎設辦事處有助於法國的銷售，但也會很花錢。

男：對，你說得對。我不確定傑若米的數據是否正確，可是這無疑會是一筆大投資。另一方面，它卻能讓公司在歐洲市場擁有一個據點。

女：我想我們可以請個顧問來做個詳細的財務分析。那，好，我們就告訴傑若米，我們會考慮。

題目&選項翻譯

1. 說話者在討論什麼事？
   (A) 出差
   (B) 降低海外成本
   (C) 設立分公司
   (D) 購買大樓

2. 男子暗示了什麼？
   (A) 提案太花錢，所以不予考慮。
   (B) 傑若米的計算可能不正確。
   (C) 該公司在歐洲頗具勢力。
   (D) 應該找個會計師。

3. 女子建議什麼事？
   (A) 把辦公室搬走
   (B) 提供資金投資
   (C) 聘請一個顧問
   (D) 接受提案

□ costly [ˋkɔstlɪ] *adj.* 昂貴的；代價高的

□ foothold [ˋfʊt.hold] *n.* 立足點；據點

□ accurate [ˋækjərɪt] *adj.* 精確的

Questions 4~6

4. 答案：(A)

> 破題　Who/woman ⇨ 聽女子的「身分」。

> 解析　由女子第一次發言中的 I'd like some information about... student internship program 及男子第一次發言說的 ... If your application is successful... 可推斷，本題答案為 (A)。

5. 答案：(B)

> 破題　What/woman/ask ⇨ 聽女子問的事情（聽名詞）。

> 解析　由女子第二次發言中的 ... how long will it take to hear back from you? 可知，本題答案為 (B)。

6. 答案：(B)

> 破題　When/woman probably/be contacted ⇨ 聽女子被告知的「時間」。

> 解析　由男子第二次發言中說的 ... but I can probably have an answer for you by tomorrow 可知，本題答案為 (B)。

錄音內容

Questions 4 through 6 refer to the following conversation.

W: Hi, I'd like some information about your student internship program.

M: Well, we offer two types of internships, but there's only one form to fill out. If your application is successful, you'll either be offered an unpaid position as an office assistant or a paid position as a financial researcher. Both are excellent learning opportunities.

W: That sounds interesting. And if I turn in my application today, how long will it take to hear back from you? I've already been offered another paid position, and I have to give them my decision by the day after tomorrow.

M: It usually takes three days, but I can probably have an answer for you by tomorrow.

錄音翻譯

題目 4~6 請參照以下對話。

女：嗨，我想問一些有關你們的學生實習的訊息。

男：嗯，我們有兩種實習，可是要填的表格只有一種。假如妳順利申請到，將會被派去擔派任無給職的辦公室助理，或是有給職的金融研究員。兩個都是非常好的學習機會。

女：那聽起來很有趣。假如我今天遞交申請表，多久能得到你們的消息？我已經獲得另一個有給職，而我後天之前就必須告訴他們我的決定。

男：通常要三天，不過我或許可以在明天之前給妳答案。

題目&選項翻譯

4. 女子最有可能是什麼人？
   (A) 學生
   (B) 招募人員
   (C) 金融研究員
   (D) 辦公室助理

5. 女子詢問的是什麼？
   (A) 工時
   (B) 回覆時間
   (C) 有給職
   (D) 工作必須條件

6. 女子大概何時會得到消息？
   (A) 當天下班
   (B) 明天
   (C) 後天
   (D) 一週後

☐ internship [ˋɪntɝnˌʃɪp] *n.* 實習（期間）
☐ recruiter [rɪˋkrutɚ] *n.* 招聘人員
☐ requirement [rɪˋkwaɪrmənt] *n.* 必要條件；資格
☐ turn in 繳交

Questions 7~9

7. 答案：**(B)**

破題　When/woman/go on a trip ⇨ 聽女子啟程的「時間」。

解析　由女子的第一次發言中的 ... I'm leaving for New York on Friday... 可知，本題答案為 (B)。

8. 答案：**(C)**

破題　What/man/imply ⇨ 聽男子話中的「暗示意圖」。

解析　由男子第一次發言中的 Would you like to come along? It would be a good chance to meet some new clients. 可知，去參加研習營可以認識新客戶，而認識新客戶即表示對她的職涯可能會有幫助，故選 (C)。

9. 答案：**(C)**

破題　Why/woman/go/New York ⇨ 聽女子去紐約的「原因」。

解析　由女子第二次發言中的 ... We're having a big family reunion... 可知，她要參加家族聚會，而家族聚會屬私人活動，故選 (C)。注意，不可選 (D)，因為該活動先前已計畫好了。

錄音內容

Questions 7 through 9 refer to the following conversation.

M: I'm going to be speaking at a company retreat this Saturday. Would you like to come along? It would be a good chance to meet some new clients.

W: I would love to go, but I'm leaving for New York on Friday, and won't be back until the following Thursday.

M: Oh, you'd better rest up. The New York office is really busy around this time of year.

W: Actually, I'm not going on business. We're having a big family reunion on Sunday, so I'm just going to relax.

録音翻譯

題目 7~9 請參照以下對話。

男：我這個星期天要到公司的度假研習營演講。妳要不要一起來？這是認識一些新客戶的好機會。

女：我很想去，不過我星期五要去紐約，下週四才會回來。

男：哦，你最好好好休息。紐約辦事處在每年的這個時候都忙得不得了。

女：事實上，我不是去洽公。我們星期天有個大型的家族聚會，所以我只是要去輕鬆一下。

題目&選項翻譯

7. 女子什麼時候要啓程？
   (A) 星期四
   (B) 星期五
   (C) 星期六
   (D) 星期日

8. 男子暗示什麼？
   (A) 公司的研習營會讓人覺得疲憊。
   (B) 他希望女子去演講。
   (C) 公司的研習營對她的職涯可能有幫助。
   (D) 他從來沒去過紐約。

9. 女子為什麼要去紐約？
   (A) 為了處理一些業務
   (B) 為了跟同事輕鬆一下
   (C) 為了出席一項私人活動
   (D) 為了計畫一次家族聚會

□ retreat [rɪ`trit] *n.* 靜修所；（公司舉辦之）度假研習營；度假村
□ reunion [ri`junjən] *n.* （親友等的）團聚

Questions 10~12

10. 答案：(A)

破 題 What/speakers/discuss ⇨ 聽取二人所說的「主旨」。

解 析 由女子第一次發言中的 She's an important client, and I'd really like you to meet her at the airport. 及男子回應中的 Yes, I should be able to make it. 可知，「接人」為對話的主旨，故選 (A)。

11. 答案：(C)

破 題 What/woman/ask/man/do ⇨ 聽取女子要男子做的「動作」。

解 析 由女子第一次發言後半部的 I'd really like you to meet her at the airport. 可知，答案為 (C) Greet a client。注意，此處的 greet 相當於 meet。

12. 答案：(C)

破 題 What time/training/end ⇨ 聽取訓練結束的「時間」。

解 析 由男子發言中的 I have a conference call from five o'clock until six, and a quick session immediately afterwards, but that won't take longer than an hour. 可知，答案為六點再加一小時，故正確答案為 (C)。

錄音內容

Questions 10 through 12 refer to the following conversation.

W: Hi, Bill. Did you get my message about Nancy Chen's travel schedule? She's an important client, and I'd really like you to meet her at the airport.

M: Yes, I should be able to make it. I have a conference call scheduled from five o'clock until six, and a quick training session immediately afterwards, but that won't take longer than an hour.

W: OK, that should still leave you plenty of time. Her plane doesn't arrive until eight o'clock, and it'll take her some time to clear customs.

錄音翻譯

題目 10~12 請參照以下對話。

女：嗨，比爾。你有沒有收到我關於南茜・陳出差行程的留言？她是個重要客
　　戶，我非常希望你去機場接她。

男：有，我應該可以去。我預定要在五點到六點開電話會議，緊接著有一場簡短
　　的訓練講習，但是不會超過一小時。

女：好，那你應該還有充裕的時間。她的飛機八點才會到，而且她還要花一點時
　　間通關。

題目&選項翻譯

10. 說話者在討論什麼？
　　(A) 安排接人
　　(B) 預訂海外班機
　　(C) 籌辦訓練講習
　　(D) 預訂晚餐的位子

11. 女子要男子做什麼？
　　(A) 訂位
　　(B) 更改他的行程
　　(C) 接一位客戶
　　(D) 載她去機場

12. 訓練講習什麼時候結束？
　　(A) 下午五點
　　(B) 下午六點
　　(C) 下午七點
　　(D) 下午八點

☐ conference call　電話會議
☐ customs [ˈkʌstəmz] *n.* 海關

Questions 13~15

13. 答案：(C)

破題 What/man/do ⇨ 聽男子的「動作」字眼。

解析 從男子的第一次發言：I have a package here for Nancy Porter. 即可知答案為 (C)。

14. 答案：(A)

破題 What/woman/imply/Nancy Porter ⇨ 聽女子話中的意圖。

解析 從女子話中的 Another one? 可推斷，Nancy Porter 之前已經收到過一件包裹，故本題應選 (A)。注意，通常句子語調上升表「驚訝」，也常是出題重點。

15. 答案：(D)

破題 What/woman/do/next ⇨ 聽女子接下來可能會去做的「動作」。

解析 由男子第二次發言中的 Actually, I need Ms. Porter's signature... Could you see if she's in? 可推知，接下來女子應該會聯絡她，故選 (D)。

（錄音內容）

Questions 13 through 15 refer to the following conversation.

M: Good morning. I have a package here for Nancy Porter.

W: Another one? I wonder what's going on. Here, let me sign for it.

M: Actually, I need Ms. Porter's signature to release the parcel. I'm sorry, but I'm on a very tight schedule. Could you see if she's in?

（錄音翻譯）

題目 13~15 請參照以下對話。

男：早安，我這裡有個包裹要交給南茜‧波特。

女：又一件嗎？真不知道是怎麼回事。好，我來簽個名。

男：事實上，我需要波特小姐簽名才能交件。很抱歉，不過我的時間很趕。妳能不能幫我看看她在不在？

題目&選項翻譯

13. 男子在做什麼？
(A) 郵寄包裹
(B) 接受訂貨
(C) 送件
(D) 安排會議時間

14. 女子暗示南茜‧波特的什麼事？
(A) 她已經收到了一個包裹。
(B) 她忙得不可開交。
(C) 她已經走出了辦公室。
(D) 她排定了另一場約會。

15. 女子接下來大概會怎麼做？
(A) 要男子解釋情況
(B) 把包裹送到南茜‧波特的辦公室
(C) 替南茜‧波特簽文件
(D) 聯絡南茜‧波特

□ signature [ˋsɪɡnətʃɚ] *n.* 簽名
□ release [rɪˋlis] *v.* 解放；釋出
□ parcel [ˋpɑrsl] *n.* 包裹（相當於 package）
□ tight [taɪt] *adj.* （時間）緊湊的

Part 4

Short Talks
簡 短 獨 白

題型簡介

Part 4「簡短獨白」共有 10 篇獨白，每段獨白對應 3 道題目，共 30 題。獨白由一人唸出，錄音內容不會出現在試題本上，但會印出問題和選項。獨白內容通常很簡短，多在一分鐘以內的長度。

出題預覽

1. What will the CEO's presentation be about?
   (A) The introduction of new board members
   (B) The schedule for media day
   (C) The importance of confidentiality
   (D) The launch of a new product

2. What is true about the event?
   (A) Journalists will be divided into two groups.
   (B) Employees must never discuss the new product.
   (C) Project leaders will join the speaker's tour.
   (D) Board members will sign new agreements.

3. Where will the speaker's tour start?
   (A) The fulfillment center
   (B) The north suite
   (C) The R&D lab
   (D) The production area

1. 答案：(D)   2. 答案：(A)   3. 答案：(C)

As you all know, Friday is media day here at G-Tech. Starting from nine o'clock, we'll be hosting journalists from all over the world, introducing them to our team, and unveiling our newest product, code-named "Starfire." I will take print reporters on a tour of our facilities—starting in the research and development lab, then moving to the production area, and finally to the fulfillment center. Meanwhile, the television reporters will set up in the meeting rooms in the north suite and conduct individual on-camera interviews with project leaders and members of the board. At 11:30 we will all gather in the main auditorium for the highlight of the day—the official launch of Starfire by CEO Dicello. Remember, you have all signed confidentiality agreements, so I don't need to remind you not to discuss Starfire with reporters until after the CEO's presentation. In the afternoon, reporters will then have several hours to use Starfire, at which time you may freely speak with them about it.

各位都知道，星期五是我們 G-Tech 的媒體日。從九點開始，我們將招待來自世界各地的記者，向他們介紹我們的團隊，並公開我們最新的產品，代號是「Starfire」。我會帶平面記者參觀我們的廠房，從研發實驗室出發，然後前往生產區，最後再到發貨中心。同時，電視記者則會到北廂房的會議室，以便跟專案領導人及各位董事做個別的電視訪問。十一點半的時候，全體人員將到大禮堂集合，以迎接今日的重頭戲——由執行長迪羅正式發表 Starfire。記住，各位都簽了保密協定，所以我不需要提醒各位，在執行長發表之前，不可以跟記者討論 Starfire。下午的時候，記者們會有機會使用 Starfire 幾個小時，屆時各位就可以和他們自由討論。

題目＆選項翻譯

1. 執行長的發表與什麼有關？

(A) 介紹新董事

(B) 媒體日的行程

(C) 保密的重要性

(D) 新產品的推出

2. 關於這場活動，何者為真？

(A) 記者會被分成兩組。

(B) 員工絕對不可以討論新產品。

(C) 專案領導人會參加發言人的導覽。

(D) 董事們會簽署新協定。

3. 發言人的導覽會從哪裡開始？

(A) 發貨中心

(B) 北廂房

(C) 研發實驗室

(D) 生產區

□ journalist [ˋdʒɜnəlɪst] n. 新聞記者

□ unveil [ʌnˋvel] v. 揭開；展示

□ fulfillment center 發貨中心

□ conduct [kənˋdʌkt] v. 實施；管理；進行

□ auditorium [ɔdəˋtorɪəm] n. 禮堂

□ launch [lɔntʃ] n./v.（產品）推出；上市

□ confidentiality [ˌkɑnfədɛnʃɪˋælətɪ] n. 機密

題型透析

獨白類型

Part 4「簡短獨白」出現的內容涵蓋各種不同的商業或生活主題，大致說來可歸納為五大類：

① 新聞報導
如電視或廣播中聽到的新聞、氣象報導，或其他公益簡報等。

② 廣播
如在飛機上、百貨公司、戲院等地方所播放的注意事項或訊息通知等。

③ 廣告
如在廣播、電視或百貨商場裡的促銷折扣或特價訊息等。

④ 演說
如就職、離職感言、宣布政策、頒獎典禮、專題演說或旅遊導覽等。

⑤ 語音留言
如電話答錄機的留言或其他事先錄好的語音指示等。

出題形式

Part 4 每段獨白都只唸一次，時間長達 30 秒以上，每段獨白對應三個問題。由於「不能重覆聽」及「不能做筆記」，因此在獨白播放前所做的題目預測，決定了你接下來要聆聽的重點。題目沒問的地方，可不用去聽；換言之，聽到和題目不相關的部分忽略即可。但是當聽到與題目有關的內容時，要立刻去看該題的「答案選項」，並在確定答案後立即作答，否則就算聽懂了內容，之後再回來圈選各題的答案時，重點可能已忘得差不多了。

因此，要在 Part 4 拿高分，就得在錄音播放前先做題目預測，決定聆聽獨白時的重點。以下是針對多益測驗歷年考題及最新出題趨勢所作的詳盡分析，只要按照這些全真題的出題模式「見招拆招」並反覆練習，就有機會在 Part4 順利作答，取得滿分。

① 「地點」考題

全真題 <u>Where</u> is + <u>sb.</u>?

某人在哪裡？

<u>Where</u> will the next <u>board meeting</u> take place?

下次的董事會在哪裡開？

<u>Where</u> are the <u>speakers</u>?

說話者在哪裡？

<u>Where</u> are the <u>people</u> who are <u>listening</u> to this talk?

聽這段談話的人在哪裡？

<u>Where</u> is this <u>announcement</u> most likely being <u>made</u>?

這則公告最可能是在哪裡發布？

<u>Where</u> is the <u>shop</u> located?

商店位在哪裡？

注意 全真題中劃底線部分為題目預測之重點字，請特別留意。

破解重點 由題目所問的「人」或是與該地點有關的兩、三個名詞，推知正確地點。

如：由 students, chalk, blackboard 即可推知地點為 classroom。

② 「動作」考題

全真題 <u>What</u> will + <u>sb.</u> + <u>do</u>?

某人會做什麼？

<u>What</u> will <u>happen</u> <u>next</u>?

接下來會發生什麼事？

<u>What</u> is + <u>sb.</u> + <u>told</u> to <u>do</u>?

某人被告知要做什麼？

<u>What</u> does the <u>speaker</u> <u>recommend</u>?

說話者推薦了什麼？

<u>What</u> are the <u>audience members</u> <u>asked</u> to <u>do</u>?

觀眾被要求做什麼？

<u>What</u> does the <u>caller</u> <u>suggest</u> the <u>man/woman</u> to <u>do</u>?

打電話的人建議男子／女子做什麼？

What does the corporation hope to do?

公司希望做什麼？

What should employees do if they are planning to attend the retirement dinner?

假如員工打算參加退休晚宴，他們應該做什麼？

What does Mary do?

瑪莉是做哪一行的？

破解重點 基本上，「動作」考題當然要去聽「動作字眼」，亦即「動詞」，但要注意下列幾點：

(1) 問某人的動作，就注意聽該人的動作字眼。

(2) 題目是「被動」問法時，獨白中常以「主動」用法表達，反之亦然。

(3) 有「建議」、「推薦」字眼的題目時，要注意聽「祈使句」或「命令句」。

③「主旨」考題

全真題 What is being discussed?

在討論什麼事？

What is being announced?

在公告什麼事？

What is the main topic of the talk?

這則談話的主題為何？

What is the talk mainly about?

這則談話主要跟什麼有關？

What is the purpose of the meeting/the announcement/the speech?

開會／公告／演講的目的是什麼？

What is the message mainly about?

這則訊息主要跟什麼有關？

破解重點 獨白題中通常前三句（最多至第五句）會提到主旨。要注意聽其中的「名詞」。

④「人物角色、職稱、所屬單位」考題

全真題 <u>What</u> is the <u>man's</u> <u>occupation</u>?

男子從事什麼職業？

<u>Whose</u> sales <u>figures</u> <u>increased</u> <u>most</u> in the <u>previous</u> month?

前一個月誰的銷售數字提高最多？

<u>What</u> most likely is the <u>speaker</u>?

說話者最可能是做什麼的？

<u>What</u> is the <u>job</u> being advertised?

登刊廣告的工作是什麼？

<u>Who</u> is the <u>speaker</u>?（⇨ 聽發言者）

說話的人是誰？

<u>Whom</u> is the <u>speaker</u> probably <u>addressing</u>?（⇨ 聽觀眾）

話說者大概在對誰講話？

<u>Who</u> is the intended <u>audience</u> for this talk?（⇨ 聽觀眾）

這則談話的對象是誰？

<u>What</u> is Mrs. Lee's <u>current</u> <u>position</u>?

李太太目前的職位是什麼？

<u>Who</u> is <u>Marc Wise</u>?

馬克懷斯是誰？

破解重點 此類題目要去聽題目所問「人名」、「職稱」或「所屬單位」。但問到「說話者」或「觀眾、聽者」是誰這類問題時，則要從獨白中與「身分屬性」有關的名詞來推敲答案。比方說，聽到 orientation（新生訓練), training package（訓練課程）時，可推知聽者為 new employees（新進員工）。

⑤「時間、數字、日期」考題

全真題 <u>What time</u> will the <u>bus</u> leave?

公車什麼時候會開？

For <u>how long</u> will <u>arrivals</u> be <u>delayed</u>?

到達的時間會延後多久？

<u>When</u> will the <u>program</u> be broadcast?

節目什麼時候會播？

<u>When</u> should <u>prices</u> <u>increase</u>?

價格應該在什麼時候調漲？

How many stores does Walton's have?

華頓有多少家店？

When should the project be completed?

案子應該在什麼時候完成？

How much experience is needed for the job?

這份工作需要多少經驗？

破解重點 此類題目一定要在聽到重點時立刻去點選答案，否則容易忘記或搞混。多益測驗常在此類考題中故意唸出二或三個不同的時間、數字或日期來混淆視聽，千萬不要中計，一定要聽清楚與該題所指之「人、事、物」相關的資訊，再選答案等。

⑥「原因、理由」考題

全真題 According to the announcement, why will the plant be temporarily shut down?

根據公告，工廠為什麼會暫時停工？

Why has the price of the tickets been reduced?

票價為什麼調降了？

Why does the speaker mention November 20?

說話者為什麼提到 11 月 20 日？

Why does the man have to work early in the morning?

男子為什麼必須一大早上班？

Why is Mr. Kim not playing?

金恩先生為什麼不玩？

Why is Indira not in the office?

英德瑞為什麼不在辦公室？

破解重點 注意題目所問特定之人或事的「原因、理由」字眼，這類題目的答案通常緊跟在表「目的」或「原因、理由」的句型之後，如：

(1) 目的句型：to V / in order to V / so as to V / for the purpose of + V-ing / with a view to + V-ing / so that + S + V / in order that + S + V

(2) 原因句型：because of / due to / owing to / as a result of / on account of

⑦「推論」考題

全真題 What does the <u>speaker</u> <u>imply</u> about the <u>audience</u>?

話說者暗指聽眾怎麼樣？

<u>What</u> can be <u>said/inferred</u> about the <u>situation</u>?

關於這個情況可以推論出什麼？

<u>What</u> is probably <u>true</u> about...?

關於……，何者大概為真？

<u>What</u> had the <u>speaker</u> probably <u>told</u> the <u>audience</u> <u>last month</u>?

說話者上個月大概對聽眾說了什麼？

破解重點 此類型題目本身並無任何可據以作答的線索，因此難度較高，但可利用聽「特殊字眼」或「特殊句型」的方式找出答案。常見的特殊字眼如 but 或 however 這類「轉折語」，或其他表「比較」或「差異點」等的句型。

⑧「What」的考題

▐「單一名詞」考題

全真題 <u>What</u> <u>season</u> is it now?

現在是什麼季節？

<u>What</u> is <u>included</u> in the <u>group rate</u>?

團體價中包含了什麼？

<u>What</u> does the <u>shop</u> <u>sell</u>?

這家店所賣的東西是什麼？

<u>What</u> are on <u>display</u> at the <u>museum</u>?

博物館在展覽什麼？

According to the speech, what <u>quality</u> helped <u>Mr. Kim</u> <u>succeed</u>?

根據這則發言，什麼樣的特質幫助了金先生成功？

What does the <u>man</u> <u>give</u> the <u>woman</u>?

男子給了女子什麼？

<u>What</u> will the <u>legal department</u> <u>send</u>?

法務部會寄出什麼？

破解重點 聽取與該題目中所提到之人、事、物相關的「單一名詞」。但要注意「詞性變化」，比方說，題目問某人有那些特質，聽到的內容是「形容詞」 dependable（可靠的），選項中的正確答案可能會替換成「名詞」reliability（可靠）。

2 「密集性排列名詞」考題

全真題　What does the <u>company</u> produce?

這家公司生產什麼？

What can be <u>bought</u>?

有什麼東西可以買？

<u>Which</u> of the following was <u>not</u> <u>mentioned</u>?

下列何者沒有被提到？

<u>Which</u> of the following is <u>not</u> <u>available</u> at the time this talk is being given?

在這段談話進行時，下列何者買不到？

破解重點　錄音員在獨白中提到一連串的同屬性的名詞，但問題常會問何者「沒有」被提到，此時要邊聽邊看選項來作答。

⑨ 「特殊字眼」考題

1 強烈字眼與特殊字眼

全真題　What is <u>unusual</u> about... <u>exhibit</u>?

……展覽有什麼不尋常之處？

What <u>surprising</u> <u>trend</u> was reported?

報導提到什麼令人意外的趨勢？

破解重點　聽到像 particularly（尤其地）、especially（特別地）、amazingly（令人驚訝地）等這類強烈字眼時，之後出現的「名詞」或「形容詞」常是答題重點。

2 改變與差異點

全真題　<u>What</u> will be <u>different</u>?

會有什麼不同？

<u>How</u> is <u>Toronto</u> <u>different</u> from other cities?

多倫多跟其他城市有何不同？

What <u>change</u> does the <u>speaker</u> announce?

說話者宣布什麼變革？

<u>How</u> do <u>summer</u> <u>hotel</u> <u>rates</u> <u>compare</u> to <u>winter</u> rates?

夏季的飯店價格跟冬季價格比起來怎麼樣？

破解重點　聽與原來敘述不同的名詞、動詞，尤其是在 from... to...、vary、turn... into 或 change... into 這類句型之後出現時，常是答題重點。

⑩「方法」考題

全真題 <u>How</u> will the <u>winner</u> be <u>selected</u>?

優勝者會如何挑選？

<u>How</u> are the <u>doors</u> <u>marked</u>?

門是怎麼標示的？

<u>How</u> did <u>Beth</u> <u>spend</u> her <u>dinner</u> hour?

貝絲是怎麼度過晚餐時光的？

<u>How</u> will the <u>salary</u> be <u>determined</u>?

薪水會怎麼決定？

<u>How</u> will <u>someone</u> <u>know</u> if he/she <u>wins</u> an <u>item</u> from the <u>silent</u> <u>auction</u>?

要怎麼知道自己在靜態拍賣中得標了？

破解重點 注意題目針對特定人或事的提問方式，通常答案也是聽動詞、名詞或形容詞。注意，「by + 方法」是常見的句型。如：... by <u>cutting down on</u> the number of employees（靠減少員工人數）。

⑪「否定、負面字眼」考題

全真題 What <u>restriction</u> does the <u>man</u> <u>mention</u>?

男子所提到的限制是什麼？

<u>What</u> is <u>wrong</u> with the <u>apartment</u>?

公寓有什麼問題？

<u>Why</u> is the <u>woman</u> <u>unable</u> to <u>attend</u> the staff <u>meeting</u> tomorrow morning?

女子明天早上為什麼無法出席員工大會？

<u>Why</u> is the <u>caller</u> <u>unable</u> to <u>speak</u> to anyone?

打電話來的人為什麼找不到人講話？

<u>What</u> is the <u>problem</u> about the <u>bicycle</u>?

腳踏車有什麼問題？

Word List
- [ ] restriction [rɪ`strɪkʃən] *n.* 限制
- [ ] auction [`ɔkʃən] *n.* 拍賣

破解重點 只要題目中有出現「否定、負面」的字眼時，一定要去聽與該「人、事、物」相關的「否定、負面」問題之後的字詞，這些字詞通常即為答案。

此類考題常見的否定、負面字眼有：hardly, barely, scarcely, not, no, problem, worried, concerned, sad, unhappy, difficult, difficulty, hard time。

⑫「正面、好處字眼」考題

全真題 What special offer does the speaker make?

說話者提供什麼特惠？

What is one of the benefits of working at Vera?

在微拉工作有什麼好處？

What is good news?

好消息是什麼？

破解重點 聽取題目所問的「人、事、物」所得到的「好處」字眼，例如：benefit, special, excellent, wonderful。

Example

MP3 053 ▶▶ MP3 057

1. How did industry analysts react to the announcement?
   (A) They were pleased.
   (B) They were aggressive.
   (C) They were enthusiastic.
   (D) They were surprised.
   Ⓐ Ⓑ Ⓒ Ⓓ

2. Where is TRZ Research's current data storage facility?
   (A) Berlin
   (B) Zurich
   (C) Gdansk
   (D) Frankfurt
   Ⓐ Ⓑ Ⓒ Ⓓ

3. What reason was NOT given for TRZ Research's decision?
   (A) Decreased energy costs
   (B) Lower share prices
   (C) Reduced labor costs
   (D) Lower taxes
   Ⓐ Ⓑ Ⓒ Ⓓ

4. What is the purpose of this announcement?
   (A) To alert passengers to new boarding information
   (B) To assist passengers who want to change their flight
   (C) To inform passengers about a customer service program
   (D) To reschedule passengers with connecting flights Ⓐ Ⓑ Ⓒ Ⓓ

5. Where are passengers asked to go?
   (A) Gate 7
   (B) Gate 17
   (C) Gate 116
   (D) Gate 118   Ⓐ Ⓑ Ⓒ Ⓓ

6. What should passengers with connecting flights NOT do?
   (A) Proceed to Concourse B.
   (B) Board the flight at 7:15.
   (C) Contact ground staff in Toronto.
   (D) Call customer service.   Ⓐ Ⓑ Ⓒ Ⓓ

7. What is the purpose of this message?
   (A) To reschedule a business trip
   (B) To suggest a cheaper alternative
   (C) To communicate accommodation options
   (D) To solve a transportation problem   Ⓐ Ⓑ Ⓒ Ⓓ

8. What is the problem with the hotel Melanie requested?
   (A) It is not where the conference is located.
   (B) The rates are higher than the company will pay.
   (C) It is not close enough to the conference site.
   (D) There are not any rooms available.   Ⓐ Ⓑ Ⓒ Ⓓ

9. What is the speaker's relationship to Melanie?
   (A) A coworker
   (B) A travel agent
   (C) A conference organizer
   (D) A hotel receptionist   Ⓐ Ⓑ Ⓒ Ⓓ

10. What is the main focus of the tour?
    (A) Buildings
    (B) Gardens
    (C) Boats
    (D) Museums   Ⓐ Ⓑ Ⓒ Ⓓ

11. What does the speaker say about the Old Firehouse?
    (A) It is Springfield's oldest building.
    (B) Its garden will be open for viewing.
    (C) It is located in the residential district.
    (D) It is a very well-known place.   Ⓐ Ⓑ Ⓒ Ⓓ

12. How long is the tour?
    (A) Less than one hour
    (B) Slightly over one hour
    (C) Nearly two hours
    (D) Over two hours   Ⓐ Ⓑ Ⓒ Ⓓ

13. What is being announced?
    (A) The launch of a specialty market
    (B) The relocation of a restaurant
    (C) The building of a branch office
    (D) The opening of a new location   Ⓐ Ⓑ Ⓒ Ⓓ

14. What is different about Rizzo's in Sunset Park?
    (A) It serves twice as many dishes.
    (B) It is suitable for large gatherings.
    (C) It offers traditional Italian meals.
    (D) It provides live music on Saturdays.   Ⓐ Ⓑ Ⓒ Ⓓ

15. What special offer does the speaker make?
    (A) There will be no charge for desserts.
    (B) Balloons will be given to all patrons.
    (C) Free drinks will be provided.
    (D) Gourmet pizzas will be served.   Ⓐ Ⓑ Ⓒ Ⓓ

Questions 1~3

1. 答案：(D)

[破　題] How/analysts/react/announcement ⇨ 聽 analysts 對主題的「反應」。

[解　析] 第二行的 announced 後接主旨，因此接著講的內容即為對主題的反應。由第三行的 The news came as a surprise to industry analysts... 可知，正確答案為 (D)。

2. 答案：(A)

[破　題] Where/TRZ/current/data storage facility ⇨ 聽 TRZ 資料儲存廠的「地點」。

[解　析] 由第四行 ... TRZ to expand capacity at its facility in Berlin... 可知，答案為 (A)。注意，本句後面 or to open... in Zurich 為陷阱，Zurich 這個個地點代表另外可能設的廠，而非題目所指的 data storage facility。

3. 答案：(B)

[破　題] What/reason/not/TRZ Research's decision ⇨ 聽「沒有」提到的理由，通常會從一群「密集性排列」的名詞出題。

[解　析] 第五行及第六行 TRZ Research confirmed that lower taxes—as well as reduced labor and energy costs—were the key factors behind the decision，說明了決定的關鍵原因，其中並沒有提到較低的股價，故本題應選 (B)。

[錄音內容]

Questions 1 through 3 refer to the following report.

TRZ Research, providers of data backup and storage solutions to many of Europe's leading banks, announced today that it will open a major new data storage facility in Gdansk, Poland. The news came as a surprise to industry analysts who had expected TRZ to expand capacity at its facility in Berlin or to open an additional facility in Zurich. TRZ Research confirmed that lower taxes—as well as reduced labor and energy costs—were the key factors behind the decision. Gdansk, a major port and shipbuilding center, has been aggressively wooing electronics, telecommunications, and information technology companies. TRZ Research is the third major IT company this year to announce new operations in the city. News of the announcement was not enthusiastically received at the Frankfurt Stock Exchange, where TRZ Research is traded. Shares were down two percent and closed at just over forty-one Euros.

録音翻譯

題目 1~3 為以下報導的相關問題。

為歐洲許多頂尖銀行提供資料備份與貯存解決方案的業者 TRZ 研究今天宣布，它將在波蘭的但斯克設立大型的新資料貯存廠。這個消息跌破了業界分析師的眼鏡，他們原以為 TRZ 會擴充柏林廠的容量，或是在蘇黎世另外設一個廠。TRZ 研究證實，稅率較低加上勞動和能源成本減少是這個決定的關鍵因素。但斯克是主要港口兼造船中心，它一直積極招攬電子、電信和資訊科技公司。TRZ 研究是今年宣布要在該市設立新據點的第三家重要的資訊科技公司。法蘭克福證交易所對這項消息的發布反應並不熱烈，而 TRZ 研究即是在此交易。它的股價跌了百分之二，收盤時只略高於四十一歐元。

題目&選項翻譯

1. 業界分析師對這項宣布的反應為何？
   (A) 他們很高興。
   (B) 他們很積極。
   (C) 他們很熱切。
   (D) 他們很意外。

2. TRZ 研究目前的資料貯存廠在哪裡？
   (A) 柏林
   (B) 蘇黎世
   (C) 但斯克
   (D) 法蘭克福

3. 什麼「不」是 TRZ 研究做出決定的理由？
   (A) 能源成本降低
   (B) 較低的股價
   (C) 勞動成本減少
   (D) 較低的稅率

☐ facility [fəˋsɪlətɪ] *n.* 設備；場所
☐ woo [wu] *v.* 懇求；爭取
☐ aggressively [əˋgrɛsɪvlɪ] *adv.* 積極地
☐ share [ʃɛr] *n.* 股票；股份

Questions 4~6

4. 答案：(A)

> **破題** What/purpose/announcement ⇨ 聽「目的」，即「主旨」，通常會出現在獨白前三句。

> **解析** 由第二、三行的 Due to... problem... at gate7, the <u>boarding gate</u>... <u>changed</u>，可知，本題應選 (A)。

5. 答案：(B)

> **破題** Where/passengers/asked/go ⇨ 聽旅客「被」要求去的「地點」。

> **解析** 由第四行的 Transcon Air 118 passengers <u>should proceed</u> to <u>gate17</u> in Concourse B 可知，正確答案為 (B)。注意，此類問「特定數字」的考題，要在聽到答案之後立刻去點選答案。

6. 答案：(C)

> **破題** What/passengers/connecting flight/not do ⇨ 聽「沒提到」或特別要求「不要做」的動作。

> **解析** 由第四行 ... should proceed to gate 17... 和第七行 Passengers with connecting flights in Toron to... should... contact a membeer of the... ground staff...，以及第九行 ... or call Transcon customer service by dialing... 可知，未提到的動作為 (C)。

(錄音內容)

Questions 4 through 6 refer to the following announcement.

Good evening. This announcement is for passengers for Transcon Airlines flight 118 scheduled to depart for Toronto at six. Due to a mechanical problem with the jetway at Gate 7, the boarding gate for this flight has been changed. Transcon Air 118 passengers should proceed to Gate 17 in Concourse B. Due to the gate change, the flight will be delayed by approximately one hour and fifteen minutes. The new boarding time is seven fifteen. Passengers with connecting flights in Toronto who may be affected by the delay should immediately contact a member of the Transcon ground staff at Gate 17 or call Transcon customer service by dialing one-one-six on any of the white courtesy phones in the terminal. We apologize for the inconvenience and thank you for flying with Transcon Air.

錄音翻譯

題目 4~6 為以下廣播的相關問題。

晚安，本公告是針對洲際航空一一八號班機預定於六點飛往多倫多的旅客。由於七號門的空橋發生了機械故障，本班機的登機門已更改。洲際航空一一八號班機的旅客應前往 B 大廳的十七號門。由於登機門更改，班機大概會延後一小時又十五分鐘。新的登機時間是七點十五分。要在多倫多轉機而可能會受到延後影響的旅客應立刻聯絡洲際航空位於十七號門的地勤人員，或是用航站內任何一具白色服務電話撥打一一六給洲際航空的客服部。造成您的不便，我們深感抱歉。感謝您搭乘洲際航空。

題目＆選項翻譯

4. 這則廣播的目的是什麼？
   (A) 提醒旅客新的登機訊息
   (B) 協助想要更換班機的旅客
   (C) 把一項客服方案告知旅客
   (D) 幫需要轉機的旅客重訂時間

5. 旅客被要求改去哪裡？
   (A) 七號門
   (B) 十七號門
   (C) 一一六號門
   (D) 一一八號門

6. 要轉機的旅客「不」應該做什麼？
   (A) 前往 B 大廳。
   (B) 在七點十五分登機。
   (C) 聯絡多倫多的地勤人員。
   (D) 打電話給客服部。

☐ proceed [prəˋsid] *v.* 繼續進行
☐ concourse [ˋkɑnkors] *n.*（車站、機場的）中央大廳
☐ approximately [əˋprɑksəmɪtlɪ] *adv.* 大約
☐ courtesy phone（機場或大賣場等的）免費電話

Questions 7~9

7. 答案：(C)

破題 What/purpose/message ⇨ 聽「主旨」，通常出現在前三句。

解析 由第一～三行 I'm <u>afraid</u> I have bad news regarding your coming trip to New York. You requested a room... but <u>unfortunately</u>... <u>fully booked</u>. 及第五行 <u>Basically</u> there are three things we can do. I could... 可看出，說話者先提出問題，再提出解決方案，故本題應選 (C)。

8. 答案：(D)

破題 What/problem/hotel/Melanie requested ⇨ 聽關於 Melanie 要求的 hotel 之「負面」字眼。

解析 第二行 You requested a <u>room</u>... but <u>unfortunately</u>... <u>fully booked</u>. 可知，本題應選 (D)。要特別注意的是，出現強烈字眼 "Unfortunately" 之後，通常會有出題重點。

9. 答案：(A)

破題 What/speaker's relationship/Melanie ⇨ 聽二者「互動」的字眼或「稱謂」。

解析 由第一行 Hi, <u>Melanie</u>. This is <u>Ted</u> in travel department. 說話者直呼對方名字且提到了自己的部門可推知，兩人在同一家公司上班，故應選 (A)。

錄音內容

Questions 7 through 9 refer to the following message.

Hi, Melanie. This is Ted in the travel department. I'm afraid I have some bad news regarding your upcoming trip to New York. You requested a room in the hotel where the conference is being held, but unfortunately it's fully booked. And because it's right downtown, the room rates for other hotels in the area are higher than the limit allowed by the company. Basically there are three things we can do. I could book you into a more expensive hotel downtown, and ask you to make up the amount that exceeds the company's budget. Or I could book you into a hotel farther away, but that would require at least a one-hour trip to the conference site. Finally, I could issue you a check for the company's maximum hotel allowance—that's $200 per night—and let you make your own arrangements. Time is getting short, so I'd appreciate it if you could get back to me by tomorrow morning. If I don't hear from you by noon, I'll stop by your cubicle on my way to lunch.

(錄音翻譯)

題目 7~9 為以下訊息的相關問題。

嗨，梅蘭妮，我是差旅部的泰德。關於妳即將去紐約的事，恐怕我有一些壞消息。妳要求在開會的飯店住宿，但可惜飯店都訂滿了。而且因為它就在市區，所以當地其他飯店的住宿費也比公司允許的上限高。基本上，我們有三個辦法。我可以幫妳訂比較貴的市區飯店，並請妳自付超過公司預算的差額。或者我可以幫妳訂遠一點的飯店，不過從那裡到會議現場最少要一個小時的路程。最後，我可以依照公司最大額度的飯店津貼開張支票給妳，也就是每晚兩百美元，然後由妳自行安排。時間緊迫，所以要是妳能在明天早上前回電給我，我會很感謝。假如我在中午前沒收到妳的消息，我會在去吃午餐時到妳的隔間找你。

(題目&選項翻譯)

7. 這則留言的目的是什麼？
   (A) 重訂出差的時間
   (B) 建議比較便宜的方案
   (C) 傳達住宿選擇
   (D) 解決交通問題

8. 梅蘭妮要住的飯店有什麼問題？
   (A) 那不是開會的地方。
   (B) 費用高過公司所會支付的金額。
   (C) 離開會的地方不夠近。
   (D) 沒有任何空房。

9. 話說者跟梅蘭妮是什麼關係？
   (A) 同事
   (B) 旅行社職員
   (C) 會議主辦人
   (D) 飯店接待人員

□ upcoming [`ʌpˌkʌmɪŋ] *adj.* 即將來臨的
□ make up 補足
□ exceed [ɪk`sid] *v.* 超過
□ allowance [ə`lauəns] *n.* 津貼；零用金
□ get back to sb. 回電給某人
□ cubicle [`kjubɪkl] *n.* 小隔間
□ accommodation [əˌkɑmə`deʃən] *n.* 膳宿

Questions 10~12

10. 答案：(A)

破題 What/main focus/tour ⇨ 聽此 tour 的「主要焦點」，通常即指「目的」。

解析 由第二行 We're going to start right here... and visit serveal houses... to see how residential architecture has evolved in the city over the last 120 years. 可知，正確答案為 (A)。注意，不定詞（to + V）後接「目的」，通常為答題重點。

11. 答案：(D)

破題 What/speaker/say/the Old Firehouse ⇨ 聽 the Old Firehouse 的相關訊息。

解析 由第十一、十二行 ... and finally the Old Firechouse, spring field's most famous landmark 可知，答案應選 (D)。

12. 答案：(D)

破題 How long/tour ⇨ 聽 tour 的「總長時間」。

解析 本題需要將 tour 各項參觀的時間加起來才能得出答案。將第六、七行 ... the tour will take approximately 45 minutes. After a short 15-minute break, we'll take a 20-minute ferry ride... 以及第八行 Our one-hour downtown walk... 中的四項劃底線的時間加起來，一共超過二小時，故選 (D)。

（錄音內容）

Questions 10 through 12 refer to the following short talk.

Welcome to the Architecture of Springfield Tour. My name is Alex and I'll be your guide this morning. We're going to start right here in West Springfield and visit several homes along Grant St. to see how residential architecture has evolved in the city over the last 120 years. We won't be able to enter all of the homes, but we have arranged to tour the first floor and gardens of Astor Place, Springfield's oldest home. This part of the tour will take approximately 45 minutes. After a short 15-minute break, we'll take a 20-minute ferry ride across the river to East Springfield and visit the highlights of the busy commercial district. Our one-hour downtown walk will take us by the Bixby Bank Tower, the Ancient History Museum, the Springfield Theater, and finally the Old Firehouse,

Springfield's most famous landmark. I'll be sharing stories about the history of each of these buildings as we walk. If you have questions at any point along the tour, please just go ahead and ask.

録音翻譯

題目 10~12 為以下簡短獨白的相關問題。

歡迎參加春田建築之旅。我的名字叫艾力克斯，今天早上就由我來擔任各位的導遊。我們將從西春田這裡出發，並沿著格蘭特街參觀幾戶民宅，以了解過去一百二十年來，本地住宅區的建築如何地演化。我們沒辦法進入所有的民宅，但我們安排了去看亞斯特廣場的一樓和花園，這是春田最古老的民宅。這個部分的參觀大約要花四十五分鐘。在十五分鐘的短暫休息後，我們會搭二十分鐘的渡輪跨河到東春田，並參觀繁忙商業區的重要景點。我們會在市區步行一小時，前往畢克斯比銀行大樓、古代歷史博物館、春田戲院，最後到老消防站，這是春田最著名的地標。在我們一面走路時，我會把這些大樓的歷史一一述說給各位聽。如果各位在沿途參觀時有問題，請隨時發問。

題目&選項翻譯

10. 此次參觀的主要焦點是什麼？
    (A) 建築
    (B) 花園
    (C) 船
    (D) 博物館

11. 說話者提到老消防站的什麼事？
    (A) 它是春田最古老的建築。
    (B) 它的花園將開放參觀。
    (C) 它位於住宅區。
    (D) 它是非常知名的地點。

12. 此次參觀要多久？
    (A) 不到一小時
    (B) 比一小時略久
    (C) 將近兩小時
    (D) 超過兩小時

☐ **residential** [ˌrɛzəˈdɛʃəl] *adj.* 居住的
☐ **architecture** [ˈɑrkəˌtɛktʃə] *n.* 建築
☐ **ferry** [ˈfɛrɪ] *n.* 渡輪

☐ **highlight** [ˈhaɪˌlaɪt] *n.* 最突出（或最精彩）的部分

Questions 13~15

13. 答案：(D)

破 題 What/announced ⇨ 聽「主旨」。

解 析 由第二句 Rizzor's is proud to <u>announce</u> the <u>opening</u> of our <u>second restanrant</u> this Saturday. 可知，本題應選 (D)。注意，通常 announce 之後即是主旨。

14. 答案：(B)

破 題 What/different/Rizo's/Sunset Park ⇨ 聽在 Sunset Park 分店與原店的 不同處，特別要注意「比較級」字眼。

解 析 由第六行 location has all of the dishes... but it <u>twice as spacious</u> 可 知，答案為 (B)。But 後面經常有出題重點，而「倍數」字眼也是常考重點。

15. 答案：(A)

破 題 What/special offer/speaker/make ⇨ 聽「特惠」字眼，要注意「否定 字」、「比較級」及「強烈字眼」。

解 析 第 十 二 行 And to make your visit extra <u>special</u>, everyone dining at Rizzor's... will <u>receive</u> a <u>complimentary dessert</u>. 中的 special 即為重 點，故本題應選 (A)。另，no charge 與 complimentary 同義。

録音內容

Questions 13 through 15 refer to the following advertment.

Come on down to Rizzo's Italian Food in Sunset Park this Saturday and be part of the fun. Rizzo's is proud to announce the opening of our second restaurant this Saturday. For anyone who hasn't tried Rizzo's gourmet pizzas or traditional pasta dishes, you're in for a treat. With recipes handed down through generations of the Rizzo family, you'll know you're eating the real thing. Our new Sunset Park location has all of the dishes you've come to know and love at our original North Beach location but is twice as spacious. Our second-floor events room is large enough to seat over 150 and is a perfect location for your wedding reception, class reunion, or business meeting. For the grand opening, there will be live Italian music, two-for-one drink specials, and free balloons for the kids. And to make your visit extra special, everyone dining at Rizzo's in Sunset Park on Saturday will receive a complimentary dessert. So, don't wait! Come to Rizzo's and enjoy a taste of Italy!

(錄音翻譯)

題目 13~15 為以下廣告的相關問題。

本週六請來日落公園的瑞佐義大利餐館開心一下。瑞佐很驕傲地宣布，我們的第二家餐廳將在本週六開幕。凡是沒有試過瑞佐美味披薩或傳統義大利麵的人，都可以來享受一下。從瑞佐家族相傳好幾代的烹飪中，您會知道什麼才叫吃東西。我們在日落公園的新館有您在原本北灘館所熟知及喜愛的各種菜色，但空間卻有兩倍大。我們二樓的活動廳大到足以容納超過一百五十人，並且是舉辦婚宴、同學會或商業會議的絕佳地點。盛大開幕當日會有現場演奏的義大利音樂、買一送一的飲料特惠，以及送給小朋友的免費氣球。而且為了讓您的光臨格外地特別，星期六來日落公園瑞佐用餐的人都可以獲得免費的甜點。所以別等了！到瑞佐來享受一頓義大利餐吧！

(題目&選項翻譯)

13. 此廣告在宣布什麼事？
    (A) 成立名產市場
    (B) 餐廳遷移
    (C) 蓋新分公司
    (D) 新地點開幕

14. 日落公園的瑞佐有什麼不同之處？
    (A) 它所賣的菜色有兩倍之多。
    (B) 它適合大型聚會。
    (C) 它賣傳統的義大利餐。
    (D) 它週六都有現場演奏的音樂。

15. 說話者提供什麼特惠？
    (A) 甜點不收費。
    (B) 所有的主顧客都會拿到氣球。
    (C) 提供免費飲料。
    (D) 供應美味披薩。

☐ gourmet [ˋgʊrme] *n.* 美食家
☐ recipe [ˋrɛsəpɪ] *n.* 食譜
☐ spacious [ˋspeʃəs] *adj.* 寬敞的

☐ complimentary [͵kɑmpləˋmɛtərɪ] *adj.*
免費贈送的
☐ patron [ˋpetrən] *n.* 主顧（尤指老顧客）

答題基本對策

① 事先瀏覽題目

儘量在錄音內容播放前先做題目預測，以快、狠、準的方式，快速瀏覽題目之疑問詞、主詞、動詞、名詞、受詞及特殊字眼。

② 善用「影音對照法」

聽到人名、地名、專有名詞時，除非與題目有關，否則先不理會。若是題目中問到的專有名詞，則用「影音對照法」，不要去翻譯它。

③ 注意重複出現的重點字

獨白中一再重複強調的重點字（通常為名詞），常是答案線索之指標字。

④ 利用選項反推答案

題目走向不清楚時，可瀏覽一下答案，推測出可能的內容。

⑤ 當心選項陷阱

題目之選項答案愈長，愈有可能是陷阱，務必小心檢視作答。

⑥ 緊盯題目「關鍵字」

聽到獨白出現與題目有關的關鍵字時，立刻去看該題目並圈選相關答案。

⑦ 留意開頭的「介紹說明」

注意聽獨白開始前的介紹說明（the introductory announcement），例如：由 Questions 71 to 73 refer to this commercial message... 可知，這則獨白是有關「廣告訊息」的內容，將有助於預測出題方向。

⑧ 前三句必有考題

獨白前三句最重要，經常會有出題關鍵，一定要注意聆聽。

9 **注意「同義字」**

獨白中的重點敘述在題目選項中常替換成意思相似的同義字詞或片語，務必特別留意。比方說，題目提到商店有 complimentary dessert（免費甜點）的特惠，但選項可能換句換說成 no charge for desserts（甜點不收費）。

10 **注意「訊號字」**

獨白中常會出現一些「訊號字」（Signal Words），可藉以掌握獨白後面的出題重點或發展方向。

大師 **關鍵指引**

簡短獨白中常見的訊號字句：

1. 演講架構

- There are three kinds of... 有三種……
- We'll be looking at a couple of ways to... 我們會列出幾種方式來……
- First, ... 首先，……
- Then, ... 接著，……
- That brings us to... 接下來我們……
- There are two points of view... 有兩種觀點……
- Next I want to mention... 其次我想談一談……
- First, let's look at... 首先，我們來看……
- Next, let's consider... 接著，我們來思考……
- Okay, now let's talk about... 好，現在我們來談談……
- Now, what about...? 那，……怎麼樣？
- Finally, ... 最後，……

2. 方向改變

- On the other hand, ... 另一方面，……
- However, ... 不過，……
- But... 可是……

3.加強或重要性

- Most importantly, ... 最重要的是，……
- One important point/issue/problem/question/concept is...
  有一個重點／爭議／問題／疑問／觀念在於……

- Especially... 尤其是，……
- Significantly, … 重要的是，……
- Be sure to note that... 一定要注意，……
- Pay special attention to... 要特別注意……

4. 描述與舉例

- consists of... 包含
- Namely, ... 也就是，……
- Take... for example... 以……為例
- Specifically, ... 明確地說，……
- Let's consider the case of... 就……情況而言
- For example, ... 例如，……
- That is... 那就是……
- For instance, ... 例如，……

5. 定義

- is... 是……
- is called... 被稱為……
- means... 意思是……
- is known as... 即所謂的……
- refers to... 指的是……

6. 分類

- groups of... ……的分群
- properties of... ……的屬性
- varieties of... 不同的……種類
- types of... ……的樣式
- parts of... ……的部分
- characteristics of... ……的特徵
- kinds of... ……的種類
- classes of... ……的類別

7. 時間順序或過程

- step 步驟
- phase 時期
- Before 在……之前
- At the same time 在此同時
- Now 現在
- Later 後來
- Eventually 最後
- First, ... Second, ... Third, ... 第一，……。第二，……。第三，……。
- Next, ... then, ... last, ... 其次，……接著，……最後，……。
- stage 階段
- Finally 最後
- After 在……之後
- Meanwhile 同時
- As soon as 一旦
- Subsequently 隨後

8. 比較和對照

- like... 像……
- similarly... 同樣地
- similar to... 與……類似
- in the same way 以同樣的方式

- in contrast 相較之下
- compared with 與……相比
- whereas 卻；而
- Although 雖然
- Conversely 相反地
- Even though 縱使
- Instead 而是
- On the other hand 另一方面

- differ from 有別於
- in comparison 相較
- 形容詞 + -er 更……
- But 可是
- In spite of 不管
- However 然而
- On the contrary 相反地
- Despite 儘管

9. 因與果
- Thus 如此一來
- Because 因為
- For this reason 基於這個原因
- Since 既然
- As a consequence 因之
- Hence 因此

- Therefore 因此
- Because of 由於
- Consequently 因而
- So 所以
- As a result 結果

破題關鍵要領

要在 Part 4 拿到高分，除了熟悉獨白類型與出題形式外，更要熟習命題的關鍵句型，要能一聽到獨白的特定句型，就知道要選取的答案指標，這樣就能快速作答，並利用剩下的時間預覽下段獨白的題目。

① Who 考題

● **關鍵句型** ⇨ Welcome aboard... Air Flight 787 from... to....

答案指標 ⇨ Flight attendant（⇨ 考說話者）

● **關鍵句型** ⇨ Welcome to... Company. I'm... and I'll be conducting the tour today.

答案指標 ⇨ A company employee（⇨ 考說話者）

● **關鍵句型** ⇨ ... we have been holding interviews for a new editor to join our team. Mr. Katz has been chosen for the position.

答案指標 ⇨ An editor（⇨ 考此人職業）

● **關鍵句型** ⇨ Thank you for preregistering for the... Expo, which will run from...

答案指標 ⇨ Those who had preregistered（⇨ 考收到信的人）

● **關鍵句型** ⇨ On July 8 we will welcome the financial planner... as our keynote speaker for the annual employee appreciation luncheon.

答案指標 ⇨ Employees（⇨ 考參加者）

● **關鍵句型** ⇨ Though we have no official dress code for traveling while on business, employee should remember that their physical appearance may affect....

答案指標 ⇨ A company administrator（⇨ 考說話者）

Word List
- □ keynote [ˋkiˌnot] *n.* （演講的）主旨
- □ dress code 服裝規定

● 關鍵句型 ⇨ I've called this meeting because, since the beginning of the year, our store has been losing 2000 euros a month due to the theft.

答案指標 ⇨ A store supervisor（⇨ 考說話者）

● 關鍵句型 ⇨ Instead of..., this division offers brief, needs-oriented courses offered by specialist consultants.

答案指標 ⇨ Specialist consultants（⇨ 考課程提供者）.

● 關鍵句型 ⇨ This is Radio Talk Today. My name is... and this evening we'll be talking with... about yesterday's election results.

答案指標 ⇨ A radio show host（⇨ 考說話者）

● 關鍵句型 ⇨ I'm happy to report that there are no major traffic delays.... Stay tuned for an update in ten minutes.

答案指標 ⇨ A radio announcer（⇨ 考說話者）

● 關鍵句型 ⇨ Good afternoon, New York. This is meteorologist... with the Christmas's Eve forecast.

答案指標 ⇨ A meteorologist（⇨ 考報導者）

● 關鍵句型 ⇨ Hello, my name is.... I'll be serving you tonight. Let me tell you about some of our specials.

答案指標 ⇨ A waiter（⇨ 考說話者）

● 關鍵句型 ⇨ This is probably a good time to start discussions.... We just agreed to lower our interest rate this morning.

答案指標 ⇨ Banker（⇨ 考說話者）

Word List
☐ tuned [tjund] *adj.* 調整好頻道的
☐ meteorologist [ˌmitɪəˈrɑləgɪst] *n.* 氣象學者
☐ forecast [ˈforˌkæst] *n.* 預報

② Topic（主旨）考題

● 關鍵句型 ⇨ It is with great pride that I announce that.... Thanks for coming to our staff meeting today.

答案指標 ⇨ Staff meeting

● 關鍵句型 ⇨ In today's business news, it has been reported that sb. will retire next month.

答案指標 ⇨ Retirement

● 關鍵句型 ⇨ Welcome to this year's national championship tournament.

答案指標 ⇨ Tournament/Competition

● 關鍵句型 ⇨ We are pleased to announce that the company will be opening its own cafeteria for employees next morning.

答案指標 ⇨ Cafeteria Opening

● 關鍵句型 ⇨ As you know, our lease on this building is due to expire at the end of the year, and I've been looking for new premises.

答案指標 ⇨ The expiration of the lease

● 關鍵句型 ⇨ Welcome to +〈公司名〉+ industries' new employee orientation.

答案指標 ⇨ New employee orientation

● 關鍵句型 ⇨ Ladies and gentlemen, I have two announcements relating to this afternoon's conference program. First, ... Second, ...

答案指標 ⇨ Conference

● 關鍵句型 ⇨ Attention, travelers, we regret to inform you that because of a security situation, all entrances to and exists from Terminal 1 are temporarily closed.

答案指標 ⇨ Terminal shutdown

Word List

□ premise [ˋprɛmɪs] *n.* 經營場地

● 關鍵句型 ⇨ Good morning, and welcome to our "First-Day-on-the-Job" at.... As you know, this is the first of the four-day orientation...

答案指標 ⇨ Orientation for the new employees

● 關鍵句型 ⇨ Welcome to the... International Visitors' Center. I am Vicky, your guide for today's tour. As you may know, Lion Mountain is the third highest mountain in the world.

答案指標 ⇨ Attraction of the tour

● 關鍵句型 ⇨ This is Peter King in New York with an update on that crash near Triangle Airport.

答案指標 ⇨ Plane crash

● 關鍵句型 ⇨ Hello. This is... calling about the... Well, I finally have the arrangements for the party settled, so I'd like to confirm the order....

答案指標 ⇨ Confirming the order

③ Action（動作）考題

● 關鍵句型 ⇨ Now, I am going to describe all of the problems in detail. After that, I'll explain the work that...

答案指標 ⇨ Introducing the new system

● 關鍵句型 ⇨ Now let't welcome.... He'll talk about this year's tournament and answer question.

答案指標 ⇨ Introducing tournament.

● 關鍵句型 ⇨ Tune in again tomorrow when we'll talk about vacation destinations that both adults and children will enjoy.

答案指標 ⇨ Talking about vacation destinations

Word List
□ tournament [`tɝnəmənt] *n.* 錦標賽

● 關鍵句型 ⇨ To celebrate our achievement, and to show you our appreciation, we will be having a company picnic in... on...

答案指標 ⇨ Having a company picnic.

④ Where（地點）考題

● 關鍵句型 ⇨ Thank you for calling Macy's Florist. Our office is currently closed. Our regular business hours are...

答案指標 ⇨ A flower shop（⇨ 問打電話聯絡的營業單位）

● 關鍵句型 ⇨ Good morning shoppers and welcome to Sunny's. We offer one-stop shopping for all your food needs.

答案指標 ⇨ At a supermarket（⇨ 問廣播的所在地）

● 關鍵句型 ⇨ Hello, Mr. Perez. This is Kelly Wang from PTB pharmacy.

答案指標 ⇨ A pharmacy（⇨ 問電話從那打來的）

● 關鍵句型 ⇨ We are pleased to announce that the company will be opening its very own cafeteria for employees next week. Each week on Friday afternoon, the chef will post the menu on the bulletin board near the entrance.

答案指標 ⇨ Near the entrance to the cafeteria（⇨ 問資訊被張貼在何處）

● 關鍵句型 ⇨ Attention, passengers waiting to board flight 165 to Tokyo. Your flight has been delayed due to...

答案指標 ⇨ At an airport（⇨ 問廣播發生的地點）

高頻字彙和情境用語

① 日常對話高頻用語

- (a) short cut 捷徑
- (a) dead end 困境
- (a) drawback 缺點
- (a) first impression 第一印象
- (a) matter of opinion 見仁見智的問題
- (a) second opinion 其他人的意見
- (a) step forward 往前一步
- (a) value judgment 價值判斷
- (a) vicious circle 惡性循環
- at random 隨機地；隨便地
- be taken aback 吃驚；措手不及
- (an) open mind 開闊的心胸
- in touch with 和……有接觸
- (the) end product 最後產品
- (the) first step 第一階段
- (the) pros and cons
  正反的論點；贊成和反對的意見
- a good/great deal of
  許多（接不可數名詞）
- a matter of
  取決於……的情況、問題、事情
- a matter of fact 事實上
- a safe bet 較有把握的選擇、行動等
- a snap decision 倉促之間的決定
- above all 最重要地
- according to 根據……
- account for 解釋；對……負有責任
- agree on 對……取得共識
- agree to 同意去……
- agree with 同意……

- ahead of time 提早
- aim at 以……為目標
- all important 最重要的
- all in all 總的說來
- all or nothing 非全有即全無
- all systems go 一切就緒；萬事皆備
- allow for 考慮；斟酌
- amount to 等於
- and so on 等等
- argue against 對……提出相反的意見
- arise from 由……而來
- arrange for 為……做安排
- as a rule 通常
- as a whole 整體來看
- as far as 盡……，就……
- as long as 只要
- as such 就本身而論
- as to 關於；至於
- as usual 照例
- as we have seen 如同我們所見到的
- as well as 以及
- as yet 迄今為止
- at a glance 一瞥
- at all 絲毫；根本
- at first 首先
- at first sight 乍看之下
- at least 至少
- at once 馬上
- at will 任意
- at/from the outset 在／自最初

- at (the) most 最多
- average out 平均算來
- back against the wall 處境困難
- back and forth 來來回回地
- back down 讓步
- back out (of) 退出（協議或計畫等）
- based on 基於……
- be against 反對
- beside the point 不相關
- be specific 明確地說
- be in line with 與……一致
- be in the dark 不知情
- be in the picture 狀況內
- be/go out of action 不能運轉
- be/fall short of 短少
- begin/start with 由……開始
- better safe than sorry
  保險一點總比遺憾好
- bit by bit 一點一點地；漸漸地
- break down 失敗；拋錨
- break new/fresh ground 開闢新領域
- break off 突然停止；中斷
- break the ice 打破僵局；打破沈默
- break through 突破
- bring about 引起
- by the same token 同樣地
- by the way 順便一提
- carry out 實行
- change one's mind 改變心意
- check over 檢查
- come to the point 直截了當地說
- come up with 想出、提出（點子）
- common ground 共識
- common sense 常識

- compete against 與……競爭
- compromise with 妥協；讓步
- consist of 由……組成
- cope with 處理
- crystal clear 清晰明瞭的
- cut corners 走近路
- cut one's losses
  （及早放棄）以免造成更大損失
- do business with 和……做生意
- do with 忍受；處理；跟…有關
- draw up 起草（文件）；制訂
- either way （兩者之中）任一樣都可
- every other 每隔
- face up to 勇於面對
- first and foremost 首要的是
- focus on 專注於
- for sale 待售
- for sure 確切地
- for the most part
  在大多數情況下；主要地
- for the time being 暫時
- for and against 贊成和反對
- game plan （比賽前的）戰略計畫
- get across (to sb.) 使人瞭解
- get down to business 開始辦正事
- get to the bottom of 弄清……的真相
- get to/reach first base (with)
  邁向成功的第一步
- get one's priorities 決定優先順序
- give and take 互相遷就
- give rise to 引起
- go ahead 先行
- go along with 認同
- go for it 努力爭取；大膽一試

- go wrong　出錯
- hand in hand　手牽手；聯合
- hard facts　明確的事實
- have an effect　有影響
- have doubts about　對……存疑
- hit or miss　孤注一擲地
- hold good　有效；適用
- in a moment　立刻
- in a nutshell　概括來說
- in a word　簡言之
- in accordance with　與……一致
- in addition to　除了……以外
- in agreement with　同……一致
- in all　總共
- in all probability　很可能
- in any case　無論如何
- in brief　簡言之
- in case　萬一
- in conjunction with
　與……共同運作或行動
- in connection with　有……關
- in contrast to/with　與……對照
- in depth　深入地
- in detail　詳細地
- in effect　實際上
- in essence　本質上
- in excess of　超過……
- in fact　事實上
- in full　全部地
- in future　從今以後
- in general　一般而言
- in itself　就其本身而言
- in lieu of　代替……
- in order to　為了……

- in other words　換句話說
- in passing　順便一提
- in place of　代替……
- in principle　原則上
- in reality　事實上
- in so far as　在……的範圍內
- in terms of　就……方面；用……字眼
- in that case　既然那樣
- in the black　有盈餘
- in the course of
　在……期間；在……過程中
- in the final analysis　歸根究底
- in the first place　首先
- in the future　未來
- in the light of　鑑於
- in the long run　最終
- in the long/short/medium term
　從長／短／中期來看
- in the meantime　同時
- in the nature of　有……的性質
- in the red　虧損；出現赤字
- in the same way　同樣地
- in the shape of　以……的形式
- in theory　理論上
- in time　及時
- in turn　依次
- in vain　白費
- in view of　鑑於；考慮到
- in my opinion　我的看法是
- in/of all shapes and sizes　各式各樣的
- in/under the circumstances
　在這種情況下
- in this respect　就這一點而言
- insist on　堅持……

- it/that depends 看情況而定
- It/That remains to be seen. 仍有待觀察。
- as simple as that 就這麼簡單
- keep an eye on 留意
- Keep one's options open. 暫不作選擇。
- last but not least 最後但並非最不重要的
- leave it open 暫緩
- look forward to 期待……
- look into 調查……
- make a loss 虧損
- make a profit 獲利
- make clear 解釋清楚
- make do 勉強滿足或接受
- make headway 進展；進步
- make money 賺錢
- make progress 進步
- make sense 合理
- make sure/certain 確認
- make up one's mind 下定決心
- make one's point 表達意見
- make a deal with 與……達成協議
- make sth. work 讓某事能運作
- meet someone halfway. 與某人妥協。
- moment of truth 關鍵時刻；緊要關頭
- more or less 或多或少
- nine times out of ten 十次中有九次
- no exception 沒有例外
- no problem 沒問題
- of course 當然
- of its own accord 自動地；自然地
- on a large scale 大規模地
- on average 平均
- on balance
  （在考慮過所有因素後）總的來說
- on behalf of 代表……
- on condition that
  只要……；以……為條件
- on paper 理論上；未經實踐
- on purpose 故意
- on second thought 進一步考慮後
- on the basis of 基於……
- on the blink （機器等）故障、失靈
- on the contrary 相反地
- on the face of it 顯然地；從表面判斷
- on the ground(s) of/that 以……為理由
- on the one hand..., on the other (hand)
  一方面……，另一方面……
- on the surface 表面上
- on the whole 整體而言
- on time 準時
- open doors for 為……準備
- out of the question 不可能
- pay a price 付出代價
- pay back 償還
- pay one's way 自給自足；不負債
- plan ahead 事先計畫
- point out 指出
- prove the case/point of 證明……的論點
- put it differently 用另外一個方式來說
- put together 拼湊
- put (the) pressure on 施壓於
- refer to 參照
- rely on 依賴
- result in 導致
- right/straight away 立刻
- rule out 排除
- run into 遇見
- save the situation 挽回頹勢

- see eye to eye with　與……看法一致
- see the light　領悟
- set up　建立
- settle differences　消除歧見
- shift the blame/responsibility　規避責任
- sleep on　徹夜思考
- smooth out　消除歧見
- so far　迄今
- soften up　軟化
- split the difference　互相讓步
- stand to　居於（有利或不利）的位置
- stand out　引人注目
- stem from　起源於
- step in　干涉
- take a firm line (or stand) on/over　採取堅定的態度
- take action　採取行動
- take effect　生效
- take sth. into account/consideration　考慮某事
- take note of　注意……
- take one's chance　碰碰運氣
- take place　發生
- take risks　冒險
- take shape　體現
- take steps　採取步驟
- take the consequences　承擔的後果
- take the initiative　採取主動
- take the long view　長遠來看
- take the view that　意見是……

- take upon oneself　承擔（責任等）
- talk over　商討
- talk sb. into　說服某人去做某事
- talk sb. out of　說服某人別做某事
- that is to say　也就是說
- the fact of the matter is　事實是…
- the facts speak for themselves　事實證明一切
- the ins and outs of sth.　某事的細節
- the long and the short of it　要言之
- think out　想出
- think over　仔細考慮
- thrash out　研討解決
- throw light on　有助說明某事
- tie in with　使與……結合
- time out　暫停
- trigger off　觸發；引起
- try out　試驗
- up to　忙於
- vary from　與……相異
- weigh up　衡量；斟酌
- what if　假使……的話，不知怎樣
- What's more　再者
- with a view to　以……為目的
- with hindsight　後見之明
- with regard to　關於……
- without fail　必定
- without prejudice　沒有偏見
- worth doing　值得做

② 經濟、貿易高頻字彙

- accelerated (adj.) 加速的；早熟的
- account (n.) 帳單；帳戶；客戶
- accumulation (n.) 累積
- affiliate (v.) 使加入（加盟）
- affluent (adj.) 富裕的
- aid (v.) 援助　(n.) 援助
- allocate (v.) 分配
- analyst (n.) 分析者
- appreciate (v.)（土地、貨幣等）增值
- auction (n.) 拍賣
- audit (n.) 查帳　(v.) 審核
- ban (v.) 禁止　(n.) 禁令
- banking (n.) 銀行業（務）
- bankruptcy (n.) 破產
- bargain (n.) 交易；買賣　(v) 討價還價
- barter (n.)（物和物的）交換
  (v.) 以物易物
- bid (n.) 投標；出價　(v.) 出價
- bilateral (adj.) 雙邊的
- bill of lading (n.)【英】提貨單
- boom (n.)（商業等）繁榮　(v.) 迅速
  發展；興旺
- boost (n.)【口】（價格等）提高
  (v.) 提高
- bottom line (n.) 結算數字
- boycott (n.) 杯葛；聯合抵制
  (v.) 杯葛；聯合抵制
- breakthrough (n.) 突破
- budget (n.) 預算　(v.) 編列預算
- bullish (adj.)（股票等）看漲的
- buoyant (adj.) 看漲的
- calculate (v.) 計算
- capitalism (n.) 資本主義

- commodity (n.) 商品
- compensate (v.) 賠償；補償
- compete (n.) 競賽
- conglomerate (adj.) 聚合的　(n.) 企業集團
- consignee (n.) 受託人
- consolidate (v.) 結合；合併
- consumption (n.) 消費
- contractor (n.) 承包商
- cooperate (v.) 協力；合作
- cost of living (v.) 生活費用
- cost-effective (adj.) 符合成本效益的
- costly (adj.) 昂貴的；代價高的
- credible (adj.) 可信的
- creditor (n.) 貸方
- currency (n.) 貨幣
- dealer (n.) 商人；業者
- debtor (n.) 借方
- decline (v.) 傾斜；下降；下跌　(n.) 衰退
- decrease (v.) 減少　(n.) 減少
- deduction (n.) 減除；扣除額
- deficit (n.) 赤字
- deflation (n.) 通貨緊縮
- depression (n.) 不景氣；蕭條
- depreciate (v.) 貶值；跌價
- dramatic (adj.) 戲劇性的
- distribute (v.) 分發；分配
- dip (v.) 下跌
- diversify (v.) 使多樣化
- dividend (n.) 股息（錢）
- downturn (n.) 衰退
- drop (v.) 下降
- dumping (n.) 傾銷
- earnings (n.) 所得；工資

- economic (adj.) 經濟上的
- embargo (n.) 禁運
- enterprise (n.) 企業
- estate (n.) 地產
- evaluate (v.) 評估
- excess (n.) 過度；過量；過剩
- expire (v.) 到期
- exploitation (n.) 開發；利用
- export (n.) 出口；輸出　(v.) 出口；輸出
- extravagant (adj.) 奢侈的；浪費的
- fashion industry　流行服裝業
- fluctuate (v.) 波動
- fluctuation (n.) 波動
- fiscal (v.) 會計的
- foreign exchange　外匯
- fund (n.) 資金
- gain (v.) 獲得
- general strike　總罷工
- gloomy (adj.) 黯淡的
- guarantee (n.) 保證（書）　(v.) 保證
- haggle (v.) 討價還價　(n.) 討價還價
- headquarters (n.) 總部
- hike (v.) 突然提高　(n.) 提高（價錢）
- increase (v.) 增加　(n.) 增加
- imbalance (n.) 不平衡
- import (n.) 進口；輸入　(v.) 進口；輸入
- impose (v.) 課徵（稅金或罰款）
- income (n.) 收入
- indicate (v.) 指示
- index (n.) 指標
- inflation (n.) 通貨膨脹
- infrastructure (n.) 基礎建設
- IT industry　資訊科技業
- insure (v.) 投保

- interest rate　利率
- inventory (n.) 庫存；存貨盤點
- letter of credit　信用狀
- liberalization (n.) 自由化
- long-range (adj.) 長期的；遠程的
- manufacturing industry　製造業
- mass production　大量生產
- merge (v.) 合併
- minimum wage　最低工資
- moderate (adj.) 穩健的；中等的
- monopoly (n.) 獨占；壟斷
- mushroom (v.) 如雨後春筍般湧現
- multinational (n.) 跨國企業　(adj.) 多國的
- nationalization (n.) 國有化
- level off　趨於平穩
- on the rise　（物價等）上升中；（人）地位提升中
- order (n.) 訂單　(v.) 訂購
- output (n.) 出產；生產量
- payment (n.) 支付；付款
- pending (adj.) 懸而未決的
- percentage (n.) 百分比
- plummet (v.) 筆直下滑
- plunge (v.) 猛跌；驟降　(n.) 猛跌
- productivity (n.) 生產力
- profitable (adj.) 獲利的
- promote (v.) 促進；促銷；擢升
- property (n.) 財產
- prosper (v.) 繁榮
- protectionism (n.) （貿易）保護主義
- purchase (v.) 購買　(n.) 購買
- quality control　品質管理
- quota (n.) 定量；配額
- quote (v.) 報價　(n.) 報價
- real estate　不動產

- rebound (v.) 回升　(n.) 回升
- rebuild (v.) 重建
- recall (v.) 召回；收回　(n.) 召回
- recede (v.) 向後退
- recession (n.) 不景氣
- reconstruct (v.) 重建
- recover (v.) 恢復
- reform (v.) 改革
- reimbursement (n.) 退款；賠償
- resource (n.) 資源
- reveal (v.) 顯示
- revenue (n.)（國家的）收入；歲收
- revitalization (n.) 復甦
- rise (v.) 上升
- rundown (n.) 減縮
- sabotage (n.) 蓄意破壞
- service industry　服務業
- sharp (adj.) 急遽的；激烈的
- slide (v.) 下滑 (n.) 滑落
- slip (v.)（品質等）變壞、下降
- slow down　減速；減緩
- sluggish (adj.) 緩慢
- slump (v.) 暴跌；不景氣　(n.) 衰退；暴跌

- soar (v.) 暴漲
- stable (adj.) 穩定的
- stimulate (v.) 刺激
- stock (n.) 存貨
- subcontractor (n.) 轉包商
- substantial (adj.) 大量的
- subsidy (n.) 津貼；補助金
- supplier (n.) 供應者
- surge (v.) 激增　(n.) 激增
- syndicate (n.) 企業聯合組織　(v.) 組成聯合組織
- tariff (n.) 關稅；稅率
- trade off　交易
- trade union　工會
- trademark (n.)（註冊）商標
- transact (v.) 交易
- tumble (v.)（物價等）暴跌
- uncertainty (n.) 不確定性
- union (n.) 合併；聯合
- upsurge (v.) 高漲　(n.) 高漲
- walkout (n.) 聯合罷工
- warehouse (n.) 倉庫
- work force　勞動人口

③ 旅遊、購物高頻字彙

- affordable (adj.) 負擔得起的
- aircraft (n.) 飛行器
- aviation (n.) 航空；飛行
- baggage claim　行李提領處
- board (v.) 登機或車船等交通工具
- bargain (n.) 便宜貨；買賣　(v.) 討價還價
- brochure (n.) 小冊子
- buckle up　繫安全帶
- cabin (n.) 小屋

- cargo (n.) 貨物
- carry-on (n.) 隨身行李
- confirmation (n.) 確認
- conveyance (n.) 運輸
- cruise (n.) 航行
- customs (n.) 海關
- delay (n.) 延遲　(v.) 延遲
- deluxe (adj.) 豪華的
- destination (n.) 目的地

- embark (v.) 上船（或飛機等）
- en route (adv.)【法】在途中
- excursion (n.) 遠足；遊覽
- exotic (adj.) 異國情調的；奇特的
- expedition (n.) 探險；遠征
- fare (n.)（交通工具之）票價
- ferry (n.) 渡輪　(v.)（乘渡輪）渡過
- festival (n.) 節慶
- flight attendant　空服員
- freight (n.) 貨運
- ground crew　地勤人員
- intersection (n.) 十字路口
- itemize (v.) 詳細列舉
- itinerary (n.) 行程表
- jaywalk (v.) 不守規則穿越馬路
- jet lag　時差
- journey (n.) 旅程
- label (n.) 標籤
- life vest　救生衣
- lodge (n.) 小屋　(v.) 住宿
- luxurious (adj.) 豪華的
- modify (v.) 變更；修正
- navigate (v.) 航行
- pack (v.) 包裝
- patron (n.) 主顧；（老）顧客

- peak season　旺季
- pickpocket (n.) 扒手
- pilot (n.) 飛行員
- porter (n.) 門房
- refund (n.) 退款　(v.) 退還
- reimburse (v.) 償還
- round-trip (adj.) 來回的
- route (n.) 路徑
- runway (n.) 飛機跑道
- schedule (n.) 時間表
- shortcut (n.) 捷徑
- sightseeing (n.) 觀光
- snapshot (n.) 快照
- stopover (n.) 中途停留
- suite (n.)（旅館的）套房
- take off　起飛
- timetable (n.) 時間表
- transit (n.) 運輸
- transport (n.) 運輸；運送　(v.) 運送
- vacant (adj.) 空的
- vehicle (n.) 交通工具
- vender (n.) 小販
- via (prep.) 經由；取道
- VIP (n.) 貴賓 (= Very Important Person)
- voyage (n.) 旅行；旅程

❹ 餐飲、社交、娛樂高頻字彙

- acquaintance (n.) 相識的人
- amuse (v.) 使歡樂
- anniversary (n.) 週年紀念日
- appetite (n.) 食慾
- appetizer (n.) 開胃菜
- applaud (v.) 鼓掌
- banquet (n.) 宴會

- beverage (n.) 飲料
- buffet (n.) 自助餐
- celebrity (n.) 名人
- chef (n.) 主廚
- cinema (n.) 電影院
- compliment (n.) 恭維
- composer (n.) 作曲家

- concert (n.) 音樂會
- conductor (n.) 指揮家
- courtesy (n.) 禮貌;禮儀
- cuisine (n.) 烹飪;烹調法
- distinguished (adj.) 傑出的;卓越的
- drama (n.) 戲劇
- eloquent (adj.) 口才好的
- entrée (n.) 主菜
- farewell (n.) 告別
- flavor (n.) 味道
- get-together (n.) 聚會
- gymnasium (n.) 健身房
- hilarious (adj.) 狂歡的
- hors d'oeuvre (n.)【法】開胃小菜
- ingredient (n.) 成分;原料
- instrument (n.) 樂器
- intermission (n.)【美】(戲劇等)中場休息
- leftovers (n.) 剩菜
- leisure (n.) 閒暇(時間)
- media (n.) 媒體
- musician (n.) 音樂家
- napkin (n.) 餐巾

- newscast (n.) 新聞廣播
- palatable (adj.) 美味的
- pass up【口】放過;錯過
- pastry (n.) 用麵團和油酥烤成的小甜點心
- performance (n.) 表演
- periodical (n.) 雜誌;定期刊物
- premiere (n.) 首次公演   (v.) 首次公演
- preservative (n.) 防腐劑
- rate (v.) 分級
- reception (n.) 招待會
- recipe (n.) 食譜
- recommend (v.) 推薦
- recreation (n.) 消遣;娛樂
- refreshments (n.) 茶點
- scenario (n.)【義】戲劇的情節
- seasoning (n.) 調味料
- spice (n.) 香料
- stadium (n.) 體育場
- subscribe (v.) 訂閱
- symphony (n.) 交響曲
- ticket office 售票處
- vegetarian (n.) 素食者

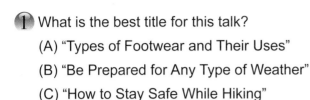

Exercises

1 What is the best title for this talk?

(A) "Types of Footwear and Their Uses"

(B) "Be Prepared for Any Type of Weather"

(C) "How to Stay Safe While Hiking"

(D) "New Developments in Footwear Technology"

2 What does the speaker say about hiking boots?

(A) They are the least expensive.

(B) They are designed for rocky terrain.

(C) They are useful for walking on ice.

(D) They are intended for serious adventurers.

3 What kind of footwear would the speaker recommend for someone who walks in rainy weather?

(A) Walking shoes

(B) Hiking boots

(C) Mountaineering boots

(D) Crampons

4 What is the main purpose of this talk?

(A) To announce school and office closures

(B) To forecast a change in food prices

(C) To provide information about a storm

(D) To compare crop damage throughout the region

5 What does the speaker suggest about the storm?

(A) Its direction is unpredictable.

(B) It is becoming increasingly dangerous.

(C) Its strength is diminishing.

(D) It is major hurricane.

6 Which crop has the storm NOT affected yet?

(A) Oranges

(B) Sugar

(C) Coffee

(D) Tobacco

Ⓐ Ⓑ Ⓒ Ⓓ

7 Where is this introduction being made?

(A) In a university lecture hall

(B) At a regular breakfast meeting

(C) In a private consulting office

(D) At a government conference

Ⓐ Ⓑ Ⓒ Ⓓ

8 Which is NOT one of Megan Frank's current responsibilities?

(A) Director of human resources

(B) Adjunct professor

(C) Partner in a consulting firm

(D) Advisor to a government official

Ⓐ Ⓑ Ⓒ Ⓓ

9 Who is the speaker addressing?

(A) Executives at a financial services company

(B) Partners in a consulting firm

(C) Students in a graduate seminar

(D) Members of the mayor's commission

Ⓐ Ⓑ Ⓒ Ⓓ

10 What is being announced?

(A) The building of an urban rail system

(B) The launch of an airport shuttle

(C) The opening of a new commuter route

(D) The construction of an additional train station

Ⓐ Ⓑ Ⓒ Ⓓ

11 How many stations does the Orange Line stop at?

(A) Five

(B) Six

(C) Seven

(D) Eight   Ⓐ Ⓑ Ⓒ Ⓓ

12 At which station can passengers transfer to another line?

(A) Civic Center

(B) Hoover Ferry

(C) Hoover Airport

(D) Waverly State Park   Ⓐ Ⓑ Ⓒ Ⓓ

13 What is the purpose of the meeting?

(A) To train recently hired employees

(B) To distribute employee ID cards

(C) To explain a new procedure

(D) To encourage workers to be on time   Ⓐ Ⓑ Ⓒ Ⓓ

14 What does the speaker say about the old system?

(A) It was not reliable enough.

(B) It caused some inconveniences.

(C) It was too complicated.

(D) It required a password.   Ⓐ Ⓑ Ⓒ Ⓓ

15 When will the new system go into service?

(A) Immediately

(B) The next day

(C) On Friday

(D) The following week   Ⓐ Ⓑ Ⓒ Ⓓ

Questions 1~3

1. 答案：(A)

破 題 What/title ⇨ 聽「主旨」，通常在獨白的前三句。

解 析 由第一行 The <u>type</u> of <u>footwear</u> you <u>choose</u> <u>depends</u> entirely on the <u>type</u> of <u>hiking</u> you will be <u>doing</u>. 即可知，本題答案為 (A)。

2. 答案：(B)

破 題 What/speakers/say/hiking boots ⇨ 聽有關 hiking boots 的「特質」字眼。

解 析 由三～五行 If, <u>however</u>, you plan to be hiking on <u>uneven trails</u> or crossing <u>rocky</u> terrain, you'll want... <u>hiking boots</u> 即可知，本題答案為 (B)。

3. 答案：(B)

破 題 What/kind/footwear/recommend/walks/rainy ⇨ 聽取與 rainy 相關字眼前後的鞋子「種類」。

解 析 第五行 In addition to being <u>waterproof</u>, <u>this</u> kind of foot wears provides... toward preventing injuries. 中的 waterproof（防水的）與題目重點字 rainy 有關，故後面敘述即為答案，而句中 this 指的就是上一句的 hiking boots，故選 (B)。

(錄音內容)

Questions 1 through 3 refer to the following short talk.

The type of footwear you choose depends entirely on the type of hiking you will be doing. For fair-weather walking along paved roads or well-maintained dirt paths, inexpensive walking shoes are more than adequate. If, however, you plan to be hiking on uneven trails or crossing rocky terrain, you'll want to invest in a pair of hiking boots. In addition to being waterproof, this kind of footwear provides extra padding for the hiker's feet and support for the ankles, both of which go a long way toward preventing injuries. For serious adventurers, for example those who expect to be hiking for extended periods through the snow, mountaineering boots are essential. These are extremely durable boots with a firm, thick sole. Mountaineering boots also allow the hiker to attach crampons, which are metal frames with spikes on them, to make walking on ice easier.

題目 1~3 為以下簡短獨白的相關問題。

你要選用什麼樣的鞋子完全取決於你要做什麼樣的健行。假如是在晴天走鋪面道路或維護良好的泥土路，便宜的步鞋會非常恰當。但要是你打算走不平的小道或橫越多岩石的地形，就需要買雙健走鞋。除了防水外，這種鞋子還為健行者多加了墊子來保護足部並支撐腳踝，讓走遠路也能避免受傷。如果是熱衷冒險的人，例如預計要長期在雪地中行走的人，登山鞋就不可或缺。這是十分耐用的鞋子，鞋底既堅固又厚實。登山鞋還能讓健行者裝上帶釘鞋底，也就是上面有釘子的金屬框，使得在冰上行走較容易。

1. 這段談話最合適的標題是什麼？
   (A)「鞋子的種類及其用途」
   (B)「為任何一種天氣做好準備」
   (C)「如何在健行時保持安全」
   (D)「製鞋科技的新發展」。

2. 說話者說健行鞋怎麼樣？
   (A) 它們最便宜。
   (B) 它們是為多岩石地形所設計的。
   (C) 它們適合用於冰上行走。
   (D) 它們適合熱衷冒險的人。

3. 說話者會推薦哪種鞋給在雨天行走的人？
   (A) 步鞋
   (B) 健行鞋
   (C) 登山鞋
   (D) 釘鞋

□ adequate [ˋædəkwɪt] *adj.* 足夠的；恰當的
□ terrain [tɛˋren] *n.* 地形；地域
□ waterproof [ˋwɔtɚͺpruf] *adj.* 防水的
□ injury [ˋɪndʒərɪ] *n.* 傷害
□ mountaineering [ͺmauntəˋnɪrɪŋ] *n.* 登山（運動）

□ durable [ˋdjurəbl] *adj.* 耐用的
□ crampon [ˋkræmpən] *n.*（防滑）帶釘鞋底
□ spike [spaɪk] *n.* 鞋底釘

Questions 4~6

4. 答案：(C)

破 題 What/purpose/talk ⇨ 聽「目的」，即「主旨」，通常出現在前三句。

解 析 第 一 ～ 三 行 After passing over..., <u>Tropical storm</u>... <u>heading</u> north and <u>expected</u> to make <u>landfall</u>... Florida... early tomorrow afternoon. 即提供了風暴的相關演變消息，故本題應選 (C)。

5. 答案：(C)

破 題 What/speaker/suggest/storm ⇨ 聽與 storm「特質」相關的字眼。

解 析 第三行 A <u>spokesperson</u> from the National Hurricane Center... said it's likely that Olaf will be <u>downgraded</u> to <u>tropical depression</u>... 明白指出暴風雨將減弱為熱帶性低氣壓，故本題應選 (C)。

6. 答案：(A)

破 題 Which/crop/strom/not/affected ⇨ 聽「沒有」被影響的 crop 種類，通常要去聽一連串「密集性排列」的名詞組合。

解 析 由第十一行 ... but <u>crop damage</u>, especially to <u>sugar</u> and <u>coffee</u> fields... and <u>tobacco</u> plantations... 可知，沒有提到的名詞為 (A)。通常在強烈字眼，如 especially 之後常為答案出處，需特別留意。

（錄音內容）

Questions 4 through 6 refer to the following report.

After passing over Jamaica and Cuba, Tropical Storm Olaf is heading north and expected to make landfall here in southern Florida sometime early tomorrow afternoon. A spokesperson from the National Hurricane Center in Miami has said it's likely that Olaf will be downgraded to tropical depression later tonight or tomorrow morning. Schools and government offices will remain open, but residents of Miami-Dade and Monroe counties are advised to avoid unnecessary travel and to stay away from beaches and rivers. With major fruit harvests still weeks away, citrus farmers are preparing for the worst. Last year, a similar storm wiped out nearly 15 percent of the orange and grapefruit crops. As of this afternoon, no deaths and relatively few injuries have been reported, but crop damage, especially to sugar and coffee fields in Jamaica and tobacco plantations in Cuba, is significant.

題目 4~6 為以下報導的相關問題。

在掃過牙買加和古巴後，熱帶風暴歐拉福正往北移動，並預計在明天中午過後就會在南佛羅里達本地登陸。邁阿密國家颶風中心的一位發言人說，歐拉福在今天深夜或明天早上可能會減弱為熱帶性低氣壓。學校和政府機關照常上課、上班，邁阿密——戴德和蒙羅郡的居民最好避免不必要的外出，並遠離海邊和河邊。由於離水果大量收成還有好幾週，柑農正準備因應最壞的情況。去年有一場類似的暴風雨把將近百分之十五的柳橙和葡萄柚作物給吹毀。到今天下午為止，獲報的死亡人數為零，傷者也相當少，可是農作損失慘重，尤其是牙買加的糖和咖啡田，以及古巴的菸草種植場。

題目&選項翻譯

4. 這段談話的主要目的是什麼？
   (A) 宣布學校和機關停班停課
   (B) 預測糧價的變化
   (C) 提供暴風雨的相關消息
   (D) 比較整個地區的農作損失

5. 說話者表示暴風雨將會如何？
   (A) 它的方向無法掌握。
   (B) 它變得愈來愈危險。
   (C) 它的強度正在減弱。
   (D) 它是個大型颶風。

6. 暴風雨還「沒有」影響到哪種作物？
   (A) 柳橙
   (B) 糖
   (C) 咖啡
   (D) 菸草

☐ head [hɛd] *v.*（向特定方向）出發
☐ landfall [ˋlændfɔl] *n.* 登陸
☐ spokesperson [ˋspoksˏpɜsn̩] *n.* 發言人
☐ downgrade [ˋdaʊnˏgred] *v.* 使降級
☐ depression [dɪˋprɛʃən] *n.*【氣】低氣壓

☐ harvest [ˋhɑrvɪst] *n.* 收割季節
☐ citrus [ˋsɪtrəs] *n.* 柑橘屬植物
☐ diminish [dəˋmɪnɪʃ] *v.* 減小
☐ hurricane[ˋhɜɪken] *n.* 颶風

Questions 7~9

7. 答案：(B)

破題　Where/introduction/made ⇨ 聽「場合地點」。

解析　由第一行 It is a distinct <u>pleasure</u> to <u>welcome</u>... to... Wedgewood Investment's <u>monthly</u> Leadership <u>Breakfast</u>. 即可知，本題應選 (B)。通常在 Welcome... 之後就會提到獨白的「主旨」或「地點」。

8. 答案：(A)

破題　Which not/Megan Frank's/current responsibilities ⇨ 聽所有與該人士有關的「工作職務」字眼。

解析　由第七行開始的 Since that time she has returned to... as an <u>adjunct</u> <u>professor</u>... She is also a founding partner of... a <u>consulting</u> firm... And... she has recently <u>accepted</u> the <u>mayor's</u> invitation to join the city's equal opportunity commission. 可知，只有 (A) 的職務沒有提及。注意，由於本題問的是 current responsibilities（目前職務），第五行中提到的 the Director of Human Resources 是 late 90s（90年代末期）的事。

9. 答案：(A)

破題　Who/speaker/addressing ⇨ 聽「聽眾」為誰。

解析　由第一句 It is... welcome... to Wedgewood <u>Investment's</u>... Breakfast. 及第二句 Dr. Frank will be speaking... about new trends in <u>executive</u> <u>compensation</u>... 中的關鍵字 Investment 及 executive compensation，可推知答案為 (A)。

録音内容

Questions 7 through 9 refer to the following short talk.

It is a distinct pleasure to welcome Megan Frank to Wedgewood Investment's monthly Leadership Breakfast. Dr. Frank will be speaking to us this morning about new trends in executive compensation, a topic that I know is dear to the heart of every one of us here today. Old timers like myself will remember Megan from when she served as the Director of Human Resources here at Wedgewood Investments for several years in the late 90s. Since that time she has returned to the academic world as an adjunct professor at Waheila University, where she teaches a course in performance evaluation as well as graduate seminars in collective bargaining. She is also a founding partner of Tully, Frank, and Holmes, a consulting firm specializing in executive placement, executive training, and workplace arbitration. And if that weren't enough, she has recently accepted the mayor's invitation to join the city's equal opportunity commission. So, without further ado, please join me in a round of applause for Dr. Frank.

録音翻譯

題目 7~9 為以下簡短獨白的相關問題。

非常高興請到梅根‧法蘭克來參加威吉伍投資每月一次的領導早餐會。法蘭克博士今天早上要跟我們談談主管薪酬的新趨勢，我知道今天在座的每個人心裡都很關心這個主題。像我這種老一輩的都記得，梅根在九○年代末期時，在威吉伍投資這裡當過好幾年的人力資源主任。後來她回到學術界擔任瓦赫拉大學的助理教授，並在該校教授績效評估課程，以及集體協商的研究所專題研討。她也是 TFH 的創始合夥人，這家專門提供主管配置、主管訓練和職場仲裁顧問的公司。假如這樣還不夠的話，她最近應市長之邀加入了本市的平等機會委員會。所以，我們不再贅述，請跟我一起以掌聲來歡迎法蘭克博士。

題目&選項翻譯

7. 這段介紹詞是在哪裡提出的？
   (A) 大學演講廳
   (B) 一般的早餐會
   (C) 私人顧問公司
   (D) 政府會議

8. 哪一個「不」是梅根‧法蘭克目前的職務？
   (A) 人力資源主任
   (B) 助理教授
   (C) 顧問公司的合夥人
   (D) 政府官員的顧問

9. 說話者在對誰講話？
   (A) 金融服務公司的主管
   (B) 顧問公司的合夥人
   (C) 專題研討會的研究生
   (D) 市長委員會的委員

□ compensation [ˌkɑmpənˈseʃən] *n.*
【美】報酬；薪水
□ adjunct [ˈædʒʌŋkt] *n.* 助手；副手
□ placement [ˈplesmənt] *n.* 人員配置

□ arbitration [ˌɑrbəˈtreʃən] *n.* 仲裁
□ commission [kəˈmɪʃən] *n.* 委員會
□ ado [əˈdu] *n.* 騷動；辛勞

Questions 10~12

10. 答案：(C)

> **破 題** What/announced ⇨ 聽「主旨」，以前三句中的「名詞」為重點。

> **解 析** 由第一行 Today marked the <u>opening</u> of the Orang Line, a <u>commuter</u> light <u>rail</u> <u>route</u> that connects... 即可知，正確答案為 (C)。

11. 答案：(C)

> **破 題** How many/station/Orange Line/stop ⇨ 聽 Orange Line 的站別「數量」。

> **解 析** 第一行有提到 the Orange Line，之後第四行的 The line runs through <u>two</u> exsiting downtown <u>stations</u> 以及第五、六行的 There are <u>five</u> Waverly County <u>stations</u> 可知，2 + 5 = 7，故本題應選 (C)。

12. 答案：(A)

> **破 題** Which station/passengers/transfer/another line ⇨ 聽乘客轉車的「站名」。

> **解 析** 由第七行 Passengers can <u>connect</u> to the... lines at the <u>Civic Center hub</u>. 可知，正確答案為 (A)。注意，可以 connect 即代表可以 transfer。

(錄音內容)

Questions 10 through 12 refer to the following report.

Today marked the opening of the Orange Line, a commuter light rail route that connects Waverly County and downtown Hoover. The new line is expected to relieve traffic congestion on Highway 4 and ease rush-hour bottlenecks on the Hoover City Bridge. The line runs through two existing downtown stations, Civic Center and Hoover Ferry, before crossing the river into Waverly. There are five Waverly County stations, including Morristown, Hoover Airport, and the terminus, Waverly State Park. Passengers can connect to the Blue, Yellow, and Green lines at the Civic Center hub. Hoover mayor Enrique Montero presided over the grand opening ceremony, which included a ribbon cutting, speeches from government and union officials, and a concert by the Hoover High Marching Band. Mayor Montero remarked that although the line was primarily intended to help weekday commuters, he expected that Hoover residents would take advantage of the new line to enjoy the spectacular natural scenery of Waverly State Park.

題目 10~12 為以下報導的相關問題。

今天是橘線的通車日，這條通勤輕軌路線連接了韋佛里郡和胡佛市區。這條新線可望紓解四號公路的交通壅塞，並減輕胡佛市大橋在尖峰時間的交通瓶頸。這條線會經過市區兩個現有的車站——市中心站和胡佛渡口站，然後跨河進入韋佛里。韋佛里郡有五個車站，包括摩里斯鎮站、胡佛機場站和終點站韋佛里州立公園。乘客可以在市民中心轉運站連接藍、黃、綠線。胡佛市長安立奎·蒙特羅主持了盛大的揭幕儀式，其中包括剪綵、政府和工會官員演說，以及胡佛高中鼓號樂隊的演奏。市長蒙特羅表示，雖然這條線主要是為了協助平日上下班的人，但是他也期待胡佛市民會利用這條新線前往韋佛里州立公園欣賞壯觀的自然景色。

10. 此報導在宣布什麼？
    (A) 城市鐵路系統的建構
    (B) 機場接駁車的推出
    (C) 新的通勤路線的開啓
    (D) 額外火車站的建造

11. 橘線停幾個站？
    (A) 五個
    (B) 六個
    (C) 七個
    (D) 八個

12. 乘客可以在哪個車站轉搭別的線？
    (A) 市民中心
    (B) 胡佛渡口
    (C) 胡佛機場
    (D) 韋佛里州立公園

☐ commuter [kə`mjutə] *n.* 通勤者　　☐ hub [hʌb] *n.* 中心；中區
☐ route [rut] *n.* 路線　　☐ preside [prɪ`zaɪd] *v.* 主持
☐ congestion [kən`dʒɛstʃən] *n.* 壅塞　　☐ ribbon cutting　剪綵
☐ terminus [`tɜmənəs] *n.* 終點　　☐ spectacular [spɛk`tækjələ] *adj.* 壯觀的

Questions 13~15

13 答案：(C)

破題 What/purpose/meeting ⇨ 聽「主旨」，即此 meeting 的「目的」。

解析 由第一行 Stacey Chen asked me to give a brief talk to everyone about the new time card system. 可知，答案為 (C)。

14. 答案：(B)

破題 What/speaker/say/old system ⇨ 聽關於 old system 的「特質」字眼。

解析 第四行 Because there is <u>only one</u> machine, howerver, this <u>resulted</u> in <u>long lines</u>, especially after our lunch berak. 中出現表「獨一性」的 "only" 及轉折語 "however"，其後 resulted in long lines（大排長龍）即是造成的結果，故應選 (B)。

15. 答案：(D)

破題 When/new system/service ⇨ 聽 new system 的啓用時間。

解析 第十一、十二行 We won't switch to the new system until <u>next Monday</u>... 可知，本題應選 (D)。注意，通常聽到 not... until...（直到……才……）會有出題重點。

錄音內容

Questions 13 through 15 refer to the following announcement.

Good afternoon. Stacey Chen asked me to give a brief talk to everyone about the new time card system. As you know, we've been clocking in and out of work everyday by swiping our employee ID cards through the card reader in the lobby. Because there is only one machine, however, this resulted in long lines, especially after our lunch break. Instead of using a single card reader, the new system is accessible from every computer in the office. As soon as you come to work, just turn on your computer, enter your employee number and password, and then click on the "Clock In" button. The time will be recorded by the computer. At the end of the day, simply click on the "Clock Out" button before going home. Remember to follow the same procedure when you leave and return from lunch. We won't switch to the new system until next Monday, so you'll still have to swipe your ID card today, tomorrow, and Friday. I've sent everyone an email with more information about the new system, and I encourage you to read it right away.

錄音翻譯
題目 13~15 為以下談話的相關問題。

午安。史黛西‧陳要我簡單跟各位說明新的打卡系統。各位都知道，我們每天上下班打卡時，都要在大廳的讀卡機裡刷一下員工識別卡。不過，由於只有一台機器，所以這也造成了大排長龍，尤其是在午休時間後。新系統不再只靠一台讀卡機，辦公室的每台電腦都能連線。你一來上班的時候，只要打開電腦，輸入你的員工號碼和密碼，然後按下「簽到」鍵即可。電腦會把時間記錄下來。到了下班的時候，只要按下「簽退」鍵就可以回家了。當你去用餐和回來的時候，記得要遵照同樣的程序。我們要到下星期一才會改用新系統，所以今天、明天和星期五還是必須刷識別卡。我寄了一封電子郵件給大家，裡面有新系統的詳細資料。我鼓勵大家立刻看看。

題目&選項翻譯

13. 這場會議的目的是什麼？
    (A) 訓練新進員工
    (B) 發員工識別卡
    (C) 解釋一項新程序
    (D) 鼓勵員工準時

14. 說話者說舊系統如何？
    (A) 它不夠可靠。
    (B) 它造成了一些不便。
    (C) 它太複雜。
    (D) 它需要密碼。

15. 新系統何時開始啟用？
    (A) 立刻
    (B) 隔天
    (C) 星期五
    (D) 下星期

☐ swipe [swaɪp] *v.* 擦過；刷（卡）

☐ accessible [æk`sɛsəbl] *adj.* 可進入的

2

New TOEIC

模擬測驗

Answer Sheet

模擬試題
答案卡

NAME 姓名	

Test 1

Part 1		Part 2						Part 3						Part 4					
No.	ANSWER A B C D	No.	ANSWER A B C D	No.	ANSWER A B C D	No.	ANSWER A B C D	No.	ANSWER A B C D	No.	ANSWER A B C D	No.	ANSWER A B C D	No.	ANSWER A B C D	No.	ANSWER A B C D	No.	ANSWER A B C D
1	Ⓐ Ⓑ Ⓒ Ⓓ	11	Ⓐ Ⓑ Ⓒ	21	Ⓐ Ⓑ Ⓒ	31	Ⓐ Ⓑ Ⓒ	41	Ⓐ Ⓑ Ⓒ Ⓓ	51	Ⓐ Ⓑ Ⓒ Ⓓ	61	Ⓐ Ⓑ Ⓒ Ⓓ	71	Ⓐ Ⓑ Ⓒ Ⓓ	81	Ⓐ Ⓑ Ⓒ Ⓓ	91	Ⓐ Ⓑ Ⓒ Ⓓ
2	Ⓐ Ⓑ Ⓒ Ⓓ	12	Ⓐ Ⓑ Ⓒ	22	Ⓐ Ⓑ Ⓒ	32	Ⓐ Ⓑ Ⓒ	42	Ⓐ Ⓑ Ⓒ Ⓓ	52	Ⓐ Ⓑ Ⓒ Ⓓ	62	Ⓐ Ⓑ Ⓒ Ⓓ	72	Ⓐ Ⓑ Ⓒ Ⓓ	82	Ⓐ Ⓑ Ⓒ Ⓓ	92	Ⓐ Ⓑ Ⓒ Ⓓ
3	Ⓐ Ⓑ Ⓒ Ⓓ	13	Ⓐ Ⓑ Ⓒ	23	Ⓐ Ⓑ Ⓒ	33	Ⓐ Ⓑ Ⓒ	43	Ⓐ Ⓑ Ⓒ Ⓓ	53	Ⓐ Ⓑ Ⓒ Ⓓ	63	Ⓐ Ⓑ Ⓒ Ⓓ	73	Ⓐ Ⓑ Ⓒ Ⓓ	83	Ⓐ Ⓑ Ⓒ Ⓓ	93	Ⓐ Ⓑ Ⓒ Ⓓ
4	Ⓐ Ⓑ Ⓒ Ⓓ	14	Ⓐ Ⓑ Ⓒ	24	Ⓐ Ⓑ Ⓒ	34	Ⓐ Ⓑ Ⓒ	44	Ⓐ Ⓑ Ⓒ Ⓓ	54	Ⓐ Ⓑ Ⓒ Ⓓ	64	Ⓐ Ⓑ Ⓒ Ⓓ	74	Ⓐ Ⓑ Ⓒ Ⓓ	84	Ⓐ Ⓑ Ⓒ Ⓓ	94	Ⓐ Ⓑ Ⓒ Ⓓ
5	Ⓐ Ⓑ Ⓒ Ⓓ	15	Ⓐ Ⓑ Ⓒ	25	Ⓐ Ⓑ Ⓒ	35	Ⓐ Ⓑ Ⓒ	45	Ⓐ Ⓑ Ⓒ Ⓓ	55	Ⓐ Ⓑ Ⓒ Ⓓ	65	Ⓐ Ⓑ Ⓒ Ⓓ	75	Ⓐ Ⓑ Ⓒ Ⓓ	85	Ⓐ Ⓑ Ⓒ Ⓓ	95	Ⓐ Ⓑ Ⓒ Ⓓ
6	Ⓐ Ⓑ Ⓒ Ⓓ	16	Ⓐ Ⓑ Ⓒ	26	Ⓐ Ⓑ Ⓒ	36	Ⓐ Ⓑ Ⓒ	46	Ⓐ Ⓑ Ⓒ Ⓓ	56	Ⓐ Ⓑ Ⓒ Ⓓ	66	Ⓐ Ⓑ Ⓒ Ⓓ	76	Ⓐ Ⓑ Ⓒ Ⓓ	86	Ⓐ Ⓑ Ⓒ Ⓓ	96	Ⓐ Ⓑ Ⓒ Ⓓ
7	Ⓐ Ⓑ Ⓒ Ⓓ	17	Ⓐ Ⓑ Ⓒ	27	Ⓐ Ⓑ Ⓒ	37	Ⓐ Ⓑ Ⓒ	47	Ⓐ Ⓑ Ⓒ Ⓓ	57	Ⓐ Ⓑ Ⓒ Ⓓ	67	Ⓐ Ⓑ Ⓒ Ⓓ	77	Ⓐ Ⓑ Ⓒ Ⓓ	87	Ⓐ Ⓑ Ⓒ Ⓓ	97	Ⓐ Ⓑ Ⓒ Ⓓ
8	Ⓐ Ⓑ Ⓒ Ⓓ	18	Ⓐ Ⓑ Ⓒ	28	Ⓐ Ⓑ Ⓒ	38	Ⓐ Ⓑ Ⓒ	48	Ⓐ Ⓑ Ⓒ Ⓓ	58	Ⓐ Ⓑ Ⓒ Ⓓ	68	Ⓐ Ⓑ Ⓒ Ⓓ	78	Ⓐ Ⓑ Ⓒ Ⓓ	88	Ⓐ Ⓑ Ⓒ Ⓓ	98	Ⓐ Ⓑ Ⓒ Ⓓ
9	Ⓐ Ⓑ Ⓒ Ⓓ	19	Ⓐ Ⓑ Ⓒ	29	Ⓐ Ⓑ Ⓒ	39	Ⓐ Ⓑ Ⓒ	49	Ⓐ Ⓑ Ⓒ Ⓓ	59	Ⓐ Ⓑ Ⓒ Ⓓ	69	Ⓐ Ⓑ Ⓒ Ⓓ	79	Ⓐ Ⓑ Ⓒ Ⓓ	89	Ⓐ Ⓑ Ⓒ Ⓓ	99	Ⓐ Ⓑ Ⓒ Ⓓ
10	Ⓐ Ⓑ Ⓒ Ⓓ	20	Ⓐ Ⓑ Ⓒ	30	Ⓐ Ⓑ Ⓒ	40	Ⓐ Ⓑ Ⓒ	50	Ⓐ Ⓑ Ⓒ Ⓓ	60	Ⓐ Ⓑ Ⓒ Ⓓ	70	Ⓐ Ⓑ Ⓒ Ⓓ	80	Ⓐ Ⓑ Ⓒ Ⓓ	90	Ⓐ Ⓑ Ⓒ Ⓓ	100	Ⓐ Ⓑ Ⓒ Ⓓ

Test 2

Part 1		Part 2						Part 3						Part 4					
No.	ANSWER A B C D	No.	ANSWER A B C D	No.	ANSWER A B C D	No.	ANSWER A B C D	No.	ANSWER A B C D	No.	ANSWER A B C D	No.	ANSWER A B C D	No.	ANSWER A B C D	No.	ANSWER A B C D	No.	ANSWER A B C D
1	Ⓐ Ⓑ Ⓒ Ⓓ	11	Ⓐ Ⓑ Ⓒ	21	Ⓐ Ⓑ Ⓒ	31	Ⓐ Ⓑ Ⓒ	41	Ⓐ Ⓑ Ⓒ Ⓓ	51	Ⓐ Ⓑ Ⓒ Ⓓ	61	Ⓐ Ⓑ Ⓒ Ⓓ	71	Ⓐ Ⓑ Ⓒ Ⓓ	81	Ⓐ Ⓑ Ⓒ Ⓓ	91	Ⓐ Ⓑ Ⓒ Ⓓ
2	Ⓐ Ⓑ Ⓒ Ⓓ	12	Ⓐ Ⓑ Ⓒ	22	Ⓐ Ⓑ Ⓒ	32	Ⓐ Ⓑ Ⓒ	42	Ⓐ Ⓑ Ⓒ Ⓓ	52	Ⓐ Ⓑ Ⓒ Ⓓ	62	Ⓐ Ⓑ Ⓒ Ⓓ	72	Ⓐ Ⓑ Ⓒ Ⓓ	82	Ⓐ Ⓑ Ⓒ Ⓓ	92	Ⓐ Ⓑ Ⓒ Ⓓ
3	Ⓐ Ⓑ Ⓒ Ⓓ	13	Ⓐ Ⓑ Ⓒ	23	Ⓐ Ⓑ Ⓒ	33	Ⓐ Ⓑ Ⓒ	43	Ⓐ Ⓑ Ⓒ Ⓓ	53	Ⓐ Ⓑ Ⓒ Ⓓ	63	Ⓐ Ⓑ Ⓒ Ⓓ	73	Ⓐ Ⓑ Ⓒ Ⓓ	83	Ⓐ Ⓑ Ⓒ Ⓓ	93	Ⓐ Ⓑ Ⓒ Ⓓ
4	Ⓐ Ⓑ Ⓒ Ⓓ	14	Ⓐ Ⓑ Ⓒ	24	Ⓐ Ⓑ Ⓒ	34	Ⓐ Ⓑ Ⓒ	44	Ⓐ Ⓑ Ⓒ Ⓓ	54	Ⓐ Ⓑ Ⓒ Ⓓ	64	Ⓐ Ⓑ Ⓒ Ⓓ	74	Ⓐ Ⓑ Ⓒ Ⓓ	84	Ⓐ Ⓑ Ⓒ Ⓓ	94	Ⓐ Ⓑ Ⓒ Ⓓ
5	Ⓐ Ⓑ Ⓒ Ⓓ	15	Ⓐ Ⓑ Ⓒ	25	Ⓐ Ⓑ Ⓒ	35	Ⓐ Ⓑ Ⓒ	45	Ⓐ Ⓑ Ⓒ Ⓓ	55	Ⓐ Ⓑ Ⓒ Ⓓ	65	Ⓐ Ⓑ Ⓒ Ⓓ	75	Ⓐ Ⓑ Ⓒ Ⓓ	85	Ⓐ Ⓑ Ⓒ Ⓓ	95	Ⓐ Ⓑ Ⓒ Ⓓ
6	Ⓐ Ⓑ Ⓒ Ⓓ	16	Ⓐ Ⓑ Ⓒ	26	Ⓐ Ⓑ Ⓒ	36	Ⓐ Ⓑ Ⓒ	46	Ⓐ Ⓑ Ⓒ Ⓓ	56	Ⓐ Ⓑ Ⓒ Ⓓ	66	Ⓐ Ⓑ Ⓒ Ⓓ	76	Ⓐ Ⓑ Ⓒ Ⓓ	86	Ⓐ Ⓑ Ⓒ Ⓓ	96	Ⓐ Ⓑ Ⓒ Ⓓ
7	Ⓐ Ⓑ Ⓒ Ⓓ	17	Ⓐ Ⓑ Ⓒ	27	Ⓐ Ⓑ Ⓒ	37	Ⓐ Ⓑ Ⓒ	47	Ⓐ Ⓑ Ⓒ Ⓓ	57	Ⓐ Ⓑ Ⓒ Ⓓ	67	Ⓐ Ⓑ Ⓒ Ⓓ	77	Ⓐ Ⓑ Ⓒ Ⓓ	87	Ⓐ Ⓑ Ⓒ Ⓓ	97	Ⓐ Ⓑ Ⓒ Ⓓ
8	Ⓐ Ⓑ Ⓒ Ⓓ	18	Ⓐ Ⓑ Ⓒ	28	Ⓐ Ⓑ Ⓒ	38	Ⓐ Ⓑ Ⓒ	48	Ⓐ Ⓑ Ⓒ Ⓓ	58	Ⓐ Ⓑ Ⓒ Ⓓ	68	Ⓐ Ⓑ Ⓒ Ⓓ	78	Ⓐ Ⓑ Ⓒ Ⓓ	88	Ⓐ Ⓑ Ⓒ Ⓓ	98	Ⓐ Ⓑ Ⓒ Ⓓ
9	Ⓐ Ⓑ Ⓒ Ⓓ	19	Ⓐ Ⓑ Ⓒ	29	Ⓐ Ⓑ Ⓒ	39	Ⓐ Ⓑ Ⓒ	49	Ⓐ Ⓑ Ⓒ Ⓓ	59	Ⓐ Ⓑ Ⓒ Ⓓ	69	Ⓐ Ⓑ Ⓒ Ⓓ	79	Ⓐ Ⓑ Ⓒ Ⓓ	89	Ⓐ Ⓑ Ⓒ Ⓓ	99	Ⓐ Ⓑ Ⓒ Ⓓ
10	Ⓐ Ⓑ Ⓒ Ⓓ	20	Ⓐ Ⓑ Ⓒ	30	Ⓐ Ⓑ Ⓒ	40	Ⓐ Ⓑ Ⓒ	50	Ⓐ Ⓑ Ⓒ Ⓓ	60	Ⓐ Ⓑ Ⓒ Ⓓ	70	Ⓐ Ⓑ Ⓒ Ⓓ	80	Ⓐ Ⓑ Ⓒ Ⓓ	90	Ⓐ Ⓑ Ⓒ Ⓓ	100	Ⓐ Ⓑ Ⓒ Ⓓ

Test 1

模擬試題

Part 1

LISTENING TEST

The Listening test allows you to demonstrate how well you understand spoken English. The listening test has four parts, and you will hear directions for each of them. The entire Listening test is approximately forty-five minutes long. Write only on your answer sheet, not the test book.

PART 1

Directions: For each question in Part 1, you will hear four statements about a photograph. Select the statement that best describes what you see in the photo and mark your answer on the answer sheet. The statements will only be spoken once, and do not appear in the test book.

Example

Sample Answer

Statement (C), "They are sitting around the table," is the best description of the photograph, so you should mark (C) on your anwer sheet.

1.

Ⓐ Ⓑ Ⓒ Ⓓ

2.

Ⓐ Ⓑ Ⓒ Ⓓ

Go on to the next page. ▶

3.

4.

5.

6.

Go on to the next page. ▶

7.

Ⓐ Ⓑ Ⓒ Ⓓ

8.

Ⓐ Ⓑ Ⓒ Ⓓ

9.

10.

Part 2

PART 2

Direcitons: In Part 2, you will hear either a statement or a question and three responses. They will only be spoken one time, and do not appear in your test book. Select the best response to the question or statement and mark the corresponding letter (A), (B), or (C) on your answer sheet.

Example

Sample Answer

You will hear:　　　Does this bus go to the train station?

You will also hear:　(A) I've listened to this station for years.

　　　　　　　　　(B) No, you need to take number 75.

　　　　　　　　　(C) The train leaves in a few minutes.

The best response to the question "Does this bus go to the train station?" is choice (B), "No, you need to take number 75," so you should mark answer (B) on your answer sheet.

11. Mark your answer on your answer sheet.　　Ⓐ　Ⓑ　Ⓒ

12. Mark your answer on your answer sheet.　　Ⓐ　Ⓑ　Ⓒ

13. Mark your answer on your answer sheet.　　Ⓐ　Ⓑ　Ⓒ

14. Mark your answer on your answer sheet.　　Ⓐ　Ⓑ　Ⓒ

15. Mark your answer on your answer sheet.　　Ⓐ　Ⓑ　Ⓒ

16. Mark your answer on your answer sheet.　　Ⓐ　Ⓑ　Ⓒ

17. Mark your answer on your answer sheet.　　Ⓐ　Ⓑ　Ⓒ

18. Mark your answer on your answer sheet.　　Ⓐ　Ⓑ　Ⓒ

19. Mark your answer on your answer sheet.　　Ⓐ　Ⓑ　Ⓒ

20. Mark your answer on your answer sheet.　　Ⓐ　Ⓑ　Ⓒ

Go on to the next page. ▶

21. Mark your answer on your answer sheet. Ⓐ Ⓑ Ⓒ

22. Mark your answer on your answer sheet. Ⓐ Ⓑ Ⓒ

23. Mark your answer on your answer sheet. Ⓐ Ⓑ Ⓒ

24. Mark your answer on your answer sheet. Ⓐ Ⓑ Ⓒ

25. Mark your answer on your answer sheet. Ⓐ Ⓑ Ⓒ

26. Mark your answer on your answer sheet. Ⓐ Ⓑ Ⓒ

27. Mark your answer on your answer sheet. Ⓐ Ⓑ Ⓒ

28. Mark your answer on your answer sheet. Ⓐ Ⓑ Ⓒ

29. Mark your answer on your answer sheet. Ⓐ Ⓑ Ⓒ

30. Mark your answer on your answer sheet. Ⓐ Ⓑ Ⓒ

31. Mark your answer on your answer sheet.　　(A) (B) (C)

32. Mark your answer on your answer sheet.　　(A) (B) (C)

33. Mark your answer on your answer sheet.　　(A) (B) (C)

34. Mark your answer on your answer sheet.　　(A) (B) (C)

35. Mark your answer on your answer sheet.　　(A) (B) (C)

36. Mark your answer on your answer sheet.　　(A) (B) (C)

37. Mark your answer on your answer sheet.　　(A) (B) (C)

38. Mark your answer on your answer sheet.　　(A) (B) (C)

39. Mark your answer on your answer sheet.　　(A) (B) (C)

40. Mark your answer on your answer sheet.　　(A) (B) (C)

Part 3

MP3
105

PART3

Direcitons: In Part 3, you will hear several short conversations between two people. After each conversation, you will be asked to answer three questions about what you heard. Select the best response to each question, and mark the corresponding letter (A), (B), (C), or (D) on your answer sheet. The questions and responses are printed in the test book. The conversations do not appear in the test book, and they will be spoken only one time.

41. What does the man say about the presentation?

  (A) It is almost finished.

  (B) It can be used for marketing.

  (C) It should be more fully developed.

  (D) It is longer than their boss wanted. Ⓐ Ⓑ Ⓒ Ⓓ

42. What is learned about the presentation?

  (A) It gives a brief history of the company.

  (B) It contains information about the company's products.

  (C) It shows the increase in sales over the past five years.

  (D) It describes the various service plans the company offers.

  Ⓐ Ⓑ Ⓒ Ⓓ

43. What does the speakers' company sell?

  (A) Copy machines

  (B) Paper products

  (C) Office furniture

  (D) Flooring material Ⓐ Ⓑ Ⓒ Ⓓ

MP3
107

44. Why is the woman looking for a new cell phone service provider?

(A) She is making a lot of phone calls.

(B) She needs a different long-distance plan.

(C) She needs a cell phone plan that works in Europe.

(D) She is unhappy with her current service provider's customer service.

Ⓐ Ⓑ Ⓒ Ⓓ

45. How long has the man been with his new cell phone service provider?

(A) 1 month

(B) 4 months

(C) 6 months

(D) 1 year

Ⓐ Ⓑ Ⓒ Ⓓ

46. What does the woman want to know about the man's cell phone provider?

(A) What he pays for his plan

(B) How long the contracts are

(C) How the customer service is

(D) Which phones they have available

Ⓐ Ⓑ Ⓒ Ⓓ

Go on to the next page. ▶

47. What is the committee's purpose?

    (A) Reviewing policies

    (B) Evaluating the department's efficiency

    (C) Evaluating new products

    (D) Addressing employee concerns   Ⓐ Ⓑ Ⓒ Ⓓ

48. When will Jack return to the office?

    (A) 10:00 a.m.

    (B) At noon

    (C) 1:00 p.m.

    (D) 2:00 p.m.   Ⓐ Ⓑ Ⓒ Ⓓ

49. Why does the woman want Jack to be on the committee?

    (A) He is a regional manager.

    (B) He would bring a fresh perspective.

    (C) He can explain complex matters very easily.

    (D) He has held many positions within the company.   Ⓐ Ⓑ Ⓒ Ⓓ

50. Why is the man surprised?

(A) Steve has not paid his bill yet.

(B) Steve did not attend a meeting this morning.

(C) Steve has not picked up a package of samples.

(D) Steve did not give a reason for leaving the office. Ⓐ Ⓑ Ⓒ Ⓓ

51. What did Steve tell the man that he would do?

(A) Send a payment

(B) Help him to finish a project

(C) Place an order that afternoon

(D) Make a presentation during a meeting Ⓐ Ⓑ Ⓒ Ⓓ

52. What does the woman offer to do?

(A) Call Steve

(B) Order new samples

(C) Help the man with his work

(D) Send a payment reminder notice Ⓐ Ⓑ Ⓒ Ⓓ

Go on to the next page. ▶

53. Why did the man call?

    (A) He forgot a file.

    (B) He is running late.

    (C) He needs a projector.

    (D) He took the wrong disk.   Ⓐ Ⓑ Ⓒ Ⓓ

54. How many copies of the report does the man say he has?

    (A) 10

    (B) 20

    (C) 30

    (D) 40   Ⓐ Ⓑ Ⓒ Ⓓ

55. Where do the speakers plan to meet?

    (A) At a coffee shop

    (B) At a train station

    (C) In the conference room

    (D) At the client's office   Ⓐ Ⓑ Ⓒ Ⓓ

56. What does the man think the company should do?

(A) Hire additional staff

(B) Open an overseas office

(C) Revise its financial strategy

(D) Advertise to attract new clients

57. What claim does the man make?

(A) Advertising has attracted many clients in the past.

(B) The number of clients is up 25 percent from a year ago.

(C) Finding workers with the necessary skills will not be difficult.

(D) The rent for the current office space is above average for the area.

58. What problem does the woman see with the man's plan?

(A) A new budget will have to be written.

(B) They cannot raise enough money in time.

(C) The office will have to be closed temporarily.

(D) Some workers will have to be reassigned to new departments.

A B C D

Go on to the next page. ▶

59. What is learned about the speakers?

    (A) They are sports fans.

    (B) They both like old movies.

    (C) They like to go to the theater.

    (D) They watch a lot of television.   Ⓐ Ⓑ Ⓒ Ⓓ

60. Why do the speakers want to reduce their cable service?

    (A) The fees have gone up recently.

    (B) Their free trial period is over.

    (C) They are trying to cut their expenses.

    (D) They have more channels than they need.   Ⓐ Ⓑ Ⓒ Ⓓ

61. What does the woman suggest the man do?

    (A) Talk to a coworker

    (B) Call the cable company

    (C) Respond to a promotional offer

    (D) Switch to a new cable service provider   Ⓐ Ⓑ Ⓒ Ⓓ

MP3
113

62. What surprised the woman?

(A) That the coffee maker is so large

(B) How expensive the coffee makers are

(C) How much coffee the coffee maker can make

(D) That the coffee makers are available for rent

63. How much does it cost to have a coffee maker delivered and set up?

(A) $15

(B) $20

(C) $25

(D) $30

64. How long does the woman need the coffee maker?

(A) 1 day

(B) 2 days

(C) 3 days

(D) 5 days Ⓐ Ⓑ Ⓒ Ⓓ

Go on to the next page. ▶

65. What is learned about the man?

    (A) He travels a lot.

    (B) He is a professor.

    (C) He works long hours.

    (D) He delivers a lot of presentations.   Ⓐ Ⓑ Ⓒ Ⓓ

66. Where will the lecture be held?

    (A) At a university

    (B) At a fundraising event

    (C) At a meeting of entrepreneurs

    (D) At an engineering society meeting   Ⓐ Ⓑ Ⓒ Ⓓ

67. What does the man say he will talk about?

    (A) How decisions are made in the company

    (B) The many uses of his company's products

    (C) How the departments of the company collaborate

    (D) The opportunities his company offers its employees   Ⓐ Ⓑ Ⓒ Ⓓ

MP3
115

68. What is learned about the woman?

(A) She has stayed at the hotel before.

(B) She stayed at the hotel for 5 nights.

(C) She attended a conference at the hotel.

(D) She paid for her hotel room with a credit card.

Ⓐ Ⓑ Ⓒ Ⓓ

69. What is said to be new at the hotel?

(A) The rates

(B) The menu

(C) The carpets

(D) The furniture

Ⓐ Ⓑ Ⓒ Ⓓ

70. What does the woman say she will do?

(A) Check out at noon

(B) Stay at the hotel an extra night

(C) Come back again the following year

(D) Recommend the hotel to her friends

Ⓐ Ⓑ Ⓒ Ⓓ

Part 4

Part 4

Direcitons: In Part 4, you will hear several short talks. After each talk, you will be asked to answer three questions about what you heard. Select the best response to each question, and mark the corresponding letter (A), (B), (C), or (D) on your answer sheet. The questions and responses are printed in the test book. The talks do not appear in the test book, and they will be spoken only one time.

71. What does the man say about the archives room?
   (A) It is difficult to find.
   (B) It is on the first floor.
   (C) It is smaller than he expected.
   (D) It requires an access code to enter.   Ⓐ Ⓑ Ⓒ Ⓓ

72. What does the man say to look for?
   (A) A green door
   (B) A parking lot
   (C) The main office
   (D) A freight elevator   Ⓐ Ⓑ Ⓒ Ⓓ

73. Where are the two steps?
   (A) Outside the office
   (B) Inside the archives room
   (C) In front of the warehouse
   (D) At the end of the narrow hallway

MP3
118

74. Where does the woman probably work?

　　(A) At a flower shop

　　(B) At a grocery store

　　(C) At an office supply store

　　(D) At a photo processing center　　　　Ⓐ　Ⓑ　Ⓒ　Ⓓ

75. How much is the order?

　　(A) $13

　　(B) $20

　　(C) $120

　　(D) $230　　　　Ⓐ　Ⓑ　Ⓒ　Ⓓ

76. What does the woman offer to do for the customer?

　　(A) Mail the order

　　(B) Apply a discount to the order

　　(C) Bill the order to a credit card

　　(D) Deliver the order that afternoon　　　　Ⓐ　Ⓑ　Ⓒ　Ⓓ

Go on to the next page. ▶

77. What is expected for later that afternoon?

(A) More rain

(B) Fewer clouds

(C) An end to the rain

(D) An increase in clouds

Ⓐ Ⓑ Ⓒ Ⓓ

78. What is expected for Crafton the following evening?

(A) Snow

(B) High winds

(C) Clear skies

(D) Thundershowers

Ⓐ Ⓑ Ⓒ Ⓓ

79. What is the current temperature in Crafton?

(A) 35

(B) 46

(C) 52

(D) 60

Ⓐ Ⓑ Ⓒ Ⓓ

MP3
120

80. What event is the speaker mainly discussing?

(A) A trade show

(B) A conference

(C) A fundraiser

(D) A competition   Ⓐ Ⓑ Ⓒ Ⓓ

81. What does the speaker want her audience to do?

(A) Make a list of people to thank

(B) Create a presentation about the company

(C) Discuss a strategy to increase profits of the company

(D) Make a list of things to improve for the following year   Ⓐ Ⓑ Ⓒ Ⓓ

82. What can be inferred about the event?

(A) It lasts 10 days.

(B) It ended recently.

(C) It will be held in a different city.

(D) It is scheduled for the following week.   Ⓐ Ⓑ Ⓒ Ⓓ

Go on to the next page. ▶

83. Who does the speaker probably work for?

(A) A bank

(B) A record company

(C) A television station

(D) An advertising company   Ⓐ Ⓑ Ⓒ Ⓓ

84. Why does the speaker mention a fast food company?

(A) To illustrate what a client has done

(B) To describe who his typical clients are

(C) To give an example of what a client might do

(D) To suggest where a client should go for lunch   Ⓐ Ⓑ Ⓒ Ⓓ

85. What does the speaker claim his company has done?

(A) Developed a new financial product

(B) Helped hundreds of businesses throughout the city

(C) Signed many unknown artists who later became famous

(D) Measured traffic at different points around the city   Ⓐ Ⓑ Ⓒ Ⓓ

86. What claim does the speaker make about herself?

(A) She used to be a pilot.

(B) She has never made a mistake.

(C) She works well under pressure.

(D) She works at the busiest airport in the world.　　

87. What does the speaker say an air traffic controller must be able to do?

(A) Think like a pilot

(B) Make quick decisions

(C) Use technical language

(D) Sit for hours at a time　　

88. What does the speaker imply about herself?

(A) She will retire soon.

(B) She has helped save many lives.

(C) She can think about many things at once.

(D) She has worked at airports around the country.　　Ⓐ Ⓑ Ⓒ Ⓓ

Go on to the next page.　▶

89. What does the speaker say about hotels in Seattle?

(A) They are too expensive.

(B) They are often booked up.

(C) They usually offer discounts online.

(D) They can be surprisingly affordable.   Ⓐ Ⓑ Ⓒ Ⓓ

90. Which hotels does the speaker say he prefers to stay at?

(A) Those nearest the beach

(B) Those closest to the airport

(C) Those near the convention center

(D) Those far away from tourist sites   Ⓐ Ⓑ Ⓒ Ⓓ

91. What does the speaker say he would do if he were organizing a conference?

(A) Have it in summer

(B) Hold it in a small city

(C) Limit the number of attendees

(D) Set the dates far in advance   Ⓐ Ⓑ Ⓒ Ⓓ

92. What does Amy Dillon say she never received?

(A) A receipt

(B) An invoice

(C) A client file

(D) Spreadsheets

93. Who does Amy Dillon indicate is another resource at her office?

(A) Her boss

(B) Her partner

(C) The office manager

(D) The sales representative Ⓐ Ⓑ Ⓒ Ⓓ

94. What does Amy Dillon say she plans to do that evening?

(A) Write a report

(B) Close an account

(C) Update a database

(D) Catch up on e-mail Ⓐ Ⓑ Ⓒ Ⓓ

Go on to the next page. ▶

95. What did the speaker do in China?

    (A) Toured the company's factories

    (B) Trained factory staff how to use equipment

    (C) Met with the heads of the regional offices in China

    (D) Conducted an audit of the company's offices there   Ⓐ Ⓑ Ⓒ Ⓓ

96. How does the speaker describe the people he met on his trip?

    (A) As creative

    (B) As friendly

    (C) As energetic

    (D) As hard-working   Ⓐ Ⓑ Ⓒ Ⓓ

97. What does the speaker say he learned about his company?

    (A) Its China factories are the best run.

    (B) It produces a large volume of products.

    (C) It spends a lot of money to train the staff.

    (D) Its best products are made in its factories in China.   Ⓐ Ⓑ Ⓒ Ⓓ

98. Who is the speaker probably addressing?

(A) A client

(B) A supplier

(C) A new employee

(D) A hotel manager Ⓐ Ⓑ Ⓒ Ⓓ

99. What is the speaker mainly discussing?

(A) Renting projectors

(B) Arranging for visitors

(C) Reserving conference rooms

(D) Setting up a product demonstration Ⓐ Ⓑ Ⓒ Ⓓ

100. What is said about Sue and Peter?

(A) They will bring the equipment.

(B) They will set up the meeting room.

(C) They should be invited to the meeting.

(D) They can provide help if it is needed. Ⓐ Ⓑ Ⓒ Ⓓ

Test 2

模擬試題

Part 1

MP3 127

LISTENING TEST

The Listening test allows you to demonstrate how well you understand spoken English. The listening test has four parts, and you will hear directions for each of them. The entire Listening test is approximately forty-five minutes long. Write only on your answer sheet, not the test book.

PART 1

Directions: For each question in Part 1, you will hear four statements about a photograph. Select the statement that best describes what you see in the photo and mark your answer on the answer sheet. The statements will only be spoken once, and do not appear in the test book.

Example

Sample Answer

Statement (C), "They are sitting around the table," is the best description of the photograph, so you should mark (C) on your anwer sheet.

1.

Ⓐ Ⓑ Ⓒ Ⓓ

2.

Ⓐ Ⓑ Ⓒ Ⓓ

Go on to the next page. ▶

3.

Ⓐ Ⓑ Ⓒ Ⓓ

4.

Ⓐ Ⓑ Ⓒ Ⓓ

5.

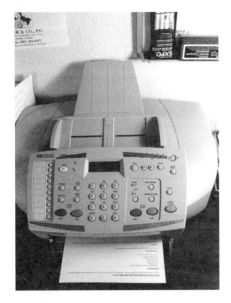

Ⓐ Ⓑ Ⓒ Ⓓ

6.

Ⓐ Ⓑ Ⓒ Ⓓ

Go on to the next page. ▶

7.

8.

9.

(A) (B) (C) (D)

10.

(A) (B) (C) (D)

Part 2

PART 2

Direcitons: In Part 2, you will hear either a statement or a question and three responses. They will only be spoken one time, and do not appear in your test book. Select the best response to the question or statement and mark the corresponding letter (A), (B), or (C) on your answer sheet.

Sample Answer

Example

You will hear: Does this bus go to the train station?

You will also hear: (A) I've listened to this station for years.

(B) No, you need to take number 75.

(C) The train leaves in a few minutes.

The best response to the question "Does this bus go to the train station?" is choice (B), "No, you need to take number 75," so you should mark answer (B) on your answer sheet.

11. Mark your answer on your answer sheet. Ⓐ Ⓑ Ⓒ

12. Mark your answer on your answer sheet. Ⓐ Ⓑ Ⓒ

13. Mark your answer on your answer sheet. Ⓐ Ⓑ Ⓒ

14. Mark your answer on your answer sheet. Ⓐ Ⓑ Ⓒ

15. Mark your answer on your answer sheet. Ⓐ Ⓑ Ⓒ

16. Mark your answer on your answer sheet. Ⓐ Ⓑ Ⓒ

17. Mark your answer on your answer sheet. Ⓐ Ⓑ Ⓒ

18. Mark your answer on your answer sheet. Ⓐ Ⓑ Ⓒ

19. Mark your answer on your answer sheet. Ⓐ Ⓑ Ⓒ

20. Mark your answer on your answer sheet. Ⓐ Ⓑ Ⓒ

Go on to the next page. ▶

21. Mark your answer on your answer sheet. Ⓐ Ⓑ Ⓒ

22. Mark your answer on your answer sheet. Ⓐ Ⓑ Ⓒ

23. Mark your answer on your answer sheet. Ⓐ Ⓑ Ⓒ

24. Mark your answer on your answer sheet. Ⓐ Ⓑ Ⓒ

25. Mark your answer on your answer sheet. Ⓐ Ⓑ Ⓒ

26. Mark your answer on your answer sheet. Ⓐ Ⓑ Ⓒ

27. Mark your answer on your answer sheet. Ⓐ Ⓑ Ⓒ

28. Mark your answer on your answer sheet. Ⓐ Ⓑ Ⓒ

29. Mark your answer on your answer sheet. Ⓐ Ⓑ Ⓒ

30. Mark your answer on your answer sheet. Ⓐ Ⓑ Ⓒ

31. Mark your answer on your answer sheet. Ⓐ Ⓑ Ⓒ

32. Mark your answer on your answer sheet. Ⓐ Ⓑ Ⓒ

33. Mark your answer on your answer sheet. Ⓐ Ⓑ Ⓒ

34. Mark your answer on your answer sheet. Ⓐ Ⓑ Ⓒ

35. Mark your answer on your answer sheet. Ⓐ Ⓑ Ⓒ

36. Mark your answer on your answer sheet. Ⓐ Ⓑ Ⓒ

37. Mark your answer on your answer sheet. Ⓐ Ⓑ Ⓒ

38. Mark your answer on your answer sheet. Ⓐ Ⓑ Ⓒ

39. Mark your answer on your answer sheet. Ⓐ Ⓑ Ⓒ

40. Mark your answer on your answer sheet. Ⓐ Ⓑ Ⓒ

Go on to the next page. ▶

Part 3

PART3

Direcitons: In Part 3, you will hear several short conversations between two people. After each conversation, you will be asked to answer three questions about what you heard. Select the best response to each question, and mark the corresponding letter (A), (B), (C), or (D) on your answer sheet. The questions and responses are printed in the test book. The conversations do not appear in the test book, and they will be spoken only one time.

41. What is true about the man?

(A) He started a small business.

(B) He failed to pay his taxes on time.

(C) He is a certified public accountant.

(D) He has relocated his business to a new city.

42. What does the woman ask the man?

(A) If he received professional tax help

(B) Whether he filed a form with the city

(C) If he has been in the city for over a year

(D) Whether he estimated how much money he owes

43. What does the woman remind the man to do?

(A) Pay a penalty charge

(B) Return the following month

(C) Pay his taxes every quarter

(D) Contact her office in September

44. What did the man do?

(A) Offered to lower a product's price

(B) Helped the woman manufacture a product

(C) Gave the woman temporary use of a product

(D) Persuaded the woman to purchase a product   Ⓐ Ⓑ Ⓒ Ⓓ

45. What does the man say is a benefit of using the product?

(A) It uses less energy to run.

(B) It is heavier and more durable.

(C) It requires less labor to assemble.

(D) It weighs less than other similar products.   Ⓐ Ⓑ Ⓒ Ⓓ

46. How does the man offer to assist the woman?

(A) By helping her with construction

(B) By arranging her government permits

(C) By reviewing her manufacturing plans

(D) By writing a customized set of guidelines   Ⓐ Ⓑ Ⓒ Ⓓ

Go on to the next page. ▶

47. Where does this conversation probably take place?

(A) At a conference

(B) At a job interview

(C) In a staff meeting

(D) In a reception area

Ⓐ Ⓑ Ⓒ Ⓓ

48. What is learned about the man?

(A) He has experience as a manager.

(B) He specializes in site analysis.

(C) He is working on a construction site.

(D) He has a degree in environmental science.

Ⓐ Ⓑ Ⓒ Ⓓ

49. What does the woman ask the man to do?

(A) Hand her a document

(B) Document his progress

(C) Clarify a point he made

(D) Examine her business plan

Ⓐ Ⓑ Ⓒ Ⓓ

50. What is the man's problem?

(A) His computer is not working correctly.

(B) He is unable to read the text on-screen.

(C) His questions were not answered by the client.

(D) He is having problems with the files he received. Ⓐ Ⓑ Ⓒ Ⓓ

51. What kind of work are the speakers probably doing?

(A) Writing a text document

(B) Taking product photographs

(C) Formulating a marketing plan

(D) Developing a computer program Ⓐ Ⓑ Ⓒ Ⓓ

52. What does the woman suggest the speakers do?

(A) Change their strategy

(B) Continue to do their work

(C) Finish their work immediately

(D) Contact Gary as soon as possible Ⓐ Ⓑ Ⓒ Ⓓ

Go on to the next page. ▶

MP3
174

53. What is the man's problem?

(A) He was not paid for a job he did.

(B) He cannot find the check he received.

(C) He sent his invoice to the wrong address.

(D) He provided the wrong contact information.

Ⓐ Ⓑ Ⓒ Ⓓ

54. What information does the man give the woman?

(A) His phone number

(B) His invoice numbers

(C) The price of his services

(D) The date he completed his job

Ⓐ Ⓑ Ⓒ Ⓓ

55. What does the woman claim to have done?

(A) Mailed the checks

(B) Signed the contracts

(C) Forgotten to send the money

(D) Written down the wrong amount

Ⓐ Ⓑ Ⓒ Ⓓ

MP3
175

56. What are the speakers discussing?

(A) A business plan

(B) A corporate logo

(C) An annual report

(D) A product design   Ⓐ Ⓑ Ⓒ Ⓓ

57. On what do the speakers disagree?

(A) Whether they should do a job

(B) When they should begin the job

(C) How much money they should spend

(D) Who they should hire to do the work   Ⓐ Ⓑ Ⓒ Ⓓ

58. What does the man say about the speakers' decision?

(A) The decision should not be made too quickly.

(B) The situation does not involve a lot of risk.

(C) More people should be involved in the decision.

(D) More work should be done before making the decision.

     Ⓐ Ⓑ Ⓒ Ⓓ

Go on to the next page. ▶

59. What does the man say is a benefit of museum membership?

    (A) Free parking

    (B) Free entry for guests

    (C) Invitations to special events

    (D) Discounts at some restaurants   Ⓐ Ⓑ Ⓒ Ⓓ

60. What does the man say regarding his membership purchase?

    (A) He bought it as a gift.

    (B) He made it while at the museum.

    (C) He had planned it for a long time.

    (D) He responded to a telephone salesman.   Ⓐ Ⓑ Ⓒ Ⓓ

61. What is probably true about the speakers?

    (A) They both work with children.

    (B) They live in the same household.

    (C) They are both interested in science.

    (D) They belong to a professional organization.   Ⓐ Ⓑ Ⓒ Ⓓ

62. What did the man do?

(A) Attended a trade show

(B) Changed his flight reservation

(C) Completed his conference registration

(D) Changed his mind about attending an event   Ⓐ Ⓑ Ⓒ Ⓓ

63. What was the man concerned about?

(A) Losing sales

(B) Traveling safely

(C) Spending too much money

(D) Losing his work benefits   Ⓐ Ⓑ Ⓒ Ⓓ

64. What does the man say he plans to do?

(A) Return to his home

(B) Remain in his office

(C) Meet with his clients

(D) Look for a cheap hotel   Ⓐ Ⓑ Ⓒ Ⓓ

Go on to the next page. ▶

65. What is learned about the man's company?

(A) It is headquartered in Asia.

(B) It has offices around the world.

(C) It opened during a downturn in the economy.

(D) It has been in business for less than 10 months.　　Ⓐ Ⓑ Ⓒ Ⓓ

66. What does the woman imply about the man's company?

(A) It has borrowed a lot of money.

(B) It needs to continue to be innovative.

(C) It faces a great deal of local competition.

(D) Its strong economic performance may not last.　　Ⓐ Ⓑ Ⓒ Ⓓ

67. What reason does the man give for his company's success?

(A) It has top-quality management.

(B) It learned from other companies.

(C) It benefited from new technology.

(D) It was well-funded when it started out.　　Ⓐ Ⓑ Ⓒ Ⓓ

68. What is the man probably doing?

(A) Confirming a previous agreement

(B) Negotiating a long-term sales contract

(C) Looking into having a design manufactured

(D) Deciding whether to purchase the woman's products Ⓐ Ⓑ Ⓒ Ⓓ

69. What does the woman say about her business?

(A) It outsells its competition.

(B) It distributes internationally.

(C) It manufacturers its own products.

(D) It only sells to the retail public. Ⓐ Ⓑ Ⓒ Ⓓ

70. What is the man concerned about?

(A) The price of the products

(B) The purity of the materials used

(C) The quality of the manufacturing

(D) The company's long-term stability Ⓐ Ⓑ Ⓒ Ⓓ

Part 4

Part 4

Direcitons: In Part 4, you will hear several short talks. After each talk, you will be asked to answer three questions about what you heard. Select the best response to each question, and mark the corresponding letter (A), (B), (C), or (D) on your answer sheet. The questions and responses are printed in the test book. The talks do not appear in the test book, and they will be spoken only one time.

71. Where does the man say he posted his resume?
(A) On his personal website
(B) On several Internet job sites
(C) On the largest Internet job site
(D) On the website of a major corporation

72. What did the man do before posting his resume online?
(A) Attended a number of job fairs
(B) Worked with several job recruiters
(C) Responded to job postings by e-mail
(D) Used the newspaper to look for jobs Ⓐ Ⓑ Ⓒ Ⓓ

73. What does the man indicate was the result of posting his resume online?
(A) He received more unwanted e-mails.
(B) He was contacted by job recruiters.
(C) He was offered a job within two days.
(D) He found better quality job prospects. Ⓐ Ⓑ Ⓒ Ⓓ

MP3
182

74. What does the woman say about her company's recent performance?

(A) Its profits have fallen significantly.

(B) Its products have not been selling well.

(C) It recently lost several regular clients.

(D) It has had to cut back production of some styles.　　Ⓐ Ⓑ Ⓒ Ⓓ

75. What does the woman say her company needs to do?

(A) Develop a new brand identity

(B) Move closer to its market base

(C) Produce more high-quality products

(D) Appeal to a wider range of customer　　Ⓐ Ⓑ Ⓒ Ⓓ

76. What does the woman imply about her company?

(A) It sells a variety of inexpensive products.

(B) Its focus is on long-term, not short-term goals.

(C) Its image has suffered as a result of falling sales.

(D) It has a reputation as a maker of high-quality products.

　　Ⓐ Ⓑ Ⓒ Ⓓ

Go on to the next page. ▶

77. How does the man plan to travel?

(A) By car

(B) By boat

(C) By bicycle

(D) By tour bus
    Ⓐ Ⓑ Ⓒ Ⓓ

78. What does the man claim about the C & O Canal?

(A) It took almost a century to construct.

(B) It was designed by non-American engineers.

(C) It was completed in the eighteenth century.

(D) It marked the birth of American civil engineering.
    Ⓐ Ⓑ Ⓒ Ⓓ

79. What does the man imply about himself?

(A) He is an amateur historian.

(B) He has a degree in engineering.

(C) He is a university history professor.

(D) He wrote a book about the C & O Canal.
    Ⓐ Ⓑ Ⓒ Ⓓ

80. What is the subject of the woman's talk?

(A) The best way to form a project team

(B) A recent project team she was a part of

(C) A performance problem she recently observed

(D) The phases that project teams normally go through

81. What does the woman claim may cause a misunderstanding on a team?

(A) Disagreements over money issues

(B) Competition between team members

(C) Lack of a clear set of expectations

(D) Team members being unfamiliar with each other

82. According to the woman, what usually happens after people have disagreements on a project team?

(A) Their work performance suffers.

(B) They develop natural work routines.

(C) They become more difficult to manage.

(D) They resist working on future projects together. Ⓐ Ⓑ Ⓒ Ⓓ

Go on to the next page. ▶

83. What can be inferred about the announcement?

(A) It is made every week at the same time.

(B) It is intended for people in several buildings.

(C) It comes directly from the head of the department.

(D) It follows other similar announcements made earlier.

84. What is going to happen during the test of the PTV system?

(A) An entire system will be shut down.

(B) The system's pressure will be raised.

(C) A toxic chemical may emerge from the system.

(D) The heat will rise to an uncomfortable level.

85. What does the announcement ask people to do?

(A) Be alert for possible hazards

(B) Leave the building immediately

(C) Shut off all computer equipment

(D) Write down everything they observe

86. How long has the repair garage been privatized?

    (A) Several weeks

    (B) Five months

    (C) One year

    (D) Five years   Ⓐ Ⓑ Ⓒ Ⓓ

87. According to the report, what resulted from the privatization of the city repair garage?

    (A) The city saved $1.5 million.

    (B) The city spent $500 thousand extra.

    (C) The city had more vehicles out of operation.

    (D) The city was audited by the federal government.   Ⓐ Ⓑ Ⓒ Ⓓ

88. What city departments is NOT mentioned as having its vehicles serviced by the city repair garage?

    (A) The fire department

    (B) The police department

    (C) The sanitation department

    (D) The motor vehicles department   Ⓐ Ⓑ Ⓒ Ⓓ

Go on to the next page. ▶

89. Why has Carolyn Rivers called Mr. O'Toole?

   (A) She told him earlier that she would call.

   (B) He left a voicemail asking her to call him.

   (C) His name was given to her by a work colleague.

   (D) He previously ordered a catalog from her company.　Ⓐ Ⓑ Ⓒ Ⓓ

90. What does Carolyn Rivers want to do?

   (A) Confirm an order

   (B) Arrange a meeting

   (C) Reschedule a delivery

   (D) Offer a line of credit　Ⓐ Ⓑ Ⓒ Ⓓ

91. What can be inferred about Mr. O'Toole?

   (A) He works near Boston.

   (B) He operates a country club.

   (C) He is a professional golfer.

   (D) He currently carries a line of Ms. Rivers' products.　Ⓐ Ⓑ Ⓒ Ⓓ

92. What information about salt does the speaker NOT provide?

(A) The total amount consumed per person

(B) The total quantity consumed worldwide

(C) The recommended quantity of salt consumption

(D) The possible links between salt and health problems   (A) (B) (C) (D)

93. What does the speaker claim about salt consumption in the U.S.?

(A) It has risen in the past ten years.

(B) It is twice as high as it ought to be.

(C) It has caused national health costs to rise.

(D) It is higher than in any other industrialized country.   (A) (B) (C) (D)

94. What does the speaker suggest should happen?

(A) The government should set new guidelines.

(B) More medical research should be conducted.

(C) People should put less salt on their foods.

(D) The food industry should put less salt in foods.   (A) (B) (C) (D)

Go on to the next page. ▶

95. Who is the woman talking about?

    (A) A client

    (B) An employee

    (C) A business partner

    (D) A friend from college   Ⓐ Ⓑ Ⓒ Ⓓ

96. In what field does the woman probably work?

    (A) Furniture sales

    (B) Interior design

    (C) Home construction

    (D) Furniture construction   Ⓐ Ⓑ Ⓒ Ⓓ

97. What does the woman claim about Ross?

    (A) He has many employees.

    (B) He is a senior citizen.

    (C) He used to work in a library.

    (D) He builds furniture entirely by hand.   Ⓐ Ⓑ Ⓒ Ⓓ

98. What advice was the man given when he first began his career?

(A) Always look professional

(B) Always carry business cards

(C) Attend professional conferences

(D) Learn how to make presentations

99. What is probably the man's job?

(A) Company trainer

(B) Corporate manager

(C) Business consultant

(D) Sales representative

100. What does the man NOT claim to do before every business meeting?

(A) Review his notes

(B) Write down his questions

(C) Examine the meeting's agenda

(D) Note who is running the meeting

國家圖書館出版品預行編目資料

New TOEIC 新多益大師指引：聽力滿分關鍵 /
王建民著. －－ 初版. －－ 臺北市；貝塔出版：
智勝文化發行, 2009. 02
　面；　　公分
　ISBN 978-957-729-720-4（平裝）
　1. 多益測驗　2. 問題集
805.1895　　　　　　　　　　　　97025267

新多益大師指引—聽力滿分關鍵
New TOEIC Master—Listening

作　　者 / 王建民
譯　　者 / 戴至中
總 編 審 / 王復國
執行編輯 / 莊碧娟

出　　版 / 貝塔出版有限公司
地　　址 / 台北市 100 館前路 12 號 11 樓
電　　話 / (02) 2314-2525
傳　　真 / (02) 2312-3535
客服專線 / (02) 2314-3535
客服信箱 / btservice@betamedia.com.tw
郵撥帳號 / 19493777
帳戶名稱 / 貝塔出版有限公司
總 經 銷 / 時報文化出版企業股份有限公司
地　　址 / 桃園縣龜山鄉萬壽路二段 351 號
電　　話 / (02) 2306-6842

出版日期 / 2013 年 3 月初版五刷
定　　價 / 500 元
ISBN: 978-957-729-720-4

喚醒你的英文語感！

對折後釘好，直接寄回即可！

| 廣　告　回　信 |
| 北區郵政管理局登記證 |
| 北 台 字 第 1 4 2 5 6 號 |
| 免　貼　郵　票 |

100 台北市中正區館前路12號11樓

 貝塔語言出版 收
Beta Multimedia Publishing

寄件者住址　□ □ □

謝謝您購買本書！！

貝塔語言擁有最優良之英文學習書籍，為提供您最佳的英語學習資訊，您可填妥此表後寄回（免貼郵票）將可不定期收到本公司最新發行書訊及活動訊息！

姓名：＿＿＿＿＿＿＿＿＿＿＿＿ 性別：□男 □女 生日：＿＿＿年＿＿＿月＿＿＿日

電話：(公)＿＿＿＿＿＿＿＿＿＿(宅)＿＿＿＿＿＿＿＿＿＿(手機)＿＿＿＿＿＿＿＿＿

電子信箱：＿＿＿＿＿＿＿＿＿＿＿＿＿＿＿＿＿＿＿＿＿

學歷：□高中職含以下 □專科 □大學 □研究所含以上

職業：□金融 □服務 □傳播 □製造 □資訊 □軍公教 □出版

　　　□自由 □教育 □學生 □其他

職級：□企業負責人 □高階主管 □中階主管 □職員 □專業人士

1. 您購買的書籍是？＿＿＿＿＿＿＿＿＿＿＿＿＿＿＿

2. 您從何處得知本產品？(可複選)

　　　□書店 □網路 □書展 □校園活動 □廣告信函 □他人推薦 □新聞報導 □其他

3. 您覺得本產品價格：

　　　□偏高 □合理 □偏低

4. 請問目前您每週花了多少時間學英語？

　　　□ 不到十分鐘 □ 十分鐘以上，但不到半小時 □ 半小時以上，但不到一小時

　　　□ 一小時以上，但不到兩小時 □ 兩個小時以上 □ 不一定

5. 通常在選擇語言學習書時，哪些因素是您會考慮的？

　　　□ 封面 □ 內容、實用性 □ 品牌 □ 媒體、朋友推薦 □ 價格□ 其他＿＿＿＿

6. 市面上您最需要的語言書種類為？

　　　□ 聽力 □ 閱讀 □ 文法 □ 口說 □ 寫作 □ 其他＿＿＿＿＿

7. 通常您會透過何種方式選購語言學習書籍？

　　　□ 書店門市 □ 網路書店 □ 郵購 □ 直接找出版社 □ 學校或公司團購

　　　□ 其他＿＿＿＿＿＿

8. 給我們的建議：＿＿＿＿＿＿＿＿＿＿＿＿＿＿＿＿＿＿＿＿＿

＿＿＿＿＿＿＿＿＿＿＿＿＿＿＿＿＿＿＿＿＿＿＿＿＿＿＿

Get a Feel for English !

喚醒你的英文語感！

Get a Feel for English !

喚醒你的英文語感！